Dear Reader,

I believe that half the fun of taking a trip is the planning you do beforehand. It's exciting to look at pictures of your destination and read about all the things you'll be able to see and do. These days, you can hop on the Internet and read firsthand accounts from other travelers, allowing you to plan the best vacation possible.

Only you can't plan for those unexpected events — the ones you won't find in travel guides. Like the time I sprained my ankle at a beach in California. Or the time my son and daughter arrived in Spain for a six-week trip, only to discover that the airport had lost their luggage (and it took a week to get it back). Maybe next time they'll listen when Mom tells them to pack a few clothes in their carry on bags.

We can never anticipate everything that is going to happen on a trip and that's part of what makes it an adventure. Aunt Edie's adventurous spirit is evident in the Secrets of Blue Hill Library series. She was an avid traveler and seemed to enjoy every moment of it. In *Mum's the Word*, a trip Aunt Edie took to Egypt forty years ago suddenly has some unexpected consequences. It's a vacation that Anne and the good folks in Blue Hill will never forget.

So buckle your seat belts for the newest adventure in the Secrets of the Blue Hill Library!

Blessings,
Kristin Eckhardt
writing as Emily Thomas

Secrets of the Blue Hill Library

Mum's the Word

Secrets of the
BLUE HILL LIBRARY

EMILY THOMAS

Guideposts

New York

Mum's the Word

CHAPTER ONE

Anne slathered a piece of wheat toast with strawberry jelly and took a quick bite as she walked toward the open doorway leading to the hall. "Hurry up, kids," she called out, "we don't want to be late for school."

To her chagrin, Anne had overslept this morning after forgetting to set her alarm clock last night. She'd been engrossed in a new mystery novel and had completely lost track of time, falling asleep well after midnight. Now, she, Ben, and Liddie were racing to head out the door on time. She'd fixed the kids a quick breakfast of cereal and toast and then packed their lunches while they finished getting ready for school.

Anne popped the last bite of toast into her mouth as the kids entered the kitchen, each carrying a backpack. "Ready to go?"

"Yep," Ben said, slinging his backpack over one shoulder and heading toward the back door. Lately, her nine-year-old son was eager to get to school every morning so he'd have time to visit with Carter Pratt, a new boy in Ben's class who had moved from Chicago to Blue Hill with his family two weeks ago.

Liddie's brow wrinkled as she stood in the middle of the kitchen. "I think I forgot something, Mommy."

"What did you forget, honey?" Anne grabbed the five-year-old's pink jacket off the back of a kitchen chair and slipped it on

Liddie. They'd been enjoying warm weather these first few days of October, but today's forecast warned of thunderstorms this morning and falling temperatures later this afternoon.

"I don't know." A shadow of worry darkened Liddie's chocolate brown eyes. "But I think it's something important."

"It can't be that important if you don't remember," Ben said impatiently. "Come on, we have to go!"

Anne reached out and placed a hand on Liddie's shoulder, gently steering her toward the door. "Don't worry, Liddie. I'm sure you'll remember eventually."

The kids walked out of their private family entrance and made their way to the silver Impala parked in the driveway.

"Wait!" Liddie shouted, coming to a stop. "I remember now!"

"What is it?" Anne asked.

Liddie spun on her heel and looked up at Anne. "I need a yellow hat, Mommy! A silly yellow hat. We're learning about the color yellow."

Anne's heart sank. They were already running late for school, and she was due to open the library in about an hour. "Are you sure you need a yellow hat today? Usually your teacher sends a note home about things like this."

"Yes," Liddie said with a resolute nod. "My teacher gave me a note, but I must have lost it."

Ben frowned at his sister. "How could you lose it?"

Liddie shrugged. "I don't know. I just did."

"Let's look in your backpack," Anne said, hoping this silly hat day was scheduled for next week. Two weeks ago, the kindergarten students had been asked to dress in all blue when they were learning that color.

Liddie handed over her backpack, and Anne quickly sorted through it. At the very bottom, she found a school library book with a piece of paper sticking out of the top. She pulled the paper out of the book and saw that it was a note from the school librarian, Francine Delaware.

Dear Parents,

We invite the kindergarten students to bring a yellow hat to school for our Friday afternoon library hour—the sillier the hat, the better! Please contact me if you have any questions.

Mrs. Delaware

Anne breathed a sigh of relief. "You don't need the hat until this afternoon. I'll find one and take it to the school at lunchtime."

Liddie nodded. "Okay, but it *has* to be a silly hat. And yellow."

"Got it," Anne said with a smile, wondering if she should try to make a hat out of craft paper or dig around in the attic for one. Aunt Edie had loved wearing hats, and Anne knew there were several stored up there, as well as a few in Liddie's bedroom, since she liked to play dress-up.

"Maybe you have a yellow hat in your toy box," Anne said as the three of them climbed into the car. She waited until the kids belted themselves into the backseat before she started the engine.

"No, I have a red one and a purple one and a pink one," Liddie told her. "No yellow."

Anne glanced at the rearview mirror as she backed out of her driveway onto Bluebell Lane, and saw Ben turn to his sister.

"You have that Tweety Bird ski hat that you could wear," Ben suggested. "It's mostly yellow."

"That's right," Anne said, heading into Blue Hill. "You look so cute in that hat."

"That's a winter hat," Liddie said. "And it's not silly enough."

"Oh, it's pretty silly," Ben countered.

"But it has to be *very* silly," Liddie insisted. "And *all* yellow."

"Don't worry, I'll figure something out," Anne said, happy that this small crisis could be solved so easily. If there wasn't a yellow hat among Aunt Edie's vast collection, Anne could fashion one out of paper. She'd stocked up on construction paper for crafts in the Children's Room of the library and knew she had plenty of yellow among the rainbow of colors.

After she dropped off the kids at Blue Hill Elementary School, Anne returned home and headed up to the attic, one flight above their third-floor family bedrooms. She switched on the attic light, figuring she had just enough time to sort through Aunt Edie's old hats before the library was due to open.

Bella Miller was scheduled to come in to work at eleven this morning, which would give Anne plenty of time to make a trip to the elementary school to deliver a hat to Liddie.

As she made her way through the maze of boxes, trunks, and crates in the cavernous attic, Anne began to hum the tune for "This Little Light of Mine," which Liddie had sung during her bath last evening. Anne knew some of Aunt Edie's old dresses and hats were stored in trunks near the northwest corner of the attic. Judging by the cobwebs in her path, Anne hadn't ventured this far into the attic for a while. She waved her hand in front of her as the path grew a little dimmer, clearing the cobwebs away.

Gray clouds filled the sky, leaving little sunlight to shine in through the leaded attic windows.

Someday she'd have to ask Alex to rewire the attic and add a few more lights, Anne decided as she reached the first trunk. She opened the lid and knelt down to sort through the clothes inside. They were neatly folded, and she did her best to keep them that way as she searched through the trunk for some hats. But she found only a few dresses from the forties and fifties, along with some old boots and shoes.

A boom of thunder sounded directly above the house, shaking the walls of the attic and making Anne jump. She took a deep breath as she closed the lid, her heart pounding. Her gaze moved to the closest window, and she saw a bolt of lightning shoot across the sky. "Looks like the forecast was right," she murmured as she moved to another trunk.

When she opened the lid, she was thrilled to see that it was filled with hatboxes. She took the first one out and opened the lid, finding a chic black hat with lace netting in the front and small red silk roses on the brim. "Very nice," she said, replacing the lid, "but not yellow."

She opened more boxes, finding a dove gray hat in one and a purple hat with a silver ribbon in the other. Only three boxes remained in the trunk. She pulled them all out and opened the first one in front of her. This one contained a green hat with a jaunty arrangement of yellow and green feathers. Anne smiled, trying to imagine where Aunt Edie would have worn such a hat. She even tried it on as another crack of thunder sounded. This time the lights in the attic flickered.

"No time for play," she murmured, quickly pulling off the hat and moving on to the next box. She gasped with delight when she saw the yellow hat inside. She lifted the frilly silk and lace pillbox hat from the box. A white silk gardenia adorned one side.

Remembering Liddie's insistence that the hat had to be entirely yellow, she glanced at the yellow feathers on the green hat. She might be able to replace the white silk gardenia with the yellow feathers. She examined the pillbox hat in her hands, determining that the white flower would be easy enough to remove. Then it was simply a matter of adding the feathers and arranging them among the yellow lace.

Raindrops hammered the roof above her, and the room grew even dimmer. She looked toward the window and saw a thick, misty fog obscuring the view.

Anne set the yellow hat back into the box and replaced the lid, then stacked it on top of the box containing the green hat with the yellow feathers. She'd take them both downstairs with her and begin the alterations after opening the library. She smiled to herself, picturing how silly *and* adorable Liddie would look wearing the yellow pillbox hat.

Her gaze moved to the last hatbox in the trunk, and curiosity made her lift the lid, just in case another yellow hat lay inside. But to her surprise, there was no hat in this box. Instead, she found an exotic scarf woven with bright red and orange threads. When she reached out to pick it up, her fingertips felt something solid underneath it. She carefully unwrapped the scarf from the object and found a piece of old pottery in the shape of a clay pot. A *very* old clay pot, judging by the color and shape.

It was reddish brown in color, with some decorative etchings along the upper rim. It stood about a foot tall and four inches wide at the base. The mouth of the pot was a little wider, the top rim slightly curled and smooth.

This clay pot was like nothing Anne had ever seen before. Neither was the scarf, which had a few faded spots on it but was otherwise in good condition. She picked up the now-empty hatbox and tilted it toward the light, noticing for the first time a small piece of ivory paper at the bottom. She picked up the small square of paper and turned it over to see Aunt Edie's familiar handwriting on the other side.

"'Egyptian clay pot,'" Anne read out loud, "'that I unearthed at an archaeological site near the palaces of Armana. Crafted during the late eighteenth dynasty (circa 1350 BC) for the Pharaoh Akhenaten. Egyptian scarf purchased at Luxor, crafted in the early twentieth century.'"

"Wow," Anne said out loud, her gaze turning back to the pot. She smoothed one palm over the surface, amazed at how soft and smooth it felt. It wasn't just old, it was an ancient artifact. Her aunt had been something of an adventurer and had traveled all over the world, but Anne didn't remember ever seeing this clay pot before.

She carefully wrapped it in the scarf once more and then placed it, along with Aunt Edie's note, back in the box. She'd take it downstairs as well, eager to examine it more closely.

After closing the trunk, she picked up all three boxes, stacking them carefully on top of each other, and then headed for the door. Another boom of thunder rattled the windowpanes, and the lights flickered for a moment before going out. The attic was now blanketed in darkness, with only a sliver of misty gray light coming through the windows.

Anne slowed her step, barely able to see the narrow path in front of her. She hoped the electricity wouldn't be out long, but she had a contingency plan in mind. She'd light some candles and retrieve some of the old lanterns from the basement to illuminate the library so she and the patrons wouldn't be wandering around in the dark.

As she turned another corner, her knee smacked hard into the brass corner of a trunk.

"Ow," Anne cried out loud, her knee buckling at the sudden impact. The hatboxes teetered in her arms, but she steadied them. Then she took a few deep, gasping breaths until the sharp pain in her knee began to fade into a dull, throbbing ache.

Finally able to walk again, Anne maneuvered her way through the cluttered attic until she reached the door. At that moment, the electricity came on again, lighting the stairway in front of her. With a sigh of relief, she walked down to the second floor and carried the boxes into the family kitchen, setting them on the table.

Then she bent down and gingerly touched her sore knee with her fingertips. She couldn't see any bruise beneath the khaki slacks she wore, but her knee felt a little tender. A quick glance at the clock told her that she didn't have time to nurse it now.

She grabbed the hatboxes once more and carried them down to the first floor, trying to ignore the ache in her knee. She breathed a quick prayer of thanks that the lights were back on and that she'd found a fun yellow hat for Liddie.

Best of all, she'd discovered an ancient Egyptian artifact that would make a wonderful display in the History Room of the library.

It was going to be a good day.

* * *

"There," Anne said, stepping back to admire her handiwork. She'd been working on the Egyptian display in the History Room for the last half hour, ever since Bella had arrived to work the checkout desk.

"That looks wonderful," Betty Bultman said, standing beside her. She'd stopped in to return some books and was intrigued by the Egyptian artifacts Anne had found. "I've always wanted to visit Egypt."

"So have I," Anne said. "ever since I started reading Elizabeth Peters's mysteries set in Egypt." Anne had placed her favorite Peters novel, *Crocodile on the Sandbank*, in the display, along with two travel books about Egypt and a nonfiction book about the Great Pyramids. She'd also arranged the woven Egyptian scarf around the display before adding the ancient clay pot in the center.

Anne walked over to adjust the scarf, her sore knee making her limp a little.

"Are you all right?" Betty asked, her brow furrowing with concern.

"Oh, I'm fine," Anne assured her. "I bumped my knee earlier while I was in the attic."

"Ouch," Betty commiserated as she began browsing the books on the shelf in front of her. "It must have been quite a bump if it still hurts. Maybe you should put some ice on it."

"That's a good idea," Anne agreed, planning to do so after lunch. But first she had an errand to run.

Anne left Betty browsing through the bookshelves in the History Room as she walked to the checkout desk.

Bella looked up as Anne approached her. "Hey, I just saw a great vintage pillbox hat in the kitchen. Is it yours?"

Anne smiled. She'd successfully replaced the white silk flower with the yellow feathers, just by using a little glue and adjusting the yellow lace on the hat. She'd left it drying on the old kitchen counter. "It belonged to Aunt Edie and is just one of several."

"I love vintage clothes and accessories," Bella said. "Are you planning to use it as part of a display?"

"Not today," Anne said. "Actually, Liddie needs a yellow hat for school."

"Oh, it must be silly hat day." Bella smiled with understanding. "Mrs. Delaware always did make the library hour so much fun."

"It is silly hat day," Anne said, her smile widening. "And I told Liddie that I'd have the hat to her by lunchtime, so I need to run to the school. Do you mind watching the library while I'm gone?"

"Not at all."

The thunderstorm had kept the library empty for most of the morning, but the sun was finally shining once more so Anne expected a busier afternoon ahead.

"Thanks. I shouldn't be gone long," Anne told Bella as she headed toward the first-floor kitchen and retrieved the hat from the counter. She carefully checked the yellow feathers, pleased to find all of them securely attached. The pair of bobby pins Anne had retrieved from her bedroom earlier would keep the hat from falling off of Liddie's cute little head. She couldn't wait to see the expression on her daughter's face when she saw the hat.

Turning around, Anne grabbed her purse off the counter and pulled the car keys out of it as she headed for the back door.

Suddenly, a high-pitched scream tore through the air, followed by a loud thump.

Anne froze for a moment, startled by the sound. It had come from inside the library. She tossed her purse, keys, and the hat onto the kitchen table, ignoring the pain in her knee as she ran toward the door leading into the library. Bella wasn't at the checkout desk anymore, but Anne could hear voices in the adjacent History Room. She raced to the open doorway and then stopped, shocked to see Mildred Farley sprawled on the floor.

The seventy-three-year-old woman lay on her back in her navy blue pantsuit, one foot twisted underneath her. Anne's gaze moved to Mildred's face, which was ghostly pale. But Mildred's eyelids fluttered as Bella and Betty knelt on either side of her, softly calling her name.

Anne hurried over to Mildred's side and knelt beside Bella, who scooted out of the way so that Anne could lean closer and talk to Aunt Edie's oldest and dearest friend. "Mildred, are you all right?"

Mildred didn't say anything, her eyes closed as she emitted a distressed moan.

Anne looked over at Betty. "What happened?"

"I don't know," Betty replied. "I was in the next room, checking out with Bella, when we both heard the scream and the fall."

Anne turned her attention back to Mildred, wondering if she should call an ambulance. She gently picked up Mildred's thin right wrist and felt for her pulse. It was fast but strong. "Mildred? Mildred, can you hear me?"

After a long moment, Mildred's eyes fluttered open. "Yes, dear, I can hear you."

"What happened?" Anne asked, now holding Mildred's hand in her own. The skin was cold and clammy. "Are you all right?"

"No," Mildred said, her gray eyes wider now and filled with fear. "No, I'm not all right. In fact, we're all in terrible danger!"

CHAPTER TWO

D anger?" Bella echoed, staring at Mildred.

Mildred nodded. "Yes, dear, danger!" Then she lifted her left hand in the air, her index finger shaking as she pointed to the Egyptian display sitting only a few feet away. "That clay pot is cursed!"

Now Anne was almost certain that Mildred had hit her head during the fall. She wasn't making any sense. "Just relax, Mildred. We're going to help you."

"The only thing that will help is to get rid of that cursed pot!" Mildred exclaimed. "I can't believe it's here." She struggled to prop herself up on her elbows and then cried out in pain.

"Are you hurt?" Anne asked, supporting the woman's left shoulder.

"It's my ankle," Mildred gasped, her face twisting in agony as she tried to move her right ankle.

Betty moved to examine Mildred's ankle, gently lifting the hem of her navy pants. "It's swelling," she announced. "It's obviously sprained, maybe even broken." She looked over at Anne. "I don't think we should try to move her."

"Neither do I," Anne said, pulling her cell phone from her pocket. She dialed 911 as Mildred shook her head.

"Please don't fuss over me," Mildred said weakly. "I'll be all right. Just give me a minute to recover."

"It's no fuss," Anne insisted. "We have to make sure you're all right.

The 911 operator answered on the second ring. "Nine one one. What's your emergency, please?"

"This is Anne Gibson at the Blue Hill Library. One of our patrons, Mildred Farley, fell and may have broken her ankle. We need an ambulance as soon as possible."

"Is the patient conscious?" the operator asked.

"Yes, but she took a bad fall, so we don't want to move her."

"Okay, I'll dispatch the ambulance. They should be there shortly."

"Thank you," Anne said before ending the call. Her heart ached for Mildred, and she wished she could do something to ease her pain. "Would you like a blanket and a pillow?" she asked, noticing a slight chill in the room.

"Yes, please," Mildred murmured, her face etched with pain.

Anne hurried upstairs to the second floor and retrieved a pillow and a warm blanket from the linen closet. By the time she took them downstairs she could hear a siren in the distance. She could also see that the clay pot was gone.

"Mildred asked us to move it," Bella explained, following her gaze, "so I placed it behind the checkout desk. It was making her upset."

"That pot is dangerous," Mildred proclaimed, her tone ominous, "more dangerous than you can ever know. "

As Anne gently placed the pillow under Mildred's head and covered her with the fleece blanket, she feared once again that Mildred might have suffered a head injury in the fall, as well as an ankle injury. There was no other reason to imagine why she'd be so afraid of a piece of old pottery.

"We're all fine," Betty assured Mildred, patting her shoulder. "And you will be too. The doctor will fix that ankle right up."

The sound of the siren grew closer, and Anne walked over to the front door and opened it. A moment later, two paramedics walked inside, carrying a stretcher between them.

"She's in here." Anne led them into the History Room.

Both Bella and Betty stood up and backed away from Mildred as the paramedics approached.

"Hello, I'm Reid," said the young man with dark hair and blue eyes. He looked about thirty and wore a white polo shirt and a pair of dark blue jeans. "And this is my partner, Kelsey." He pointed to the petite blonde, who also wore a white polo and jeans. The young woman's hair was pulled back into a short, neat ponytail.

"Thank you for coming," Mildred said, her face looking a little peaked. "Although, I wouldn't call this an emergency."

"We heard you took a fall," Reid said, "so we're glad to be here to help. Do you hurt anywhere?"

"Mainly my right ankle," Mildred told him.

Kelsey moved to examine Mildred's ankle while Reid pulled a blood pressure cuff out of the bag next to him. "Can you tell me your full name?"

"Mildred Farley."

"How did you fall, Mildred?" Ryan wrapped the cuff around Mildred's upper left arm and began to inflate it.

"I was...startled." She swallowed, and Anne could see fear shining in her eyes once more. "I guess I tried to turn around too quickly and my ankle gave way."

Reid nodded, his gaze fixed on the dial attached to the blood pressure cuff. A moment later he began unwrapping the cuff. "Well, your blood pressure is a little elevated, but that's to be expected given the circumstances. Do you have a headache or any numbness or tingling anywhere?"

"No, just the pain in my ankle. It hurts like the dickens."

Anne's distress eased a bit when she heard the familiar feistiness in Mildred's voice.

"I'm sure it does," Reid said to Mildred. Then he glanced over at his partner. "Hey, Kelsey, do we need a brace for that ankle?"

"Yes, let's put on one," Kelsey replied, rising to her feet. She smiled at Mildred. "Then it won't hurt quite so much when we move you."

Anne stepped forward. "Is there anything I can do?"

Reid shook his head as Kelsey made her way to the front door. "No, I think we'll be on our way soon. We'll transport Mildred to the medical clinic so they can check that ankle and let the doctor take a look at her."

"Oh dear," Mildred murmured, shaking her head. "I hate to be such a bother."

"It's no bother at all," Reid assured her, as Kelsey returned with an ankle brace in her hand. "That's why we're here."

Anne watched as Kelsey carefully applied the black padded brace to Mildred's rapidly swelling ankle, attaching it with Velcro straps. Then the two paramedics carefully lifted Mildred onto the stretcher and rolled it out the front door to the ambulance. Anne watched them load Mildred inside, and then Kelsey climbed in beside her as Reid headed for the driver's door.

As the ambulance drove away, Anne turned to Bella, who stood directly behind her. "I need to be there with Mildred. I know you're scheduled to leave at three, but…"

"Go," Bella interjected, "I can stay here as long as you need me."

"I can stay too," Betty offered as they all returned to the library. "Just in case Bella needs help."

Anne smiled, touched by their generosity. "Thank you both so much. And please don't mention what Mildred said about a curse to anyone."

"Don't worry, we'll handle everything here. Just let us know how Mildred is doing," Betty said.

"I will," Anne promised, heading for the kitchen to retrieve her purse.

Bella followed Anne into the kitchen. "What about the hat for Liddie?"

Anne's gaze moved to the yellow hat on the kitchen table. "Oh dear, I forgot all about it."

"I can take it to the school while Betty watches the front desk."

Anne turned to face her, so thankful for the eighteen-year-old's thoughtfulness. "Would you? That would be wonderful." She paused, not wanting her tenderhearted daughter to worry. "Just tell Liddie I was busy. I'll tell her why after she gets home from school."

"No problem," Bella said with a nod as she picked up the yellow pillbox hat.

While Bella explained her errand to Betty, Anne walked out of the library and headed toward her car. The fact that the ambulance hadn't turned on its siren when leaving reassured Anne that Mildred wasn't seriously hurt. Still, that ankle had started to look quite nasty, and Mildred's odd behavior about the clay pot still rattled her.

Why in the world would she say it was cursed? And did seeing it on display actually cause her to collapse?

Anne knew those questions would have to wait until Mildred was released from the medical center. She just hated to see the older woman in pain. The stark fear in Mildred's eyes had been real too—something Anne had rarely seen before.

* * *

When Anne arrived at Blue Hill Medical Clinic, she learned that Mildred had already been taken back to one of the examination rooms. She gave her name to the receptionist at the front desk and told her that she was a friend of Mildred Farley. Then Anne took a seat in one of the padded pea green chairs in the empty waiting area.

The minutes slowly ticked by on the wall clock as Anne waited to hear about Mildred's condition. She prayed silently for her friend, asking the Lord to watch over Mildred and heal her.

Thirty minutes later, a gust of cool air blew into the waiting area, and Anne turned to see Wendy Pyle walk through the front entrance. "Wendy," she said, happy to see her friend.

"I came as soon as I heard," Wendy said, walking over to give Anne a hug. She wore a pair of dark blue jeans and a white sweatshirt with the words *Blue Hill Panthers* embroidered in royal blue thread, along with a pair of brown penny loafers.

Wendy took a seat beside her, combing her fingers though her short black hair. "I stopped by the library to return some books, and Betty told me what happened." Concern filled her blue eyes. "Is Mildred all right?"

"She hurt her ankle, but I'm not sure if it's broken. She's been in there a while now, so I'm hoping to hear something soon."

Wendy's brow furrowed. "Betty said a piece of pottery scared her."

"Yes, as strange as it sounds, that's what happened. Mildred saw the clay pot, screamed, and tried to turn away from it, twisting her ankle in the process." Anne suppressed a shiver. "I could hear her scream and the sound of her fall all the way from the old kitchen."

"How awful," Wendy said, looking puzzled. "But Mildred Farley is one of the most sensible people I know. Why would a clay pot scare her?"

"I have no idea, but she looked terrified. She told us it was cursed."

Wendy shook her head. "That doesn't sound like Mildred at all."

"I'm worried there might be something else wrong with her," Anne confessed. "I remember my grandfather had an infection once that made him a bit...irrational. But after he started taking antibiotics, his mind was clear again."

"That's a possibility," Wendy said, leaning back in her chair. "But it's still all so strange. Where did the clay pot come from?"

Anne told Wendy about her trek to the attic earlier in the morning and the ancient treasure she'd found in one of the hatboxes. "Aunt Edie found the clay pot during a trip to Egypt, so it's quite likely Mildred has seen it before. Maybe it triggered a painful memory or something."

"Maybe," Wendy mused.

Anne stood up, tired of sitting for so long. "I'm going to get a cup of coffee. Do you want one?"

"No, thanks, I'm fine."

Anne walked over to the complimentary beverage station and poured herself a cup of coffee. Then she returned to her seat.

"Why are you limping?" Wendy asked her.

"Oh, am I?" Anne smiled. "I didn't even realize it. When I was in the attic earlier, the electricity went out for a bit and I bumped my knee on an old trunk."

"Ouch," Wendy said, grimacing in empathy. "Maybe *you* should see a doctor."

"I'm fine." Anne blew lightly on her steaming coffee before taking a cautious sip. "It's just a bit sore."

A nurse appeared in the waiting area and approached Anne and Wendy. "Anne Gibson?"

"Yes, that's me," Anne said, rising to her feet. "How is Mildred?"

The nurse smiled. "You can see for yourself. When she heard you were in the waiting room, she insisted that you come in to see her."

"Oh, good," Anne said, breathing a sigh of relief.

Wendy turned to her. "You go on back. I'll pick up Ben and Liddie after school and take them home with me. You can pick them up later, after all the dust settles."

"Oh, thank you," Anne said. "I'll be there as soon as I can."

"Take your time," Wendy told her. "And please give Mildred my best."

"I will." Anne watched Wendy walk out the door and then followed the nurse back into the patient area, where four of the six examination rooms stood open and empty.

The nurse led her into Mildred's room, closing the door behind her. "Here's your friend," the nurse told Mildred, who lay in a hospital bed.

"Anne." Mildred smiled, her color much better than it had been at the library. "It was so kind of you to come."

Anne walked over to the bedside. "I wouldn't be anywhere else." She sat down on the padded stool next to the bed. Mildred wore a white-and-blue print hospital gown, partially covered by a white bedsheet. Judging by the large bump at the end of the bed, Mildred's ankle was propped on a pillow of some sort.

A small monitor above the bed showed Mildred's heart rate and oxygen level, which both seemed normal to Anne.

"How are you feeling?" Anne asked as the nurse quietly left the room.

"Better," Mildred said with a small smile. "The doctor gave me some medicine for the pain. He took X-rays too, and I'm still waiting for the results."

Anne reached over and gently clasped Mildred's hand. Her skin was warm now, although it still felt frail. "I'm so sorry about what happened."

"It's not your fault, dear," Mildred said. "It was that horrible clay pot. Why on earth is it on display in the library?"

"I found it in the attic this morning," Anne explained. "Quite by accident, really. I was searching for a hat for Liddie, and I came across the clay pot in one of Aunt Edie's old hatboxes. It was wrapped in a lovely scarf, along with a note that said the pot was found near someplace called Armana and the scarf was from Luxor."

Mildred closed her eyes for a long moment, saying nothing. Anne glanced at the monitor and noticed that her heart rate had suddenly gone up a bit.

"I know where the clay pot is from," Mildred said at last. "I was there when Edie found it."

Before Mildred could continue, the door to the exam room opened and Dr. Tony Shields walked inside. He and Anne had graduated from Blue Hill High School together, and he worked with four other doctors at the Blue Hill Medical Clinic. He gave Anne a smile of recognition and then turned his attention to Mildred.

"Your results are back," he said, closing the door behind him. "And the good news is that your ankle isn't broken."

"Well, that's a relief," Mildred said. "And the bad news?"

"You have a severe sprain." Dr. Shields pulled up a rolling stool on the opposite side of the bed. "That means you need to pamper yourself for the next few weeks so it has plenty of time to heal."

"So I don't need a cast," Mildred said with a sigh of relief.

"No cast, but we're going to keep that padded brace on." Then his expression grew more stern. "And I mean what I said about pampering yourself, Mildred. In fact, I want that ankle propped up on a pillow during the day. That means no cooking, no cleaning, no gadding about town."

Mildred sniffed. "I don't gad about, Doctor. But I can't stay housebound for the next several weeks."

He sighed, glancing over at Anne. "Well, my suggestion is to stay at the nursing home for the next few weeks. They can take care of you and even provide some physical therapy when the time is right. You won't have to worry about anything except getting plenty of rest."

"Absolutely not," Mildred said, a flash of stubbornness in her eyes. "I'll be perfectly capable of taking care of myself."

"And I can help," Anne offered. "I can come over every day, and I'm sure others in the community will help as well."

Dr. Shields frowned as he looked at Mildred. "It's your decision, but if that ankle doesn't heal properly, it could cause trouble for years to come."

Mildred nodded. "I understand."

Anne looked at Tony, not sure if she should bring up Mildred's statement about a curse. "Does she have any other injuries? She took a pretty hard fall from the sound of it."

Dr. Shields shook his head. "I gave her a thorough examination. No head injury or other broken bones, although she will have a few bruises come morning."

"Does that mean I can go home now?" Mildred asked hopefully.

"Yes," Dr. Shields said with a smile. "But if you change your mind about the nursing home, just give me a call and I'll make all the arrangements."

"Thank you," Mildred said. "I appreciate it."

He stood up and reached over to give Mildred's forearm a gentle pat. "You take care, Mildred, and keep taking those pain pills as long as you have any discomfort."

"Thank you, Tony." Anne rose to her feet. "We'll take good care of her."

He gave them a wave as he headed for the door, almost colliding with the nurse who was on her way into the room with a folder in her hand.

"I have your discharge papers," the nurse said to Mildred as she made her way around the doctor and continued into the room. "I'll just go over these instructions with you, and you can be on your way."

"I can't wait," Mildred said, sitting up in the bed.

Anne listened to the nurse go over the instructions, committing them to memory. She felt responsible for Mildred, not only because the woman had fallen in the library, but because she was a good friend.

When the nurse was finished, she gathered Mildred's clothes from the small closet in the exam room. "I'll help you change out of that gown," the nurse told Mildred. "

Anne moved toward the door. "I'll pull my car up to the front entrance and wait for you there."

"That's fine," the nurse said. "We'll be out soon."

Anne left the room so Mildred could change into her clothes. As she walked to her car, she called Wendy to update her on Mildred's condition and let her know she'd be taking Mildred home and getting her settled in before she picked up the kids. Wendy told Anne she'd already planned on the kids joining them for supper, so she could take her time.

When Anne pulled up to the entrance, Mildred was already outside the door, sitting in a wheelchair. The nurse stood behind the wheelchair as Anne parked the Impala and then got out to open the front passenger door.

The nurse helped Mildred get settled in the front seat. "You may want to rent a pair of crutches from Thrifty's Drugstore," the nurse suggested. "That way you'll be able to get around your house without putting too much weight on that ankle."

"That's a good idea," Mildred said. "Thank you so much."

Anne rounded the car and climbed into the driver's seat. Then she turned to Mildred with a smile. "Let's get you home."

* * *

A short time later, they arrived at Mildred's house. Anne had stopped at Thrifty's along the way and rented a pair of crutches for Mildred to use. They'd also stopped by Newlands' Grocery Store so Anne could pick up a few grocery items that Mildred requested while the older woman waited in the car.

Anne helped Mildred inside her home and got her settled in her bed. She carefully propped a pillow under Mildred's ankle and then covered her with a quilt.

"Are you comfortable?" Anne asked.

Mildred nodded. "Yes, it feels good to be home. But I wish you wouldn't fuss over me. You have the library to run and the kids to look after."

Anne smiled as she perched on the edge of the mattress. "There's nowhere else I'd rather be. I just wish this had never happened."

"It's not your fault. It's that clay pot that caused this. I just hate to think what else might happen until you get rid of it."

Anne looked at her for a long moment. "You really believe it's cursed?"

"I *know* it's cursed. Edie knew it too, but she still insisted on bringing it back to Blue Hill with her even after she heard tales about it. She said it was all just silly superstition."

Anne didn't want to upset Mildred, but perhaps talking about it might relieve some of the woman's fear. "Tell me about your trip to Egypt."

Mildred smiled. "Oh, it was a long time ago. About forty years, actually. In 1975. But Edie and I had a grand time. We spent almost the entire month of April touring the pyramids and traveling along the Nile in a lovely passenger boat called a *dahabeah*. I enjoyed every moment of it until we reached Armana."

"That's where Aunt Edie found the clay pot?"

"Yes. Armana is a large archeological site that's located on the east bank of the Nile. They allow tourists a small dig area to search for artifacts. Edie found quite a treasure when she unearthed that pot, according to the head archeologist."

"Did he think the pot was cursed?"

Mildred shook her head. "Oh, goodness, no. He was British and quite proper and stuffy. But an Egyptian woman saw Edie holding the clay pot in the marketplace and became very frightened. She told us, through an interpreter, that the clay pot was cursed. She began to tell us of the terrible things that could happen, but one of the shopkeepers in the market shooed her away from us before the woman could elaborate." Mildred sighed. "At the time, I thought it was a silly superstition too, and

I encouraged Edie to keep it—which turned out to be a big mistake."

"Why do you say that?"

Mildred closed her eyes. "There are so many reasons, I don't even know where to begin. It started in Egypt and continued when we returned to Blue Hill. I finally convinced Edie to get rid of the clay pot and I never saw it again—until today."

Anne felt a twinge of guilt for her part in Mildred's distress, even if she found it irrational. She didn't believe in curses or other nonsense. "But doesn't the fact the clay pot was in Aunt Edie's attic for all these years prove that it isn't cursed?"

"It *is* cursed," Mildred said firmly, shifting under the quilt. "Maybe the curse has been dormant since the pot has been out of sight, but now that you've uncovered it again, there's no telling what might happen."

Anne could see that Mildred was getting agitated and decided they'd talked enough about the clay pot for one day. "Why don't I make you some soup?"

"Thank you, dear, but I'm not hungry." Mildred looked around the room, as if afraid that she might see something else in the shadows.

"Then at least let me get you a glass of water. The nurse said it's important for you to stay hydrated." Anne stood up and turned toward the bedroom door.

"Wait," Mildred said, her voice strained. "There's something else you should know."

CHAPTER THREE

Anne turned back to Mildred. "What is it?"

Mildred hesitated for a long moment. "I know you find this all hard to believe, Anne, and I don't blame you. I didn't believe it either when strange things started occurring forty years ago. Then something happened...."

Anne took a step closer to the bed, concerned at the color draining from Mildred's cheeks. "Look, we don't have to talk about this right now. It can wait...."

"No, it can't wait." Mildred looked up at her. "Edie wasn't the only one to find something at that dig site near Armana. I found a lovely scarab necklace, a necklace that was almost as old as Edie's clay pot. Scarabs, of course, represent scarab beetles, and they were a popular amulet in ancient Egypt. Mine was carved from soapstone and covered in a beautiful blue glaze. I hung it from a gold chain, and it was quite eye-catching—certainly like nothing you'd usually see in Blue Hill."

As Anne listened to Mildred, she wondered why she hadn't heard this story about Egypt before, from either her aunt or Mildred. Aunt Edie had traveled to so many places and told so many wonderful stories about her journeys that it might be possible Anne had forgotten a few. But she was sure she'd remember a story about a cursed Egyptian clay pot.

"When Edie and I returned to Blue Hill," Mildred continued, "my scarab necklace was quite a conversation starter. Then one day the necklace simply vanished. I'd put it in my dresser drawer after having lunch out with a friend, and the next day the drawer was empty."

"Someone must have taken it," Anne said.

Mildred shook her head. "No, that's what I thought too. But the police eventually cleared all the possible suspects. They assumed I'd lost it, but I knew I had placed it in that drawer. It's been forty years and I've never seen that necklace again. It vanished exactly three days before other strange things began happening in Blue Hill."

"What things?"

Before Mildred could reply, the telephone rang. "Excuse me." Mildred reached over to her bed stand and picked up the cordless receiver. "Hello? Oh yes, Coraline, I'm fine. Yes, I took quite a tumble."

Anne moved toward the bedroom door so that Mildred could enjoy her phone call in private. She walked to the kitchen and finished unloading the groceries she'd brought in earlier. Among them was some sliced Virginia ham from the deli counter at Newlands', a loaf of wheat bread, and some mayonnaise. She made a sandwich for Mildred, adding a dill pickle to the plate, along with a few potato chips that she found in a cupboard. Then she filled a glass with ice and added water and a straw.

As Anne wiped the bread crumbs off the counter, she noticed that Mildred's small kitchen was neat as a pin. Mildred had a housekeeper come in once a week to help keep the place tidy, so Anne didn't need to worry about Mildred trying to clean while she was recuperating.

Thankfully, everything Mildred might need while her ankle healed could be found on the first floor of the two-story bungalow. The living room and cozy dining room were just a few steps from the kitchen. The master bedroom was down the short hallway, with a master bath connected to it. Even though Mildred would have to use crutches until her ankle healed, at least her small house would make it easier to do so. A stairway off the living room led to the second story, where two spare bedrooms and a bathroom were available for guests.

Anne carried the plate and the glass back to Mildred's bedroom.

"All right, Coraline," Mildred said into the phone. "I'll see you tomorrow. Thanks again for calling."

Anne placed the plate and glass on the bedside table as Mildred hung up the phone. "I know you said you're not hungry, but I made you something to eat, just in case you change your mind."

"Thank you, Anne," Mildred said, picking up the plate and setting it on her lap. "This sandwich looks too good to resist. And it's almost time for my favorite television show." She reached for the remote control on her bedside table. "Now, you go on home. I'll be fine here until tomorrow."

"Are you sure?" Anne still wanted to ask her about the strange incidents surrounding the clay pot but noticed the fatigue in Mildred's eyes. More than anything, the older woman simply needed nourishment and rest right now.

"I'm positive," Mildred said with a faint smile. "If you could just place those crutches beside the bed, I'll be fine here on my own."

"Of course," Anne said, walking over to the corner, where she'd propped the crutches against the wall. As she carried them over to the bed, she noticed Mildred staring at her.

"Why are you limping?" Mildred asked.

"Oh, it's nothing," Anne replied. "I hurt my knee earlier today while I was in the attic. It's just a bit sore."

Mildred arched a brow. "Did it happen after you found that clay pot?"

"Well, yes," Anne admitted. "The electricity went out for a few minutes, and I was trying to find my way to the attic door in the dark. That's when I bumped into a trunk."

"And I'm guessing the electricity went out *after* you found the clay pot?"

"Yes, it did," Anne said slowly. "But that was due to the thunderstorm, not some curse."

"It's just like before," Mildred said with a resigned sigh. "And it's only going to get worse until you destroy that pot."

Anne didn't know what to say. She didn't want to let a silly superstition lead to the destruction of an ancient artifact, but Mildred was upset enough already, so she wasn't going to argue with her.

"I'd better go pick up my kids," Anne said, changing the subject. "Do you want me to get you another ice pack before I leave?"

"No, thank you," Mildred said, trying to hide a yawn. "I'm fine for now."

"Then I will see you tomorrow. Please call me tonight if you need anything, no matter what time."

"I will," Mildred promised, leaning her head against the pillow propped behind her. "Good night, Anne. And thank you again."

"Good night." Anne left the bedroom, checking the back door to make sure it was locked before leaving the house and locking the front door with the key Mildred had given her. She said a silent prayer for Mildred, asking the Lord to watch over her friend. Then she walked to her car as gray clouds filled the sky and thunder rumbled in the distance.

* * *

It was half past seven that evening when Anne picked up Ben and Liddie from Wendy's house. She filled Wendy in on Mildred's condition, explaining that she planned to visit often until Mildred recovered. Then she packed her kids into the Impala and headed home.

When Anne pulled into the driveway, she shifted the car into park with a weary sigh. *Home at last.*

Ben popped open the back door and climbed out, but Liddie stayed belted in her seat.

"Mom," Liddie said quietly, "is our house haunted?"

"Oh my goodness," Anne said, keeping her tone light, "where did you hear that?"

"Christian Pyle said a curse made Mildred fall and hurt herself. He said that means our house is haunted."

Anne climbed out of the car and opened Liddie's door to unclasp her seat belt. Then she took her daughter's hand, helping her out of the car. "And how old is Christian?"

"He's ten."

"Well, I'm thirty-four," Anne said with a smile, "which is a lot older than ten, and I'm telling you that there's no such thing as a haunted house."

Liddie grinned. "Good, because I like our house and don't want to leave."

Anne reached out to give her a hug. "We're not leaving," she promised. "Now, tell me about the silly yellow hat day. Was it fun?"

"Yes," Liddie exclaimed, "and I had one of the silliest hats! Grace even came and took our picture for the newspaper."

"Well, I can't wait to see it."

When they reached the house, Anne found Ben standing in the kitchen, digging into a bag of chips. Their chocolate Labrador, Hershey, stood next to him, waiting eagerly for some crumbs to fall to the floor. "I thought Wendy fed you supper?"

"She did, but I'm still hungry." Ben gave her a sheepish smile, one hand stuck deep in the bag of potato chips. "Can I have some chips for a snack?"

"*May* I," she corrected him.

"May I?" Ben echoed.

Anne craved a crisp, salty snack herself. It just occurred to her that she hadn't eaten anything since lunch. "Yes, you may, but why don't we save it for our movie night?"

Liddie squealed with delight, jumping up and down. "Movie night! We get to have a movie night!"

Anne smiled, certain it was the perfect way to end this strange day. "You two get into your pajamas and grab some snacks and something to drink."

"Sounds good to me," Ben said. He placed a plastic clip on the potato chip bag and then tucked it under his arm. "What movie are we going to watch?"

"*Finding Nemo!*" Liddie shouted, still jumping on her toes. "Please, *please*, let's watch *Finding Nemo*."

"Again?" Ben said with a groan, then looked over at Anne. "Mom, do we have to?"

"You can each pick a movie," Anne said. "Since it's Friday night, we'll have a double feature."

"Good," Ben said, heading out of the kitchen. "Because I want to watch *Undercover Kids*."

"That's boring." Liddie followed behind her brother. "Why don't you pick *A Little Princess*?"

"That's a girl movie."

"But it has a little monkey in it..."

Anne smiled as their voices faded down the hallway, certain that *A Little Princess* was the last movie Ben would choose. But despite his reaction to *Finding Nemo*, Anne knew that he liked that movie almost as much as Liddie. By the time it was over, she suspected that both kids would be fast asleep.

And since Anne was feeling a little sleepy herself, she decided to make sure all the lights were turned out in the library so she could settle into the sofa for the evening. First, she made her way to her bedroom and donned a warm flannel nightgown, robe, and slippers. October usually got a little chilly at night, and she hadn't turned on the heat yet.

A light rain pattered against the windowpanes as she made her way downstairs to the first floor. She checked the front door to make sure it was locked, then walked through the other rooms, straightening chairs and making sure everything was in order. When she reached the checkout desk, she saw the clay pot on the shelf below the counter.

She picked it up and carried it back to the Egyptian display in the History Room. *Funny how such a small object could cause such a big fuss,* she thought to herself. She set it in the center of the display and then stepped back to look at it.

She'd been thinking about Mildred's pleas to get rid of the clay pot. On the one hand, it would give Mildred peace of mind and, after what the woman had been through today, she deserved at least that. Yet, Aunt Edie had been faced with the same dilemma and had obviously chosen to keep the pot. She'd hidden it from view, making Mildred believe the pot had been destroyed. That told Anne that the clay pot had meant something to Aunt Edie. And how could she destroy such an interesting piece of history?

"Mom?"

Anne jumped, startled by the voice behind her. She turned around to see Ben, who now wore his Spider-Man pajamas, his bare feet silent on the floor as he approached her. She placed one hand on her chest, feeling her heart race beneath her palm. "I didn't hear you come downstairs."

"You're not scared of the pot, are you?" His hazel gaze was quizzical as he looked up at her. "Because that curse stuff is just make-believe."

Anne smiled at his serious tone. "Not scared at all. And I'm glad you know it's nonsense too."

"It's silly," Ben said, rolling his eyes. "There's no such thing as curses or haunted houses. I can't believe some people are so dumb."

Anne took a step toward him. "I wouldn't call them dumb. We each see the world in different ways, and some people are raised to believe in superstitions."

"Why?"

She reached out to gently smooth his short dark hair. "Well, in the past, it was one way of explaining things that people didn't understand. Like believing the world was flat or that tomatoes were poisonous."

He snorted. "People thought tomatoes were poisonous?"

She nodded. "Some people used to believe they were toxic and refused to eat them."

"But if we didn't eat tomatoes we couldn't have pizza," he said, his eyes round with disbelief. "Or spaghetti with meatballs, or chili soup!"

She laughed. "Well, everyone obviously didn't believe that tomatoes were poisonous, so we can enjoy those foods today. But that's just an example of how old wives' tales or superstitions can get started."

Ben's gaze moved to the clay pot. "I wonder how the story of the pot being cursed started?"

Anne wondered the same thing and was more curious than ever to discover the "strange events" around Blue Hill that Mildred had mentioned. What exactly had happened forty years ago when Aunt Edie had brought the clay pot back to Blue Hill with her?

"Maybe we can research it together," Anne told Ben. "We can look up the history of when the clay pot was made and learn about its origins."

He wrinkled his nose. "That sounds too much like homework."

She laughed. "Not to me. How about if I start the research and you can jump in and help me if you feel like it?"

"Okay," he said with a shrug. "But don't start tonight. We have two movies to watch."

Anne laughed. "All right. You head on upstairs and I'll be right behind you. I just want to make sure all the lights are off down here."

"Okay, I'll tell Liddie to get her snack and drink." Ben hurried out of the room, and a moment later she heard his footsteps on the staircase.

Anne took a last look around before finding herself once more in the History Room. She'd been debating whether to remove the clay pot from the display, but what kind of example would that set for her children? Anne had told Ben she didn't believe the pot was cursed, but removing it would give them the opposite message.

"The pot stays," she said out loud, then turned and headed out of the room, turning the light off just before she walked through the open doorway and into the foyer. She made her way to the second floor and could already hear the opening music from *Finding Nemo* drifting from the living room.

"Hey, wait for me," Anne shouted, turning off the last light in the library section of the second floor before hurrying toward their private living area.

She found Ben and Liddie already snuggled under a blanket on the living room sofa. After she retrieved an apple and a glass of tea from the kitchen, she joined them there to watch the movie. The three of them cuddled together, enjoying their snacks and laughing at some of the antics of Nemo and his friends.

When Liddie fell asleep in the middle of the movie, Anne whispered to Ben. "She's asleep. Do you want to watch *Undercover Kids* now?"

"No, that's all right," he whispered, his gaze intent on the screen. "We can finish watching this, just in case she wakes up."

Anne smiled, loving the fact that Ben was still young enough to enjoy watching an animated movie with his mom. She breathed a sigh of contentment, thanking the Lord for these precious moments with her family.

Her cell phone buzzed on the sofa next to her, indicating that she'd received a text message. She glanced at the time, noting that it was almost ten o'clock. As she picked up her phone to retrieve the message, her first thought was that Mildred needed her. Then she saw that the text message was from Alex.

She found herself smiling as she opened the message.

Hey, Anne, I heard what happened to Mildred at the library today. How are you doing?

Anne began texting her reply. *I'm fine now but was really worried about Mildred. Feel bad she hurt herself here.*

A few moments later, her cell phone buzzed again. She glanced over at Ben, but he was oblivious to the sound, his focus on the movie.

Her gaze moved to the text thread on her phone as they continued the conversation.

Not your fault, Anne.

I know, Alex. I just wish it hadn't happened. Kids and I are relaxing with movie night now.

Ryan and I doing the same. He picked Godzilla. Not too relaxing — LOL.

She chuckled softly as she began typing her reply, so thankful that they were friends. The fact that she and Alex were both single parents, with him raising his orphaned nephew, gave them a special bond.

We started with Finding Nemo *and are now watching* Undercover Kids. *If Ben falls asleep soon, I'm going to watch* The Princess Bride.

That's one of my favorites.

Anne smiled. *Mine too.*

Looks like Godzilla is about to attack, so I'd better sign off. Have a good night, Anne.

You too. She set her cell phone beside her and pulled the afghan more snugly around her shoulders, feeling more calm and relaxed than she had all day.

* * *

On Saturday, Anne worked at the library until it closed at one o'clock. Then she waited for Hannah Pyle to come to the house to watch the kids before making her way to the office of the *Blue Hill Gazette.*

The rain clouds had dissipated overnight, revealing a bright blue sky this afternoon. Even her knee felt better, although it had been a little stiff this morning.

The sun warmed her face as she parked her car in front of the office. Hannah had plans to take Liddie to the park while Ben attended his first youth membership class at the Blue Hill Community Church. Pastor Tom had organized the class to teach the fourth- and fifth-graders about the responsibilities of membership in the church and how to serve the church and their community.

Grace Hawkins, the editor of the *Gazette*, met Anne at the door. "Well, hello there. I was just on my way out."

Anne smiled. "Are you in pursuit of a hot story?"

"I'm on my way to see the largest pumpkin in the county." Grace grinned as she held up her camera. Her blonde hair, translucent complexion, and statuesque beauty always made Anne believe that Grace belonged on the other side of the camera. She easily could have worked as a model.

"That sounds fun."

"It will be. The story might even make the front page of the *Gazette*."

Anne knew Grace wasn't joking, and that was one of the reasons she loved living in Blue Hill. Most of the top stories in the *Gazette* reported good news instead of bad, like growing the county's biggest pumpkin or celebrating silly hat day at Blue Hill Elementary School.

"Although," Grace said slowly, her gaze fixed on Anne's face, "I did hear about another possible story—one involving the library."

Anne swallowed a groan. "I think I know what you're going to say."

"News travels fast around here. I heard about the curse of an Egyptian pot in the library and Mildred's fall yesterday afternoon. How is she, by the way?"

"She has a badly sprained ankle but otherwise seems to be fine."

"That's good to hear. I'm tempted to interview you about the story, but it all sounds rather far-fetched to me. Is this curse rumor real or some kind of joke?"

"I don't believe the curse is real, but Mildred has it in her head that the clay pot caused her fall. From what I gather, it's all related to something that happened forty years ago. That's why I'm here today. I'm hoping to find something in the newspaper morgue to help me understand how this curse nonsense started."

"The office is empty at the moment," Grace said as she stepped outside the open door, "but the receptionist should be back from her trip to the courthouse soon."

"No problem. I can find my way to the morgue." Anne smiled. "I've been there a few times before, as you know."

"Well, good luck with your research. And keep me posted about this alleged curse. I'm sure the pumpkin story can wait if something juicier comes along."

Anne chuckled. "I'll do that. Have fun with the pumpkin."

"I plan to."

After Grace departed, Anne walked into the empty newspaper office and headed toward the back room where the newspaper archives were stored. Once inside, she turned on one of the two microfiche machines and waited for it to warm up. Then she searched the rows of binders for a microfiche reel from April 1975.

Once she found it, Anne sat down in front of the microfiche machine and loaded the reel, eager to find information about the mysterious clay pot and the strange events that had surrounded it forty years ago.

It didn't take long for her to locate a brief news story about Mildred's stolen necklace.

EGYPTIAN NECKLACE STOLEN FROM FARLEY HOME

A valuable souvenir was taken from the home of Blue Hill resident Mildred Farley on Monday, May 5. Farley reported that a scarab necklace, an ancient Egyptian artifact she obtained during a recent trip to Egypt, mysteriously disappeared from her home. Police suspect the thief had access to the Farley house and stole the necklace, although they did not provide the name of any suspects. Farley reports that nothing else was taken from the home.

Anne sat back in the wooden chair, noting that nothing about a curse had been mentioned in the article. Then she remembered Mildred telling her that the strange incidents didn't begin until three days *after* the scarab necklace disappeared. Anne scanned the rest of the newspaper and then quickly moved onto the next edition. There, on the front page, she saw a huge headline.

MYSTERIOUS POWER OUTAGE THREATENS
TO SHUT DOWN BLUE HILL

A sudden power outage blanketed Blue Hill in darkness on Thursday, May 8. The outage was confined to the town of Blue Hill and the surrounding area. Crews worked through the night to discover the cause of the power failure. There were no storms in the area, and, according to the town electrician, Walter Ochs, no malfunctions were found at the power plant located on the outskirts of Blue Hill.

The power returned abruptly a day later, a sudden surge causing several electrical appliances to malfunction around town. The hospital lost the use of its new X-ray machine and had to postpone several elective surgeries to make certain other equipment was not affected.

More electrical surges followed throughout the next three days, all of unknown cause and origin, resulting in damage to several homes and businesses in town. The school was closed, as well as many businesses on Main Street, to prevent any further problems or mishaps. Blue Hill has experienced power outages before, but the severity of this outage is the first in Blue Hill's history and has baffled town leaders. The cost of the damage is estimated to reach nearly fifty thousand dollars, and the town council has hired an expert to study the problem and file a report within the next month to prevent such an occurrence from happening again.

According to one eyewitness, only one home, belonging to Miss Edie Summers of Bluebell Lane, was unaffected by the power outage and suffered no ill consequences from the electrical surges over the past three days.

Anne sat back in her chair, perplexed by what she'd just read. "Aunt Edie's house didn't lose power?" she murmured to herself. "How is that possible—unless the curse *is* real?"

Chapter Four

D on't be ridiculous," Anne chastised herself as soon as that thought entered her head.

Just as she'd told Ben last night, people believed in superstitions when they didn't understand why something happened. Once she figured out the reasons behind the unusual power outage and the disappearance of Mildred's scarab necklace, it would all make sense.

But how could she solve this forty-year-old mystery?

Her gaze moved back to the newspaper article she'd just read. Walter Ochs was a fellow member of the Blue Hill Community Church and lived at the Blue Hill Retirement Center. Maybe he could add some details to the story of the power outage—details that might explain why Aunt Edie's house had been spared from the mishap.

But first she needed to finish searching the newspaper archives, just to make certain she didn't miss anything else. She began scrolling through the microfiche once more, looking for any news articles about the Egyptian clay pot, the scarab necklace, or any other strange occurrences.

It didn't take her long to find one.

One week after the power outage, another headline on the front page caught her attention.

FLU OUTBREAK SHUTS DOWN BLUE HILL ELEMENTARY SCHOOL

Blue Hill Elementary School closed on Thursday, May 16, due to a large number of students and staff suffering from a strange flulike virus. According to the assistant principal, Marlys Tubbs, several students became ill during an afternoon presentation given by Miss Edie Summers, where she spoke of her recent trip to Egypt and displayed several souvenirs she'd brought back with her.

More absences the following day led school authorities to close the school in the hope of containing the virus to keep it from spreading. Miss Tubbs stated that any rumors that the virus was caused by a cursed Egyptian clay pot displayed by Miss Summers were completely false. Miss Tubbs asks parents and teachers to refrain from spreading these rumors and plans to reopen the school on Monday, May 19.

"There it is," Anne murmured to herself, quickly scanning the story again. "The first mention of the curse."

She continued her search, soon finding several letters to the editor with the same theme. The first one was written by Aunt Edie's former neighbor, Hector Mattison. Anne remembered him as a cantankerous middle-aged man who used to complain about kids plucking apples from the tree in his front yard. Anne had even done so herself once or twice when she was walking home from high school. The apple tree's branches had hung low over the sidewalk, making the luscious green fruit almost impossible to resist.

She began to read the published letter, hearing Hector's deep, querulous voice in her mind.

Dear Editor,

A scourge has fallen upon Blue Hill, and it is up to our town leaders to rid us of it. I speak, of course, of the hideous clay pot that Edie Summers brought back with her from Egypt. Nothing but trouble has happened since that cursed object appeared in our town. First the power outage, then the flu outbreak at the school, and now my new tomato plants have all withered up and died. Yes, there was a light frost last night, but I can't remember the last time it froze in May, so nobody better try to tell me any different! It's time for that pot to go back to Egypt. And if Edie doesn't like it, she can go too!

Hector B. Mattison

The other letters followed a similar theme, although the writers expressed various levels of fear instead of anger. She knew that the two emotions were really the same. She remembered her late husband, Eric, telling her once that anger was often based on fear or a feeling of helplessness. She had always tried to remember that on the few occasions when she'd been confronted by an angry patron at her library in New York. Once she'd identified their underlying fear, she could usually solve their problem and defuse the situation.

Perhaps that was the reason why Aunt Edie had hidden the clay pot away in the attic—to defuse the situation that had Hector and so many other Blue Hill residents upset. Otherwise, every bad thing that happened around town, whether a contagious flu virus or a late spring freeze, could be blamed on an ancient Egyptian artifact.

Releasing a long sigh, Anne continued to search through the May 1975 newspaper archives, but she could find no further mention of the Egyptian clay pot. She removed the microfiche reel and returned it to the binder before turning off the machine. Then she grabbed her purse and headed out of the newspaper morgue.

The receptionist was seated back at her desk, chatting on the phone. Anne gave her a friendly wave as she made her way out of the office and into the bright October sunshine. She glanced at her watch, happy to see that she had plenty of time to visit Walter Ochs before she made her way to Mildred's house. She'd called Mildred earlier and had been pleased to hear that Patty O'Hanlon, a home health aide employed by the Blue Hill Medical Clinic, had been assigned to stop by Mildred's house every day to check on her and offer assistance. Mildred told Anne that Patty had even brought a basket of blueberry muffins with her this morning.

Now that she thought about it, Anne decided that Walter might like some muffins too. She climbed into her car and headed toward Coffee Joe's to buy a dozen assorted muffins to take with her to the retirement home. Even at ninety-three, Walter was something of a ladies' man and would probably delight in sharing his muffins with some of the female residents.

A short time later, Anne arrived at the retirement home carrying a box of muffins and a few paper napkins as she walked through the door. She was about to head down the hallway to Walter's room when she spotted him sitting in the sunroom.

Alex, his great-nephew, sat next to him.

"Hello, there," Anne said as she approached them.

Walter looked up and smiled, instantly rising to his feet. "Well, this is a nice surprise!"

Alex rose too, following his uncle's example. "Hello, Anne. What brings you here?"

"I came to see Walter," Anne explained, setting the muffins and napkins on the table. "But it's nice to see you too."

A couple of older ladies sat near the television, watching a show about interior decorating. Anne recognized them as Clara Bayles and Ruby Hanes, both friends of Walter.

"Please, have a seat," Anne told the men. "I promise not to stay too long."

"You can stay as long as you like," Walter said, his blue eyes twinkling as he pulled a chair out for Anne. "I've never been one to chase away a pretty young lady—especially one bearing muffins."

Alex smiled. "Don't you think Anne's a little young for you, Uncle Walt?"

"For *me*, maybe," Walter said, grinning at his nephew.

Alex's face turned red. "Now, Uncle Walt..."

Walter chuckled. "Just teasing, my boy. Although, I'm not sure what you're waiting for." Before Alex could reply, Walter reached for a raspberry muffin and turned his attention to Anne. "Now, to what do I owe the pleasure of this visit?"

She smiled as the three of them sat down at the table. "I'm hoping you can help me with something that happened forty years ago—back in 1975 to be exact."

"1975?" Alex whistled low. "That's before you and I were born."

"I know," she said. "Apparently, there was a big power outage in Blue Hill in May of that year. I'm hoping Walter might remember it."

"I sure do," Walter said. He split the muffin in two and set it on the napkin in front of him. "I pulled a double shift and worked through the night trying to fix the problem, and when I finally got home the next morning, the telephone never stopped ringing." He looked between Alex and Anne. "You two might not remember, but back then landline phones didn't have a silent button. The only solution I had was to take the phone off the hook, and as the town electrician, I couldn't do that. So, needless to say, I didn't get much sleep for a few days."

Alex plucked a chocolate chip muffin from the box. "So tell me about this power outage. It must have been a real doozy."

"Well, I read about it in an old newspaper article," Anne said, explaining what details she knew while Walter filled in the rest. His story matched the article she'd read, including the extensive damage to electrical machines and appliances around town.

"So what's brought all this up now?" Alex asked, curiosity shining in his blue eyes.

"An Egyptian clay pot I found in the attic," Anne replied. "Apparently, it's to blame for the power outage forty years ago, along with other strange incidents."

"Ah," Walter said, nodding. "The cursed clay pot. I remember now. Most people around town truly did believe it was to blame for the power outage."

"And how about you?" Anne asked Walter.

The older man smiled. "Not for a minute. I'm not one for fairy tales. You can ask Alex if you don't believe me." He leaned back in his chair. "But it drove me crazy not knowing what caused all the trouble. Even the so-called expert that the town brought in couldn't explain why the power outage happened or the electrical surges that followed."

Alex held up both hands. "Hold on. Is this connected to Mildred's fall at the library yesterday?"

"I'm afraid so," Anne said, actually relieved that the news about the cursed pot hadn't reached everyone in Blue Hill. Then she told him about Mildred's reaction to it.

Alex stared at Anne for a long moment. "You're serious? Mildred Farley thinks that clay pot is actually cursed?"

"Yes," Anne replied. "In fact, Mildred's convinced of it. That's why I've been doing some research into what happened forty years ago that caused Aunt Edie to hide the Egyptian pot in her attic. I'm hoping I can find something to show Mildred that there's a reasonable explanation for everything that happened."

Walter reached for another muffin. "That's a tall order after all this time."

"I know," Anne admitted. "I just don't understand how the Egyptian pot came to be blamed in the first place. I'm sure Aunt Edie didn't believe it caused the power outage, and Mildred isn't one to start rumors."

The sound of chairs scraping behind her made Anne turn around. She saw Clara and Ruby approaching their table.

"We can tell you exactly who started those rumors," Clara announced.

"And why," Ruby added.

Anne stared at the two older women. Clara barely stood five feet tall and had cheerful blue eyes and dimples in her plump pink cheeks. Ruby was tall and thin, with perfectly coifed snow white hair. They both wore soft pastel track suits, Clara in pink and Ruby in lavender.

"Please join us, ladies," Walter said with a smile, rising to his feet and pulling out a chair for each woman. "Anne brought us some delicious muffins."

Ruby sat down next to Alex. "They do look good."

Clara took a seat next to Anne and reached for a blueberry muffin. "Let's split one, Ruby." She tore it in half, then placed one half on a napkin and slid it toward Ruby, keeping the other half for herself.

"Well, isn't this nice," Ruby said, a dimple dancing in each cheek. She turned to Alex. "And how is that nephew of yours doing?"

"Ryan's doing well," Alex said with a smile. "He keeps me on my toes, that's for sure." Then he turned to Anne. "Which reminds me, is it all right if Ryan comes to your place with Ben after school on Monday? I've got a job out of town, and I'm not sure I'll be back in time."

"That's fine. Ben invited a new classmate to visit after school on Monday, so he'll be thrilled to have Ryan join them." Then Anne turned to Clara, eager to steer the conversation back to the curse of the Egyptian pot. "You were saying that you knew how the curse rumors got started."

"Oh yes," Clara said with a nod, "we were there. Weren't we, Ruby?"

"We sure were." Ruby took a dainty bite of her muffin. "It happened at a meeting of the Blue Hill Garden Club. We met once a month at the community center and usually had a guest speaker. At the May meeting, Edie Summers and Mildred Farley came to speak to us about their trip to Egypt."

"It was fascinating," Clara said. "Edie was such a wonderful speaker. She really made Egypt come alive. Both she and Mildred brought souvenirs from the trip, as well as photographs, and even some pressed flowers so we could see some of the native Egyptian flora."

"Oh, this blueberry muffin is so good," Ruby said, reaching for another one. "I can't eat just half. Do you want to split this one with me, Clara?"

"Well, I can't let you eat that whole thing by yourself," Clara said with a mischievous smile. Then she turned to Walter. "You're probably sorry you invited us to join you. Soon you won't have any muffins left!"

"Not at all," Walter said with a twinkle in his eyes. "If we run out, one of you ladies can grab another fellow and the four of us can go on a double date to Coffee Joe's and buy some more."

Ruby chuckled. "A double date, indeed. Oh, Walter Ochs, you haven't changed a bit since you were a teenager. Always thinking up ways to finagle a date."

"And usually succeeding," Clara said with a reminiscent smile.

Anne enjoyed the friendly banter between Walter and the two women, but she still wanted to hear how the curse rumors got started. "So did Aunt Edie take the Egyptian pot with her to the garden club meeting?"

"Sure she did," Clara replied. "And she told us all about how she found it during an archaeological dig."

"But the best part," Ruby interjected, "was when Edie told us about the dire warnings from an Egyptian woman who claimed that the clay pot was cursed. Edie had some dramatic training, as you know, and she really set the scene."

"Edie even used a very believable Egyptian accent," Clara said. "We all applauded by the time she'd finished the story."

Anne chewed her lower lip, a bit confused. That sounded like entertainment instead of a warning about the potential danger of the clay pot.

Judging by the puzzled expression on Alex's face, he thought the same thing.

"So maybe that story scared someone at the meeting?" Alex ventured. "If that's how the rumors got started."

"I'm not sure if it was fear or a handy excuse," Ruby said wryly. "You see, Marijane Collins had a fender bender on her way home from the meeting that afternoon. She plowed her station wagon right into the back end of the mayor's Mercedes."

Clara leaned forward. "Marijane claimed that her brakes didn't work, but the mechanic who checked out her station wagon said they worked just fine. Then Marijane started telling everyone around town about the cursed clay pot that Edie had brought back from Egypt with her and blamed it for her car accident. The next day, the power outage happened."

"And then that nasty flu virus swept through the elementary school," Ruby added. "Right after Edie gave a presentation that included the Egyptian pot."

"And Hoy Miller almost cut his foot off with his lawn mower." Clara picked up a stray muffin crumb on her napkin and popped it into her mouth.

"And don't forget the mayor," Ruby said to Clara. "He tripped on a crack in the sidewalk and broke his leg."

"Wait a minute." Alex looked between the two women. "Are you saying that *all* those things were blamed on a clay pot?"

Walter nodded. "I'm afraid so. It was like a domino effect. Every time something bad or unusual happened, certain people attributed it to the Egyptian clay pot."

"Some people believed you had to come into contact with the pot, like Marijane had, for the curse to take effect," Clara explained. "Others, like Hoy Miller, thought the fact that it had been brought to Blue Hill meant the whole town was cursed."

"Poor Aunt Edie," Anne mused, picturing the hysteria. "Once the story about the curse started to spread, it would be like trying to put out a wildfire."

"You're right about that," Ruby agreed. "All the fuss didn't simmer down until Edie finally got rid of it."

Anne's gaze slowly moved around the table. "Actually, she didn't get rid of it. I found it in the attic yesterday and put it on display in the library."

Clara's eyes widened in disbelief. "Oh no! That's the last thing this town needs."

Walter smiled. "Surely, you're not superstitious, Clara?"

"Well, of course not," she said, sitting up straight in her chair. "But, why take the chance? After all, no one ever could explain all those strange incidents that happened forty years ago."

Ruby shook her head. "Now, Clara, we both know that Marijane was a terrible driver. That was her third accident that year."

"Maybe so," Clara admitted, "but what about the power outage and the flu and the mayor's broken leg?"

Anne didn't know what to say. She exchanged a glance with Alex, who gave her a small, sympathetic shrug. He didn't seem to understand this fear of an Egyptian clay pot any better than she did—especially from people she usually considered quite rational.

"Now, wait just a minute," Walter said, holding up both hands. "I do have an explanation for the power outage. Or, at least, a plausible theory."

Anne turned to him, intrigued. "You do?"

"Yes." Walter cleared his throat. "Although I didn't discover it until six months after the power outage. We were replacing one of the large transformers in the power plant, and I found a large squirrel's nest deep inside of it, along with the remnants of two other squirrel nests. Somehow the squirrels must have gotten in there and probably chewed up some wiring. We just happened to bypass those wires when we were scrambling for a way to get the power back on."

"Squirrels?" Alex said, shaking his head in disbelief. "All that trouble and expense because of squirrels?"

"Oh, they're mischievous little creatures," Clara told him. "I used to get them in my attic and had a real battle getting them out."

Anne turned to Walter. "Did you tell anyone about your theory?"

"Sure," Walter said. "I told the mayor and the town council. They came up with some plans to squirrel-proof the power plant going forward, and we haven't had another outage like that since. But some folks still believe the curse was to blame."

"Well, it *could* have caused the squirrels to do the damage," Ruby ventured. "I mean, if one believed in such a thing."

Anne planned to tell Mildred about the squirrel nests causing the power outage. The fact that there was a plausible theory about the power outage might calm Mildred's nervousness about the clay pot.

"But why wasn't Aunt Edie's house affected?" Anne asked Walter. "I read in the article that a witness reported Aunt Edie's house as the only place in Blue Hill that didn't lose electricity."

Walter snorted. "That's not true, although Hector Mattison believed it. He was probably the so-called witness. What Hector didn't know was that Edie owned her own generator and was able to restore the lights in the house until an electrician could get there to replace the fuse box."

Anne nodded, relieved *that* mystery was solved. Then she glanced at her watch, surprised to see the time. "Oh, I'd better run."

"Well, I'm certainly glad you stopped by to visit." Walter rose to his feet. "You should do so more often."

"I will," she promised, reaching out to clasp his hand in a warm handshake.

Alex stood up. "I'd better take off too, Uncle Walt. Ryan and I have a project in the backyard. We're building a tree fort."

"Just what every boy needs." Walter grinned as he clapped Alex on the shoulder. "Good to see you, kid. You bring Ryan by here for a visit soon."

"I'll do that," Alex said with a smile.

Anne and Alex said their good-byes to Ruby and Clara and then made their way out of the retirement home.

"I have to say that was one of the most interesting conversations I've had here," Alex said, holding the door open for Anne. "And that's saying something, because Uncle Walt is always full of interesting stories."

Anne smiled. "He sure is." As she walked with Alex to the parking lot, she wondered if the squirrel story would be enough to convince Mildred that the clay pot wasn't cursed. She planned to visit her after lunch and take the kids along. Hopefully both Mildred's fear and her ankle pain had subsided during the night.

Anne bid Alex good-bye as the two parted ways. She appreciated his friendship and was happy to see that he wasn't susceptible to superstition either. He'd always been a no-nonsense kind of guy, even all the way back in high school. Perhaps she'd been worried for nothing. With any luck, these newest rumors about the cursed clay pot might fade away before the weekend was over.

CHAPTER FIVE

S *moke.*

Anne smelled something burning as soon as she stepped through the back door of her house. She hurried toward the living room on the second floor. "Hannah? Ben? Liddie?" Her voice grew louder as she called out each name. "Where are you?"

"We're in here," Hannah Pyle called out, appearing in the hallway just outside the living room. "Sorry about the smell," she said sheepishly. "We burned the last batch of cookies."

Anne breathed a sigh of relief, grateful that it wasn't something more serious. "That's all right. Is everything else okay?"

"Yep," Hannah told her. "Liddie and I played at the park while Ben went to his youth membership class at church. Then we came back here and started baking cookies. The kids ate all their lunch, so I let them each have one cookie for dessert."

"That's fine," Anne said, digging into her purse. She pulled out some dollar bills and handed them to Hannah. "Thank you so much for watching the kids for me this afternoon, especially on such short notice."

"No problem." Hannah smiled as she turned back into the living room. "They're sure a lot easier to babysit than my brothers and sisters. At least they listen to me."

Anne followed her, pleased to see Ben and Liddie working together on a jigsaw puzzle. Hannah always found fun things for them to do instead of just planting them in front of the television.

"Hey, Mommy, do you want to help us?" Liddie asked, holding a puzzle piece in her hand.

"I'd love to, but first we need to visit Mildred." She watched Hannah walk over to the coffee table, where her laptop computer and a few textbooks were spread out over the surface. "Looks like you've got homework this weekend."

Hannah groaned as she placed her books inside her backpack. "Our English teacher gave us a big project that's due on Monday. I *just* finished it before you came home. I had to write a four-page paper about my favorite British author, along with a two-page book report about one of that author's novels."

"And who did you choose?" Anne asked.

"I chose Charlotte Brontë. *Jane Eyre* is one of my favorite books, so the book report was easy for me to write. And since Charlotte Brontë has two sisters who were also authors, there was plenty to write about her family and background. I wrote the rough draft of the report yesterday and polished it up today."

"I'd love to read your paper sometime," Anne said, genuinely interested.

"Okay," Hannah agreed with a smile. She reached out to pick up her laptop and then frowned. "I thought I left this on." She pushed a couple of buttons on the keyboard, and then her frown deepened. "Oh no!"

Anne took a step toward her. "What's wrong?"

"My laptop shut down." Panic flared in Hannah's eyes as she punched one of the computer keys. A moment later, the computer started again, the screen lighting up. "I don't understand what happened."

Anne glanced over at Ben and Liddie. "Did either one of you touch Hannah's computer?"

"No, Mom," Ben said. "We've just been working on the puzzle."

Hannah let out a cry of despair as she stared at the laptop. "It's gone! My report is gone."

Anne moved next to her. "How could that happen?"

"I must not have saved it, so it disappeared when my computer shut down." Hannah sunk down on the sofa and placed her head in her hands. "All that work for nothing. Now I have to write the report all over again."

"Oh, I'm so sorry," Anne said, gently patting Hannah's shoulder. "Maybe there's some way to retrieve it."

"No, there's not." Hannah lifted her head and took a deep breath. "This has happened to me before. Dad gave me a flash drive so I could always back up my work, but I forgot to bring it with me."

Anne felt so helpless. She wished there was something she could do to make Hannah feel better. "Did you save your rough draft or any notes?"

Hannah sighed. "Just some research notes." She reached over to punch some keys on her computer. "The notes are still there, at least. I guess I'll spend the rest of my weekend writing my report for a second time."

"I'm so sorry," Anne told her. "Would some cookies help?"

Hannah's mouth curved into a wan smile. "No, but thank you." Then her smile faded as she met Anne's gaze. "Did this happen because of the curse?"

The question made Anne feel a little queasy. "Oh my goodness, no. There is no curse, Hannah. Surely you know that."

Hannah gave a small shrug. "I'm sure you're right, but this is pretty weird. Why would my laptop just shut down for no reason?"

"That's happened with my computer before." Anne sat down next to her. "And you said it's happened to you before too."

"Yeah," Hannah said slowly. "But it's still strange. I mean, I only walked away from it for a minute and then…poof! My report disappeared."

"There is no curse," Anne said gently but firmly. "And I still think you should have your dad look at your laptop, just in case he might be able to salvage your project." Chad Pyle was something of an amateur computer geek and had fixed minor computer problems for Anne before.

Hannah closed her laptop and placed it in her backpack. "I will," she said, although she didn't sound very optimistic.

Anne watched Hannah say good-bye to Ben and Liddie before following her to the back door. "Are you sure you don't want some cookies?"

Hannah hesitated. "Maybe I'll take a couple with me. I'll need all the energy I can get to write that paper again."

Anne retrieved the tub of cookies that Hannah and the kids had made earlier, plucking a dozen out and placing them in a resealable plastic bag. Then she handed the bag to Hannah. "I put in enough cookies to share with your family, but the extras are all yours."

"Thanks," Hannah said, her smile widening. "I'll see you later, Ms. Gibson."

"Good-bye." Anne watched Hannah leave and then heaved a long sigh. Did everything that went wrong in Blue Hill lately have to be blamed on the clay pot?

Twenty minutes later, Anne and the kids walked up to Mildred's front door. It opened before she could even knock, and Anne saw four people seated around the living room. Mildred sat on the sofa, her injured ankle propped on a cushion on the coffee table in front of her. Dressed in a long, gold silk robe and matching slippers, Mildred almost looked like a queen holding court with her visitors.

"Hello, there," Claire Daniels, a good friend of Mildred's, greeted them. "I saw you three coming up the walk."

"Hello, Claire." Anne walked into the foyer, followed by Ben and Liddie. "How is Mildred feeling today?"

"Not too bad," Claire said. "I brought her some breakfast this morning and some of her neighbors had already stopped by with casseroles and salad. Mildred won't have to cook for weeks!"

Anne laughed. "That's one of the best things about living in a small town—there's always plenty of food." Then she held up the tub of cookies in her hand. "And we brought oatmeal cookies."

"Oh, wonderful," Claire said, clapping her hands together. Then she turned toward the sofa. "Mildred, Anne and the kids brought you some oatmeal cookies."

Mildred looked over at them as the other guests chatted with each other. "How nice. Oatmeal cookies are my favorite. Did you kids make them?"

Liddie nodded. "Yes, and so did Hannah Pyle. The curse made her computer break."

Silence descended on the room as Mildred's startled gaze turned to Anne. "What?"

"Hannah was babysitting Ben and Liddie today," Anne explained, "and she and the kids made the cookies." She placed a gentle hand on Liddie's shoulder. "Hannah's computer had a...glitch that caused her to lose a document that she'd written, but it wasn't because of any curse."

"Oh dear," Claire murmured, looking worried.

Darla Gunderson rose to her feet. "Of course there's no curse. A pot is just a pot."

"Tell that to my brother," Lars Gunderson said to his wife. "A fire took out Alfred's hay barn forty years ago after that clay pot showed up in town."

"The fire marshal said Alfred's barn was hit by lightning," Darla countered. "He should have installed a lightning rod on the barn like most farmers do."

Mildred cleared her throat, drawing everyone's attention to her. "Perhaps we should have some of those oatmeal cookies. They look delicious." Then she looked over at Claire. "Is there any coffee left?"

"I just made a fresh pot," Claire said with a nervous smile. "I'll go get it." She handed the tub of cookies to Ben. "Why don't you and your sister pass these around to everyone."

"Okay," Ben said, peeling the red plastic lid off the tub. Then he and Liddie approached each person in the room, starting with Mildred, and offered them a cookie.

Anne appreciated the respite from talking about a curse, grateful that Mildred changed the subject.

After about thirty minutes of cookies, coffee, and pleasant conversation, all of the other guests said their good-byes to Mildred and took their leave. Soon, only Anne, Ben, and Liddie remained.

"Oh my," Mildred said with a weary smile. "I don't remember when I've had so many visitors in one day."

"Are you tired?" Anne asked her.

"A bit," Mildred admitted. Then she looked at Ben and Liddie. "I'm so glad you two came to visit me. You're welcome to go outside and play on the tire swing in the backyard if you'd like. You're probably ready for some fresh air after all of this grown-up talk."

"Okay," Ben said, looking at his sister. "C'mon, Liddie. I'll push you on the swing."

Liddie skipped after her brother as he headed for the back door of the house.

When they were out of earshot, Mildred turned to Anne, her expression more serious. "I'm worried about all of you."

"We're fine," Anne assured her. "In fact, I've been looking into some of the strange events that happened forty years ago, including the power outage. I even talked to Walter Ochs, who was the town electrician at the time, and he thinks he knows what caused the outage."

Mildred arched a silver brow. "Oh?"

"It was squirrels," Anne said. "He found squirrel nests in a transformer about six months after the incident and thinks they might have caused the initial problems."

"Squirrels?" Mildred blinked. "He thinks squirrels caused all that damage?"

Anne nodded, aware that it sounded a little silly. "It's been known to happen. I read some articles about it on the Internet. Squirrels have caused that kind of damage to power plants before."

"Well, I suppose anything is possible," Mildred mused, although she didn't look convinced. "But I don't think squirrels were responsible for my scarab necklace vanishing into thin air."

"No, I'm sure they weren't." Anne looked at Mildred. "Do you have a picture of the necklace?"

"I'm afraid not." Then she held up one finger. "But you might check with my neighbor, Coraline. She didn't live in Blue Hill at the time, of course, but her sister did and Coraline used to visit her quite often."

"I didn't know Coraline had a sister."

"Yes, her name was Ada Coombs and she was quite a bit older. Ada left her house to Coraline in her will."

"So Coraline took a picture of your scarab necklace back in 1975?"

Mildred nodded. "Yes, she was visiting Ada at the time and saw me wearing it. She thought it was gorgeous and insisted on taking a photograph of it."

"But that was forty years ago. Do you think she'd still have the photo?"

Mildred chuckled. "Oh my, yes. That woman saves *everything*." Then she leaned her head back against the sofa cushion and breathed a long sigh.

"You're tired," Anne observed. "Would you like me to help you to your room so you can rest?"

"No, dear, I'm fine right here. But I might just rest my eyes for a bit, if you don't mind."

Anne rose to her feet. "The kids and I should probably go."

"Oh, not yet," Mildred protested. "They'll come in when they're ready. Let them play."

Anne wanted to give Mildred some time to herself after her full day of visitors. "Well, maybe I'll pop over to see Coraline and ask her about that photo."

"You go right ahead, Anne." Mildred closed her eyes. "I'll just rest here until you get back."

Anne moved quietly to the back door. She found Ben pushing Liddie on the tire swing and told them she was going to visit the next-door neighbor for a few minutes and that she'd be back soon. She also let them know that Mildred was resting. The kids promised to wait for her in Mildred's backyard until she returned.

Then Anne headed for Coraline's house, hoping to learn something new about the Egyptian scarab necklace that had disappeared forty years ago.

A few minutes later, Anne walked up the steps of Coraline's front porch and knocked on the door. From inside she heard Coraline say, "Just a minute." This was followed by a loud clatter. It sounded as though something had fallen.

"Is everything okay?" Anne asked, leaning her ear closer to the door.

"Yes, yes," Coraline called out. "I'll be right there."

A moment later. Anne heard the deadbolt unlock. Coraline opened the door a few inches. The older woman wore faded blue jeans and a light pink cotton blouse with short sleeves. Her short gray hair was styled into tight curls around her head.

"Good afternoon," Coraline said, smiling at Anne. "This is a pleasant surprise. Please, come in."

Anne walked inside, noting the binoculars that Coraline kept on an end table to keep a close eye on her neighbors. The sage green sofa and matching recliner were adorned with light blue pillows that matched the light blue paint on the wall. A walnut coffee table stood in front of the sofa. A vanilla-scented candle burned in the center of the coffee table, surrounded by a wreath of silk lavender flowers.

"I'm sorry to arrive unannounced like this," Anne said as Coraline closed the door behind her. "I was just visiting with Mildred, and we were talking about a scarab necklace she owned back in the seventies. She mentioned that you might have a photograph of it."

"Is that so?" Coraline clasped her hands together. "Oh, how I loved that necklace! Even after all these years, I've never seen anything quite like it." Then she headed toward the hallway. "Come with me. I think I know exactly where to find that photograph."

Anne followed Coraline down the narrow hallway until they reached a closed door at the end of it. Coraline tried to open the door, but it barely budged, almost as if something was blocking it on the other side. Coraline pushed her body against the door until it finally opened wide enough for her to kick something out of the way. Then she smiled and opened the door all the way, allowing Anne to enter ahead of her.

The room was full of boxes and crates, much like the attic in Anne's house. There were also tall stacks of books, DVDs, and sacks of clothing on the floor. In the midst of all of these piles was a white leather love seat covered with magazines. Coraline picked up the magazines from one half of the love seat and piled them on a nearby table.

"Please have a seat while I find that picture. It may take me a while."

Anne sat down, thinking it might take all afternoon if Coraline had to search through all these boxes for the photograph. She'd never realized that Coraline was something of a collector, but the unusual items in the room told her otherwise. There was even a concrete green bullfrog sitting on an old bass drum in one corner. A variety of vintage brooches were pinned to the green gingham curtains on the lone window in the room.

Anne's gaze moved slowly over the walls, which were covered with paintings of flowers, oceans, and a wide variety of wildlife. There were three mismatched chairs across from the love seat, two of them piled with empty plastic water bottles. Everything seemed to be organized into piles, giving the room an appearance of being neat, even though it was practically bursting at the seams.

"I'm not surprised you want to see that necklace," Coraline said as she opened a box in front of her and started sorting through it. "Especially after what happened to Mildred at the library. The poor woman was lucky she didn't break a bone."

Anne's gaze fell on a small, elaborately painted bowl of three white rabbits in red waistcoats having tea. Next to the bowl was a bronze-colored statue of a fish jumping out of a river. Behind this statue was a stack of three old leather-bound books. Anne couldn't see the titles of the books, but one of them had a tortoise-shell hair comb stuck in the pages.

Anne began to worry that Coraline may have crossed the line from collector to hoarder. She also wondered if Mildred's scarab necklace could be hiding in one of the many boxes in this room.

A moment later, Coraline pulled a large yellow envelope from the box in front of her. "Here it is."

She sat down next to Anne on the love seat and opened the envelope, shaking it upside down until a small pile of color photographs fell into her hand.

"I'm certain it's in this bunch somewhere," Coraline said as she flipped through the messy stack of pictures. "Ah, here we go. I have two pictures of it."

Coraline handed two of the old photos to Anne.

The first photo showed a much younger Mildred standing in her kitchen wearing a paisley pantsuit with wide bell bottom pants. Anne could see a necklace around her neck, but the shot was taken too far away to show much detail. The second photograph was a close-up shot of the necklace. The pendant was shaped like a beetle with its wings outstretched. A large green gem was embedded into the center of the pendant, and blue and green beads outlined the wings. The feathers on the wings were made of alternating green and blue gems.

"It's beautiful," Anne breathed, admiring the photograph.

"Yes, quite exquisite. Mildred was beside herself when she couldn't find it. At first, Ada and I were sure that she had simply misplaced it, but after a few days it seemed more likely that it had vanished."

Anne looked up from the photograph to meet Coraline's gaze. "So did you believe the curse was responsible?"

"I didn't know what to believe. My sister was certain a thief had come into the neighborhood. She hired someone to install extra locks on all of her doors."

"Do you mind if I borrow this photo for a while?" Anne asked, holding the close-up of the necklace.

Coraline hesitated and then said, "I suppose that would be all right, but you must take good care of it. I don't have the negatives, so I wouldn't be able to replace it."

"Of course, I will be very careful with it," Anne said, rising off the love seat. "And I promise to have it back to you very soon."

Coraline began putting the rest of the photographs back into the envelope. "That's fine. As long as I get it back, you can keep it as long as you need."

After she placed the envelope back in its box, Coraline led Anne out of the room and back down the hallway to the front door.

"Thank you again," Anne told her as she stepped onto the porch. "I really appreciate it." Then another thought occurred to her. "You'll have to come to the library soon and take a look at some of our new books. We have some lovely art books that just came in that I think you might like."

"I may just do that," Coraline said, "after the curse is lifted, of course."

Before Anne could reply, Coraline smiled at her and said, "Thanks for stopping by, Anne. You have a nice evening." Then she closed the front door.

Anne stared at it a moment, wondering why Coraline was in such a hurry. Then she saw the living room curtains part slightly and a pair of binoculars appeared between them, aimed at the Gunderson house, where Lars and Darla were raking the leaves on their front lawn.

Anne smiled to herself as she made her way down the porch steps and headed back to Mildred's house. It was time to take the kids home and do a little research on the scarab necklace. Once Anne knew more about it, maybe she could figure out who had taken it out of Mildred's house forty years ago.

CHAPTER SIX

"M ommy!"

Anne woke with a start to Liddie frantically whispering into her ear and shaking her shoulder. Liddie was in her pajamas and sitting on Anne's bed next to her. Anne sat up and turned on the lamp on her nightstand.

"Liddie, what is it?"

"I heard something downstairs." Liddie's voice trembled. "I think there is something in the library."

"It wasn't just the wind?" Anne asked, stifling a yawn as she sat up on the edge of the bed.

"No, it sounded like a loud bang. Come here, I'll show you." Liddie climbed off the bed and grabbed Anne's hand. She led Anne to the top of the stairs before stopping, then Liddie leaned into her and wrapped her small arms around Anne's waist. "Listen," she whispered.

Anne listened. Somewhere from the darkness below came a strange, clacking noise. It startled Anne for a moment and she took a step back.

"What do you think it is?" Liddie whispered.

"It's probably nothing," Anne said, trying to sound calm. "Why don't you go back to bed while I check it out?"

"Okay, but be careful, Mommy," Liddie warned. She turned and ran back down the hallway, disappearing into her bedroom.

Anne heard Liddie's bedroom door close and felt better knowing her daughter was safe.

Anne began to slowly walk down the stairs to the second floor. When she reached the landing, she started down the hall, turning on every light switch she passed. Every thirty seconds or so she would hear the clacking noise again. Each time it caused her to jump a little and then stop moving for a moment. Even though the noise made her apprehensive, she knew there must be a harmless reason for it.

Soon, she realized the sound had to be coming from the Children's Room of the library. As she moved closer, the sound grew louder.

"There's a rational explanation for this," she murmured to herself. "There has to be."

Anne straightened her shoulders, certainly not about to let herself start believing the curse was real. Determined to solve this minor mystery, she starting looking in all corners of the Children's Room and peering around each bookshelf. Then she heard the clacking noise again, the sound more distinct this time.

It was coming from the far corner of the room.

She took a deep breath and walked slowly toward the area where the sound was emanating. As she moved closer, a cool breeze drifted over her, making her shiver.

That's when she noticed one of the windows was open, the curtains fluttering in the night breeze.

Clack. Clack. Clack.

The sound was coming from behind the curtain in front of her. Anne reached out and pulled back the fabric, only to find a red yo-yo tied by its string to the window's crank handle. Each time the wind blew, the yo-yo swung back and forth, hitting the wall behind it.

Anne breathed a sigh of relief, realizing that one of the children visiting the library must have tied it there. Then she heard footsteps behind her and saw Liddie peaking around the corner.

"I thought you were in your room," Anne said.

"I wanted to make sure you weren't scared, Mommy."

"Come here," Anne said with a smile, waving Liddie over to the corner.

Liddie crept toward her, her bare feet visible beneath the hem of her pink cotton nightgown. A sudden gust of wind blew the curtains open, followed by a loud *clack, clack, clack* against the wall. The noise made Liddie yelp. She ran to Anne and wrapped her arms tightly around Anne's waist, burying her face in Anne's chest.

"Don't be afraid, Liddie." Anne gently smoothed one hand over her daughter's light brown hair. "Look, it's just a yo-yo." Anne pointed to the toy hanging outside the window. When Liddie saw it she loosened her grip around Anne.

"That's what's making the scary noise?" Liddie said. "A yo-yo?"

"It sure is." Anne reached up and unhooked the yo-yo from the window. She handed it to Liddie and then closed the window. "See, now we can sleep again. The mystery is solved."

"But I'm not feeling very tired," Liddie said, winding up the string around the yo-yo. "Maybe we should have a cookie before we go back to bed, just to help us sleep."

"A cookie?" Anne was about to say no, then remembered how brave Liddie had been to check on Anne despite her fear.

"Yes, I think we've earned a cookie. We'll split one, so the sugar doesn't keep us awake."

"Okay," Liddie agreed.

When they reached the kitchen, Anne poured them each a small glass of milk. Then Anne split a large cookie into two pieces, each of them taking half.

"I love you, Mommy," Liddie said, dipping her cookie into her milk. "And I really like my new yo-yo."

Anne smiled, cherishing this middle-of-the-night moment with her daughter. "I love you too, sweetie."

* * *

On Sunday morning, in the light of day, Anne's apprehension about last night's strange clacking noise seemed silly. Especially given Pastor Tom's message about the power of trusting in the Lord through good times and bad.

A new resolve to put an end to this silly superstition about the clay pot rose within Anne as the congregation stood to sing the closing hymn. Her voice harmonized with all of those around her as they sang "In the Garden," which just happened to be one of her favorite hymns.

A short time later, members of the congregation filled the front lawn, visiting with each other while young children stood under a large oak tree and tried to catch the falling leaves.

Ben and some of the older children played on the side lawn of the church, kicking a soccer ball back and forth between them. Anne's gaze moved to Liddie, and she watched her daughter jump into a pile of golden leaves and then laugh as she tossed the leaves into the air.

"There is no sweeter sound on earth than a child's laughter," Pastor Tom said, watching Liddie as he walked up to Anne. "I love hearing it."

"Me too," Anne agreed. "If I can hear Ben and Liddie laugh at least once a day, I'm a happy woman."

"They're wonderful children." Then he turned his full attention to Anne. "And how have you been? I visited with Mildred Farley last evening and heard what happened at the library."

"Yes, poor Mildred. I feel just awful about what happened." She met his gaze. "Did she tell you about the clay pot that my aunt Edie brought home from Egypt forty years ago?"

"Yes," he replied. "In fact, I heard about it before I went to visit Mildred. A couple of church members were concerned and asked me to talk to you about it."

Anne blinked, wanting to know who had approached him but knowing it wasn't fair to ask. "Should I assume they want me to get rid of it?"

"Yes," he said bluntly. "They're afraid, and fear can be very powerful. I remember a neighbor who lived next door to my family when I was a child. He was afraid of a lot of things, in fact the list would grow each year. Soon, he never left his home and refused to let anyone enter. My mother would take food over to his house and leave it on his doorstep for him." Pastor Tom shook his head. "Fear had made him a prisoner in his own home."

Anne glanced at the people around her, all of them chatting comfortably together. They were her church family, and it bothered her that some of them might be afraid because of the clay pot. She looked up at Pastor Tom. "Do *you* think I should get rid of it?"

"That's not my decision to make," he said gently. "But I do believe that giving in to fear just feeds it. We need to face our fears and, through faith and understanding, learn what's behind them." Curiosity gleamed in his gentle brown eyes. "So what do you think is behind Mildred's fear of that clay pot?"

"I wish that I knew. She's connected it to the mysterious disappearance of a scarab necklace she brought back from Egypt, but I don't understand how that fear has remained so strong after forty years."

He took a step closer to her, his voice a little lower now. "And how are the kids handling this? Or are they even aware of it?"

"They are aware," Anne told him. "Liddie's been asking questions and is scared when she hears strange noises." Anne smiled. "That happened last night, in fact, but it turned out to be harmless."

"And Ben?"

"Ben believes it's all nonsense and doesn't understand why anyone would be scared of an ancient Egyptian artifact."

"Well, that's good to hear," Pastor Tom said. "We missed him at the youth membership class yesterday, and I thought this business with the clay pot might have been the reason."

"Missed him?" Anne stared at the pastor. "You mean, Ben wasn't at the class?"

"No, he never showed up." His brown eyes narrowed. "Didn't you know?"

"I'm afraid not." Anne's gaze moved to the boys playing soccer on the side lawn. Her son was among them, laughing as he chased the ball across the grass. He had some explaining to do. Then she turned her attention back to Pastor Tom. "He'll be at the next class," she promised. "I'll make sure of it."

Before the pastor could reply, Marian Pauthen walked up to them.

"I'm so sorry to interrupt," Marian said with an apologetic smile, "but I wanted to ask Pastor Tom if he and Maggie would like to join Doug and me for dinner today."

"It's no problem," Anne assured her, "I need to be on my way." Then she looked at Pastor Tom. "I hope you can stop in the library sometime soon. We have some new mystery novels you might enjoy."

"Thanks, Anne, I'll do that," he replied, before turning his attention to Marian.

Anne chatted with a few more people as she slowly made her way toward her children. She needed to have a serious talk with Ben. Not only had he missed the first youth membership class, he'd lied to her about it. And he'd obviously lied to Hannah as well, since she'd believed Ben had gone to the class.

In truth, the lying bothered her more than the fact that Ben had missed the class. And the fact that she'd fallen for it unsettled her. She'd always believed that she could sense when her children weren't telling her the truth. If Ben had lied about this so easily, what other lies might he be telling?

She intended to ask him that question as soon as they got home. But she'd only taken a few steps in Ben's direction when Alex approached her. He wore a dark blue suit with a red-and-blue striped tie.

"I have some good news and some bad news," he said.

The twinkle in his eye told her she didn't need to be too worried. "I'll take the good news first," she decided.

"You don't have to cook Sunday dinner today."

She laughed and nodded. "That is good news, considering I didn't plan anything. The kids and I were just going to eat leftovers." She gazed into his blue eyes. "And the bad news?"

"Ryan invited your family to join us at the diner for lunch, and Ben accepted."

"That doesn't sound like bad news to me."

Alex winced. "You haven't heard the bad part yet. I accidentally left my wallet at the job site in Deshler yesterday and didn't realize it until just now. Which means you'll have to pay for dinner, but don't worry, I'll pay you back tomorrow."

She laughed. "No problem. But I *am* worried about your wallet. What if someone takes it?"

He shook his head. "It's probably safer at the job site than anywhere else. It's locked in my toolbox there, which is locked in the construction trailer, which has security cameras pointed in all directions.

"Security cameras?" she echoed, intrigued. "Is security really a problem at a construction site?"

"Sure," he replied. "Thieves like to steal valuable tools and sell them for money. Since most construction sites don't have anyone around at night, it usually makes for easy pickings unless you've got everything locked up."

"Have you ever had any tools stolen?"

He nodded. "Unfortunately, yes. I reported it to the police, and they were actually able to track them down using the serial numbers."

"I never realized tools had serial numbers."

"They sure do." He looked around the lawn. "Now if it was just as easy to track down our boys, life would be much easier."

Anne chuckled as she turned toward the part of the church lawn where the boys had just been playing soccer. "They were right over there a few minutes ago."

They walked toward that area, then Anne heard the sound of children. As they rounded the building, Anne saw Ryan and a few of the other boys surrounding Ben, who sat on the sidewalk holding his jaw and groaning.

Anne hurried up to him. "What happened, Ben? Are you okay?"

"Ryan and I both tried to head bump the ball, and I hurt my chin," Ben said with a moan, still holding his jaw.

Alex walked over to Ryan and placed a hand on top of his head. "Hey, buddy, what have I told you about heading the ball? That's off limits, remember?"

"Yeah," Ryan said, looking sheepish. "It's just that the other guys were doing it and I didn't want to look like a sissy."

"Me neither," Ben said.

"We can talk about that later." Anne knelt down to take a closer look at Ben. "Move your hand so I can see your chin."

Ben lowered his hand, revealing a bright red spot about the size of a quarter on his chin. "Is it bad?"

"No," Anne said, relieved that the skin wasn't broken. She tenderly touched the area, trying to ascertain if it was more serious than it looked. "Does your mouth hurt or any of your teeth?"

"No," Ben replied.

Alex moved toward them. "How about your head?"

"My head feels fine," Ben said calmly. "Is it time for lunch yet?"

Alex turned to Anne. "Well, that's a good sign. If he's hungry, then he'll probably be okay."

"I think so too," she said, although she planned to keep an eye on him. "Ben, we were going to join Alex and Ryan at the diner, but if you don't feel up to it now, we can do that some other time."

Ben jumped to his feet. "No, Mom, I'm fine. And I really want to eat with Ryan."

Liddie appeared around the corner of the building and walked up to them. "Hey, why are you all hiding from me?"

"We're not hiding, sweetie," Anne assured her. "In fact, I was just about to come and find you. We're going to the diner for lunch."

Liddie jumped in the air. "Yippee! I love the diner."

Alex laughed at her reaction. "I feel the same way. Especially about their homemade pumpkin pie."

Liddie turned to Anne. "May I have pie for lunch, Mommy?"

"Maybe you can have some pie after lunch," Anne said as she helped Ben to his feet. She brushed some grass off his khaki pants, making a mental note to apply stain remover to the knees before she put the pants in the washer. "Now, is everyone ready?"

"Looks like it," Alex said, as he and Ryan turned toward the parking lot. "We'll meet you at the diner."

Ten minutes later, Anne and the kids arrived at the diner. Anne wanted to talk to Ben about not attending the church membership class but decided to wait until they got home. Alex and Ryan had arrived just ahead of them and already snagged a table in the busy restaurant.

"The special today is fried chicken," Alex told them as Anne and the kids slid into their chairs. "That's what Ryan and I are having."

"Sounds good to me too," Anne said, pushing away the menu in front of her.

"I want a corn dog," Liddie announced.

Anne turned to Ben, who was fingering the sore spot on his chin. "How about you?"

"Fried chicken for me." Then he grinned at Ryan. "I wish someone had taken a picture of us crashing together when we were going after the ball. That would have been cool."

"I know," Ryan concurred. "I bet we looked awesome."

The waitress arrived to take their order, making short work of it since everyone but Liddie wanted the noon special. While they waited for their food, Anne and Alex chatted about the sermon while the boys continued to talk about soccer, with Liddie adding to the conversations to tell everyone that her bottom tooth was very loose.

A short time later, their meals arrived. Liddie clapped her hands together when she saw her corn dog and french fries. Anne was tempted to do the same when the waitress set her plate in front of her. It was piled high with crispy fried chicken, mashed potatoes and creamy gravy, two biscuits, and a generous portion of buttery corn.

"Yum!" Ryan exclaimed, picking up his fork.

"You said it," Alex agreed, as he and Ben dug into their food.

Anne was about to do the same when she saw Bonnie Zimmer approaching their table. The petite woman was in her mid- to late-seventies and wore a green-and-white polka dot dress with a white crochet collar.

"I don't want to interrupt your dinner," Bonnie said with a smile, "but I just wanted to thank you, Anne, for taking care of Mildred after she had her fall last Friday."

"It was the least I could do," Anne replied.

"Well, I know it made her feel better to have you there at the hospital with her." Bonne smiled. "She's so fond of you and tells me all the time that you remind her of Edie."

"Me?" Anne said, both surprised and pleased by the compliment.

Bonnie chuckled. "Of course! You've put together that wonderful library and have such nice, well-mannered children."

Her words reminded Anne about Ben's deception regarding the church membership class, but that was for another time and place. "Well, thank you very much." Then she turned to Alex. "Bonnie, do you know Alex Ochs and his nephew, Ryan?"

"Oh, sure," Bonnie said with a wave of her hand. "I used to babysit Alex whenever his parents went out."

Alex blinked. "You did? I don't remember that."

"Of course not," Bonnie said cheerfully. "You were just a baby then and cute as a button." Then she turned to Ryan. "And it's plain to see that good looks run in the family."

Ryan looked up from his mashed potatoes. "What?"

Bonnie smiled. "I was just telling your uncle that you're a handsome young man."

Before Ryan could reply, Bonnie turned and waved to a tall woman who had just walked through the door. "Now there's someone I'd like you to meet," Bonnie said to Anne, "and then I promise to leave you alone so you can enjoy your meal."

"That's fine," Anne said, hoping her mashed potatoes wouldn't get cold.

"This is my daughter, Jillian," Bonnie said as the woman reached the table. "She just moved from Portland, Oregon, to State College, so she lives much closer to me now."

Jill was a handsome woman, around fifty, with ash blonde hair and a professional air about her. Her dove gray suit and blue silk blouse only added to that impression.

"Hello," Jill said with a smile.

"It's nice to meet you," Anne told her, after Alex and the kids greeted her. "How do you like State College?"

"It's wonderful," Jill said. "I've missed Pennsylvania, so it's nice to be back."

Jill, this is Anne Gibson," Bonnie told her daughter, "the woman who runs the Blue Hill Library." Bonnie's pale blue eyes sparkled behind a pair of thick glasses. "She's Edie's great-niece."

Jill held out one manicured hand. "It's a pleasure to meet you. Edie was one of the most interesting women I've ever known."

Anne smiled. "You're right about that. How did you know her?"

"Blue Hill High School had a mentorship program back in the seventies, and Edie was my mentor. She's the one who encouraged me to pursue my dream of becoming a lawyer."

"Jill practices law in State College," Bonnie said proudly. "She's a new partner in the firm of Klove, Zimmer & Franklin."

Jill smiled. "As you can see, I don't need business cards. I just take my mother with me everywhere I go."

Bonnie laughed. "Not *everywhere*. But we do have fun together." The older woman turned to Anne. "In fact, Jill and I stopped by Mildred's house this morning before church for a nice visit. I intend to go over every day and help her out until she's back on her feet."

"That's wonderful," Anne said, touched by Bonnie's generosity. "You've known Mildred for a long time, haven't you?"

"Oh, forever," Bonnie said with a wave of her hand. "I started working as her housekeeper once a week back in the late sixties, although we've always had so much fun together it hardly seems like work."

Jill smiled at her mother. "So that's why you volunteered to do housework for Mildred every day until she recovered. You were just looking for some fun."

Bonnie laughed. "I always am!" Her gaze moved to Anne. "And Mildred should have someone with her every day until she can move around a bit better, don't you think?"

"I do." A wave of relief swept through Anne. She'd been worried about Mildred staying alone in her house, despite the myriad of visitors that brought food and well-wishes. Anne had been trying to juggle the library work schedule to allow her more time to spend with Mildred, so the fact that Bonnie planned to be there every day eased her mind.

"Mildred told us that a home health aide stopped in to see her yesterday," Jill said. "The aide will assist her with bathing and other personal needs, so Mom won't have to worry about doing any heavy lifting."

"Which means I can just do what I do best," Bonnie chimed. "Cooking and cleaning and talking Mildred's ear off."

Anne chuckled, certain that Mildred would enjoy every minute of it. "That sounds wonderful—for both of you. I'll be stopping by to visit often, so I'll probably see you there."

"Oh, I'm sure you will," Bonnie replied. "It was nice seeing you, Anne. I don't know if anyone has told you this before, but you look a bit like Edie. There's something in the eyes."

"Thank you," Anne said, flattered once more.

Bonnie and Jill bid her good-bye and then made their way to a table.

Anne watched them go, barely aware of the animated conversation between Alex and the kids. Her mashed potatoes might be cold, but the search for who stole Mildred's scarab necklace was starting to heat up.

CHAPTER SEVEN

After Anne and the kids returned from the diner, she helped Liddie change out of her Sunday clothes. Liddie had brought most of her corn dog home with her in a doggie bag and now carried it to the kitchen table and climbed onto a chair.

"I'm ready to eat the rest of my corn dog now," Liddie announced. "May I have a glass of milk, please?"

"Coming right up," Anne said, pouring a glass of milk and then grabbing a plate and carrying them both over to the table. "Put your corn dog on the plate, please."

Liddie followed Anne's instructions and then picked up her corn dog by the stick and took a dainty bite. Anne smiled to herself as she walked over to the freezer. At the rate Liddie was nibbling at her corn dog she'd still have most of it left by suppertime.

Anne retrieved a bag of frozen peas and gently placed it on Ben's chin. "How are you feeling?"

"Not so good," he admitted with a slight grimace.

Anne reached over and placed her palm on his forehead. It was cool to the touch. "Does your chin hurt? Or your head?"

He gave a small shrug. "No, just my stomach."

"That's probably because of all that fried chicken you ate for lunch. Why don't you go lie down in your room?" she suggested, noticing that he didn't quite meet her gaze. "Take the bag of frozen peas with you. That will help keep down the swelling on your chin. I'll be up there in a little while to check on you."

"Okay" Ben carried the bag of peas with him as he headed toward the stairs.

Hershey stared after him, obviously torn between following Ben and waiting for a piece of corn dog to fall on the floor.

"Mommy, can I give Hershey the rest of my corn dog?" Liddie asked. The remaining portion had already fallen off the stick and onto the plate.

"Yes, you may," Anne said, watching the Labrador's eyes light up as Liddie placed the leftover corn dog on the floor in front of him.

Hershey swallowed it in one gulp, then bounded over to the stairs in pursuit of Ben. Anne began to clear the table and place the dirty dishes in the sink, thinking about what to say to her son.

Liddie jumped up from the table and walked over to Anne. "Will you read me a book, Mommy?"

"I will after I'm done washing the breakfast dishes. Do you know what book you want to read?"

Liddie thought for a long moment. "I'll look at my bookshelf and decide. Maybe *One Morning in Maine* or *Harry the Dirty Dog*."

"All right, come and find me after you choose one."

Liddie skipped out of the kitchen and headed up the stairs to her bedroom on the third floor.

Anne filled the sink with hot water and then added a squirt of dish soap, eager for some time alone to figure out how to approach Ben. She needed to know why he'd lied to her and why he'd decided not to attend the youth membership class.

As she began to wash the dishes, a few possibilities floated through her mind. Perhaps one of the other boys had been teasing or bullying Ben. Or maybe a girl was flirting with him, which in her nine-year-old's mind could be an even worse fate than a bully.

Whatever the reason, she needed to make it clear to her son that lying was not an option in this family. As she rinsed a bowl under the sink, she wondered how Eric would handle the problem. It was times like this that most challenged her as a single mother, but she needed to trust herself and rely on her faith to see her through.

"Lord, give me wisdom," Anne prayed as she rinsed the last dish under the warm running water.

She placed the dish in the drainer and then dried her hands on a towel before turning around and heading out of the kitchen. She walked up to the third floor and headed for Ben's room. His door was half closed, so she pushed it open and walked inside.

Ben lay on his bed, staring up at the ceiling. The bag of frozen peas, wrapped in a tea towel, lay on his chin, half covering his face.

Anne closed the door behind her and walked over to the bed. "I think we can put the peas back in the freezer now," she said, lifting the towel-wrapped bag off his face and setting it on the night stand. "How does your chin feel?"

"It's really sore," he said, wincing. "I might have broken it."

"*Hmm*," she said, leaning closer to examine it. The swelling had gone down, and a faint bruise, still about the size of a quarter, now discolored his chin. Something told her that Ben was hoping his injury might elicit some extra sympathy from her. While she did feel badly that he was hurt, she worried more about the harm that lying could cause for her son.

"It actually looks a little better to me." Anne sat down on the edge of his bed. "I think the bruise will be almost gone by tomorrow."

Ben closed his eyes and emitted a long, loud yawn. "Wow, I'm really tired. Maybe I should take a nap."

"Maybe you should," Anne said evenly, "after we talk about why you missed the youth membership class and why you lied to me about it."

For the first time since she'd walked into the room, Ben met her gaze. "I don't know, Mom."

"Ben," she said, her tone gentle but firm. "You do know." Then she waited, letting the silence grow between them until he squirmed uncomfortably on the bed.

"I just didn't want to go," he said at last. "I thought it would be boring. When I saw Carter Pratt outside his house playing with a baseball, I decided to play with him instead. You're always saying we should be nice to new kids at school."

Carter's family lived a half a block from the church, but she hadn't met his parents yet. While she wanted Ben to reach out to new students, this sounded more like an excuse to skip the youth membership class than an act of kindness.

"I do want you to be nice to new kids," Anne said slowly. "But do you think I want you to lie about it?"

"No," Ben said, his gaze shifting downward.

"Lying is always wrong, Ben," she said. "And I want you to make sure you know that, in here." She placed her hand on his chest, feeling the beat of his heart beneath her palm. "The Bible tells us it's wrong too."

He looked up at her. "It does?"

"Yes, it does. "Nothing good can come from a lie. It hurts me that you lied to me, Ben. But most of all, it hurts you."

His brow crinkled. "How does it hurt me?"

"Because every time you tell a lie, you plant a little seed of guilt inside of you. That guilt grows with each lie you tell, and even worse, you have to remember all the lies so you don't get caught. Sometimes you don't even remember what's true and start lying to yourself. That's not a fun way to live."

"I'm sorry I lied, Mom," he said softly. "I didn't want to hurt you. I just didn't want you to be mad."

"I know," she said, leaning down to kiss his forehead. "From now on, if you don't want to do something, just tell me and we'll figure it out together." Anne lightly brushed his brown hair off forehead. "That doesn't mean you'll always get your way, but I promise to listen to what you have to say."

"Okay," he said meekly.

Anne gazed down at her son, sensing there was something he still wasn't telling her. "Is there anything else you want to talk about?"

"Not really," he replied. "Can I go watch television now?"

Anne hesitated and then shook her head. "No, I think you should stay in your room for a while and think about what we talked about.

His shoulders drooped. "Okay."

Anne stood up and walked to the door. "I'll let you know when you can come out."

Ben turned over on his side, his back to her, and didn't reply.

Anne sighed as she walked out of his room, hoping she'd gotten through to him. Ben had a good heart, and she prayed that he'd understand how important it was to tell the truth—especially to her.

She headed to Liddie's bedroom to see which book she'd chosen to read, but when Anne walked inside she saw her daughter sound asleep on the floor, Hershey cuddled up beside her. Smiling, she covered Liddie with a blanket and then turned around and crept quietly out of the room, finding herself with some unexpected free time on her hands.

Ever since she'd found the clay pot and the Egyptian scarf, she'd been eager to go back to the attic and see if Aunt Edie had stored any other Egyptian treasures there. Anne headed toward the stairs now and climbed up to the attic.

Once inside, she went toward the area where she'd found the clay pot. One by one, she opened trunks and crates, looking for something—anything—that might be related to Aunt Edie's trip to Egypt. She was hoping for a travel journal or diary, something that would tell her more about the clay pot and the supposed "curse" surrounding it. Perhaps if she knew the origins of the story, that could help explain it.

Twenty minutes later, Anne found a small cluster of letters buried deep inside a trunk full of travel brochures, old maps, and a khaki green pup tent. She pulled out everything but the tent, leaving it for another time. Then she carried the letters, brochures, and old maps downstairs with her. She took them into the kitchen on the second floor and placed them on the table.

The letters were wrapped in a rubber band, a total of five in all, and each one still encased in an envelope. Anne took a seat at the table and removed the rubber band, spreading the letters out in front of her.

There were five envelopes, each from the same sender: Khafra Bakari. Anne checked the date on the envelopes and noted that they were all written in 1985, ten years after Aunt Edie had brought the clay pot back to Blue Hill. She sorted the letters and placed them in chronological order. Then Anne opened the earliest one and began to read it.

Dear Miss Summers,

My family thanks you for your letter. We are all well. Mother sends her greetings and asks when you will return to Egypt.

You shall always be welcome in our home. The school does well, and Father thanks you for your generous donation. I still remember the day that I met you, when Father became your guide at Armana. I was just a child then, but now I am a teacher in the school you helped to create. I hope we shall meet again someday.

Sincerely,
Khafra Bakari

Anne lowered the letter, amazed and proud once more at the impact Aunt Edie had made on the world around her. She never knew that her aunt had helped create a school in Egypt nor that she'd corresponded with a young person who was now a teacher at that school.

Curious, Anne opened the rest of the letters, and found the content much the same. Each one thanked Aunt Edie for her generous donations to the school, including donations of books and pencils. The last letter included a photograph and ended with Khafra telling her of his future plans.

I shall soon return to the university to pursue further education so that I may one day take over running the school. You may continue to send your letters to this address, and my parents will forward them to me. Thank you for your support and friendship. It means more to me than you will ever know.

Anne wondered if Khafra and Aunt Edie had ever corresponded again. If so, the letters weren't among the bunch that she'd just found. Anne turned to the brochures and old maps, but none of them had notes or any other clues that might tell her more about Aunt Edie and Mildred's journey to Egypt.

Then her attention returned to the letters. Khafra had been a child when Aunt Edie made her trip to Egypt, which meant he'd probably be in his fifties now. Was it possible he lived at the same address? If so, maybe he could answer some of her questions about the clay pot and the supposed curse surrounding it.

Anne retrieved some stationery and a pen from a kitchen drawer and then sat down to write a letter to a man she'd never met before.

* * *

On Monday morning, Wendy Pyle arrived at the library with an armful of books and a smile on her face. "Isn't it a gorgeous day? It seems more like June than October."

"It is beautiful," Anne agreed, taking some of the books from her. The forecast promised a sunny and warm day ahead with no chance of precipitation. Ben's mood this morning seemed brighter too. He'd been chatty during breakfast, talking about an upcoming science project and asking for Anne's help. She hoped their talk yesterday had relieved some of the guilt he'd probably been feeling about his lie.

"Thanks so much for filling in this morning," Anne told Wendy, setting the books on the checkout desk. "I really appreciate it."

"Hey, I'll take any excuse to get out of the house. Besides, this will give me a chance to examine that Egyptian clay pot and scarf. I've been itching to get my hands on them."

Anne smiled. "Well, you're one of the few. I've noticed some patrons purposely avoiding the History Room. I think they wish I'd put the pot out of sight."

"What's the fun in that?" Wendy placed her purse on the shelf behind the desk. "By the way, I just started reading *Death on the Nile* by Agatha Christie. It's so descriptive, it makes me want to travel there myself."

"It would be fun, wouldn't it? We could explore the pyramids and see the Red Sea." Anne breathed a wistful sigh. "Maybe someday I'll go there."

Wendy nodded. "It's fun to dream about, isn't it? Chad and I are looking forward to traveling when the kids are grown." She chuckled. "That's more than a few years away, since the twins are only four."

"They grow up fast," Anne reminded her.

"They sure do." Wendy tucked her black hair behind one ear. "Speaking of growing, wait until you hear my plan for the children's Story Time on Wednesday. We're reading *Jack and the Beanstalk*, so I'm going to have the kids each plant their own bean seed."

Anne nodded, certain the preschoolers who attended the story hour would love it. Wendy had a way with children, and she never seemed to run out of creative ideas. "That's perfect. I may plant a bean or two myself."

Wendy moved toward the kitchen. "Right now, I could use some coffee beans. Do you mind if I make a pot?"

"Go right ahead," Anne said, following her into the kitchen. "You know where to find everything, right?"

"I sure do." Wendy opened a cupboard and pulled out a can of coffee grounds. "I've got everything handled here, so you can take off anytime. And say hello to Mildred for me."

"I will," Anne promised. "And I should be back around noon, but call me if you need anything."

Wendy smiled as she peeled the lid off the coffee can. "I have everything I need right here."

Anne laughed as she made her way to the door, eager to start her day. She looked forward to seeing Mildred, but first she wanted to pay a visit to the cold case files at the Blue Hill Police Department.

CHAPTER EIGHT

Anne entered the police station, located at the south end of the Blue Hill town hall, and saw Officer Josie Bolling standing behind the desk.

She'd known Josie as long as she could remember, and although the policewoman was two years younger than Anne, the uniform she wore gave her an air of authority.

"Hello, Anne," Josie said, holding up a blue file folder. "Believe it or not, I was able to find the file you called about. I'm surprised it's still here after all these years."

Anne walked up to her, noting that the blue file was quite thin. Still, it could contain information that would help her understand what might have happened to Mildred's scarab necklace.

Anne looked around the office and then motioned to a row of empty padded chairs near the window. "Is it all right if I just look at it over there?"

"You can use the interview room if you'd like," Josie said as she handed her the file. Josie walked toward the hallway and pointed to a door on the left. "It's empty and will give you some privacy."

"Thanks," Anne said, heading in that direction. She entered the interview room and closed the door. A square wooden table sat in the center of the room with two metal folding chairs on either side of it. The walls were painted a creamy beige, and the faint aroma of lacquer emanated from the shiny hardwood floor. Anne sat down at the table and opened the file.

Inside, she saw an incident report dated May 5, 1975. The responding officer was named Cleo Walford, who Anne knew had passed away several years ago. Officer Walford had filled out the top of the report with Mildred's name and address, along with the words *Missing Necklace* under the subject line.

Then her gaze moved down to the middle of the report.

Mildred Farley reported that a valuable necklace was taken from her home early this morning. Necklace description: eighteen-karat gold chain with an Egyptian, blue scarab pendent. Estimated value: $1,000. According to Mildred, the necklace is not insured.

Mildred stated that she placed the necklace in a drawer last evening, but it was missing when she opened that same drawer this morning. There were no signs of a break-in, and Mildred reported hearing no unusual noises or any other disturbances in the home.

Mildred reported that the following people at her residence in the last twenty-four hours:

Abel Randle – handyman.
Cleta Rinehart – boarder who rents a room on the second floor of the Farley house.
Bonnie Zimmer – housekeeper.
Coraline Watson – visiting sister of neighbor Ada Coombs.

Interviews were conducted with the possible suspects and/or witnesses but none reported seeing anything suspicious or unusual during the time in question. Mildred denies the possibility that she may have misplaced the necklace.

As per protocol, area jewelers and pawn shops have been given a description of the missing necklace and directed to contact the Blue Hill Police Department if they come across it. At this time, the case remains open, pending further investigation.

Anne pulled a small notepad out of her purse and wrote down the names in the report. Coraline had given Anne the photograph of the necklace, but she hadn't mentioned anything about being in Mildred's house on the day it disappeared. Now that she knew Coraline was something of a hoarder, with a special interest in unique items, she wondered if it was possible that a thief had moved next door to Mildred after inheriting the house from Ada.

Anne's gaze moved to the first name on the list. She didn't know anyone by the name of Abel Randle, but she'd seen a contracting company called *Randle Renovation & Repairs* in the phone book. If she recalled, it was located in Deshler but served the entire county.

The name Bonnie Zimmer didn't surprise her, since Bonnie had been Mildred's housekeeper for decades. Now Anne wished she would have asked her about the theft of the necklace. Fortunately, Bonnie lived in Blue Hill and intended to help Mildred every day until she recovered, so Anne knew exactly where to find her.

The name on the list that did surprise Anne was Cleta Rinehart. She'd had no idea Mildred had ever taken in boarders and had never heard of Cleta Rinehart before. Hopefully, Mildred could tell her more about Cleta.

Anne read the incident report once more, just to make certain she hadn't missed anything. There wasn't much to it, and something about the way the report was written suggested that Officer Walford might not have believed the necklace was actually stolen.

After placing her notepad back in her purse, Anne walked out of the interview room and handed the file to Josie. "Thank you. That was helpful."

"You're welcome." Josie tucked the file under her arm. "May I ask why you're interested in a forty-year-old case?"

Anne smiled. "I know it seems strange, but the subject of Mildred's missing scarab necklace came up again recently, and I just wanted to look into it. I know its disappearance still bothers her after all these years."

Josie hesitated. "Because of the curse?"

"Yes," Anne said slowly. "How did you know?"

Josie sighed. "We've had some phone calls. A few people around town are hearing strange noises in their house in the middle of the night or thinking they see someone outside their window. Each one has mentioned the Egyptian curse that followed Edie Summers to Blue Hill back in the 1970s. They're aware that Edie's clay pot has recently resurfaced."

"Yes, it has." Anne told her the story, including how Mildred's fall was precipitated by her seeing the clay pot on display in the library. "That's why I wanted to look into the missing necklace. Mildred is convinced that its disappearance was connected to the curse, so if I can prove otherwise..."

"You might be able to convince her that there is no curse," Josie interjected. "Well, good luck with that. In my experience, once people cling to an idea, no matter how ignorant, they have a hard time letting go of it."

"I'm just sorry that the police have to use their valuable time because of it. Hopefully things will settle down soon."

Before Josie could reply, the telephone rang on the desk between them. Josie picked it up. "Blue Hill Police Department, Officer Bolling speaking."

Anne watched as Josie listened to the caller, her brow furrowing. "I see. Yes, I'll be right there." Then she hung up the phone and looked at Anne. "Well, so much for things settling down."

"What is it?" Anne asked, a strange flutter in her stomach.

"That was Mildred Farley. She said something horrible just happened and she needs the police right away."

* * *

A few minutes later, Anne parked her Impala behind the police cruiser in front of Mildred's house. She'd followed Josie there, both concerned and curious about Mildred's phone call.

Everything seemed normal and peaceful on the outside of the house. Birds chirped in the trees, and a curl of smoke drifted from a neighbor's stone chimney. Mildred's front door was standing open behind the screen door and, as they walked up the porch steps, Anne could see Mildred seated on the sofa, her left foot propped up on a pillow.

A wave of relief swept through her at the sight. Thankfully, Mildred didn't appear hurt.

Josie rang the doorbell and, a moment later, Bonnie Zimmer appeared and opened the screen door.

"My, that was fast," Bonnie told Officer Bolling. Then her gaze landed on Anne. "And this is a nice surprise. Hello, Anne.

Mildred will be so happy to see you. She was quite upset earlier. I'm sure you'll be just the medicine she needs."

Anne followed Josie into the house, where she inhaled the sweet aroma of cinnamon. Then she walked over to Mildred. "Are you all right?"

Mildred looked up at her. "Oh, Anne, it's so disturbing. I didn't know what else to do, so I called the police."

"What happened?" Anne asked, taking a seat beside Mildred as Josie approached them.

Mildred's hand clutched a small box in her lap. She was dressed in navy blue slacks and a light blue turtleneck adorned with a single string of pearls. "The curse found me...again. I just can't believe it." She met Anne's gaze. "Oh, how I wish you would have destroyed that clay pot! I warned you, Anne. I know you don't take this seriously, but now I can prove that the curse is real."

Josie took a step closer, one hand resting on her black utility belt. "Prove it how?"

Mildred opened the box on her lap. Inside, a gold necklace with a blue scarab pendent was nestled neatly on the white velvet lining. "It came back."

Anne blinked, not believing her eyes. "Are you saying that's the same necklace that went missing in 1975?"

Mildred nodded. "Yes, it's the same one. And I found it in the same drawer that I had placed it in forty years ago." A soft pink flush colored her cheeks as she looked between Anne and Josie. "Now, do you see? It *must* be associated with the curse. There is no other explanation."

Josie leaned in for a closer look at the necklace. "I can think of one possible explanation—maybe it's a fake. People have been talking about that clay pot at the library and some of them probably remember the necklace that went missing from your home. Someone could be pulling some kind of prank."

"That is possible," Anne said slowly as she looked at Mildred. "Are you sure it's the same necklace?"

"Absolutely positive," Mildred said without hesitation. She picked up the necklace, then turned over the blue-glazed scarab, revealing a small V-shaped mark on the underbelly. "Do you see this mark? This same mark was on the scarab I found in Armana. And the gold chain belonged to my mother." She met Anne's gaze. "It's definitely the same necklace."

Josie stepped back. "That may be, but it doesn't mean its return was caused by a curse. Maybe the person who took it forty years ago thought this would be the perfect time to give it back."

"But who would do that after all this time?" Mildred asked, her brow furrowed.

"And why?" Bonnie chimed. She stood behind the sofa, looking at the necklace over Mildred's shoulder.

"We don't know that...yet," Anne mused out loud. She thought about the list of suspects from the crime report she'd read earlier. "Can you tell us who was here today?"

Mildred pursed her lips as she considered the question. "I had a few visitors. Bonnie, of course. And my home health aide was here early this morning, Patty O'Hanlon."

"She's a sweet girl," Bonnie added. "And so efficient. She was in and out of here in nothing flat."

Mildred nodded. "Patty is very thorough too. She takes excellent care of me."

"Anyone else?" Josie asked.

"Two of my neighbors, Coraline Watson and Darla Gunderson, stopped by with more food." Mildred sighed. "I'm going to blow up like a balloon at this rate, but I hate to throw out good food." She glanced up at Bonnie. "Maybe I should throw a party."

Bonnie smiled. "Not until you're up and around. The last thing you need is even more people traipsing through your house when you're on the mend."

"I suppose you're right. That young man who walked through the back door this morning almost scared me to death."

"Young man?" Josie echoed, her eyes lighting with interest. "Did you know him?"

"No, I'd never seen him before." Mildred set the scarab necklace back in the box and closed the lid. "He just waltzed right inside the house...."

"He said he knocked," Bonnie interjected, "but neither Mildred nor I heard him."

"I about jumped out of my skin when I saw him," Mildred continued. "He just walked into the living room and handed me my prescriptions."

"Oh, so he was delivering for the pharmacy?" Anne said.

Bonnie nodded. "That's right. I told Mildred that she should call Thrifty's and complain, but she didn't want to get the young man into trouble."

Mildred smiled. "Well, he just started working there, and he did apologize when I told him that he startled me. He promised to knock louder next time and not just walk inside."

"And his name?" Josie asked, her pencil poised above her notepad.

Mildred and Bonnie exchanged glances. At last Mildred said, "I believe it was Dustin, wasn't it?"

"Yes," Bonnie agreed. "Dustin Wolfe. I thought that was an unusual name, especially since he didn't resemble a wolf at all. Very tall and scrawny." She smiled at Mildred. "We probably could have fattened *him* up with some of that food in your refrigerator."

Mildred nodded. "Something to keep in mind if he makes another delivery."

The ding of an oven timer sounded in the next room. Bonnie stepped away from the sofa. "Sounds like the cinnamon rolls are done." She looked over at Anne. "Do you mind giving me a hand?"

"No, of course not," Anne said, a little surprised by the request. She followed Bonnie into the kitchen, leaving Josie and Mildred in the living room.

Bonnie grabbed an oven mitt off the kitchen counter and slipped it on. "Coraline brought over some cinnamon roll dough this morning, all ready for the oven. So we decided to go ahead and bake them up instead of sticking them in the freezer." She pulled the pan out of the oven and set them on top. "Don't they look delicious?"

Anne moved beside her, the aroma making her mouth water. "They sure do."

Bonnie leaned toward her and whispered, "Mildred is putting on a mighty fine show now, but the truth is, she was terrified when she found that necklace."

"I can imagine."

Bonnie slid the oven mitt off her hand and set it on the counter. "As I'm sure you know, Mildred doesn't scare easily.

But finding that necklace really rattled her. I encouraged her to call the police, because I was hoping that might help calm her down."

"And you have no idea how the necklace got in the drawer?"

Bonnie met her gaze, her blue eyes bewildered. "None at all! And that's what has *me* rattled. How could someone sneak in here and do such a thing without my noticing. Unless..."

"Don't tell me you think the curse is to blame?"

"I don't usually believe in such things," Bonnie replied, "but, you have to admit, this is quite strange. Do you have any other explanation?"

"Not yet," Anne said, determined to find the answers before this curse nonsense loomed any larger. She still couldn't believe people in town were calling the police because of it. And yet, she and Liddie had been spooked the other night when they'd heard a strange noise in the house. Anne had even let herself consider, for just the briefest moment, that it might have something to do with the clay pot.

Bonnie put the cinnamon rolls on a plate, and then she and Anne returned to the living room. "We've got rolls and coffee if anyone's hungry."

"Thanks for the offer," Josie said, slipping her notepad into her shirt pocket, "but I need to get back to the station." Then she turned to Mildred. "I'll make a report about today's incident, but I'm not sure we can call it a crime yet, since nothing was taken and there are no signs of forced entry. Just be sure and let us know if anything else happens that concerns you."

Mildred nodded. "I will. And thank you for coming out."

After Josie left, Anne sat down with Mildred and Bonnie to enjoy a cinnamon roll. The warm icing oozed over the flaky pastry as Anne dug into it with her fork.

"Coraline is an excellent baker," Mildred said, dabbing at her mouth with her napkin. "I'll have to get her recipe."

Anne appreciated the fact that Mildred was making small talk, especially since learning of her terror at finding the necklace. "I've been thinking," Anne began. "Would you mind if I take the scarab necklace home with me for a while? I'd like to research it and see what I can find out."

"Oh," Mildred said, looking surprised by the request. "I suppose you can. But are you sure you want it in your house?"

"Yes, it will be fine," Anne told her. "And I promise to keep it safe."

"Well, then of course." Mildred picked up the box from the coffee table and handed it to Anne. "You may keep it as long as you like."

"Thank you." Anne took another bite of her cinnamon roll and pondered the likelihood that the same person who had taken the necklace forty years ago had probably returned it—especially since Mildred had found it in the exact same place.

"You know, it was quite a coincidence," Anne said, "that I happened to be at the police station when you called. I was looking at the old file about the necklace's disappearance in 1975."

Mildred arched a brow. "Oh? Why?"

"Just curious, really, since the disappearance was so mysterious. I read the police report and saw that they had four suspects in the case. I recognized Coraline's name and Bonnie's, of course."

Bonnie grinned. "Oh my, I'd forgotten that they'd questioned me about it. Calling me a suspect makes me sound so...devious."

"I'm sorry," Anne said, although she could see by Bonnie's expression that she wasn't offended. "I'm sure it was just because you were in the house during the time the necklace disappeared."

"Who else was on the list?" Mildred asked. "I can't quite remember. Wasn't there a handyman?"

"Yes, his name was Abel Randle. Do you remember him?"

"Vaguely," Mildred replied. "He only worked here for a couple of days. My washing machine was leaking, and he came to fix it. If I remember correctly, he was something of a curmudgeon—not friendly at all. I never hired him again."

"Do you know if he's still around Blue Hill?"

"No, I don't believe so," Mildred replied. "I think he moved shortly after the necklace disappeared. Some people thought that made him look guilty, but obviously the police didn't agree."

"Did he move to Deshler?" Anne ventured, looking between Mildred and Bonnie.

"Yes, that sounds right," Bonnie said with a slow nod. "I believe his wife may have been from there."

"And what about Cleta Rinehart?" Anne asked. "I didn't recognize that name on the list."

Mildred scowled. "Cleta was the first and last boarder in this house. She was always late paying her rent and routinely raided my refrigerator."

"But did you suspect her of taking the necklace?"

"Not really," Mildred said. "Cleta allowed the police to search her room and possessions, but they didn't find anything.

She became engaged to a man from Blue Hill and moved out of my house when she married him. I believe he joined the army shortly afterward and they went to live on an army base somewhere."

Anne knew she'd probably have more questions, but she didn't want to wear out her welcome. She placed her empty plate on the coffee table and then picked up the box. "I should probably be going. Thank you for the roll and the hospitality."

"You're welcome here anytime," Mildred said with a smile.

Bonnie walked her to the front door and held it open for her. "Thanks for taking the necklace with you," Bonnie whispered. "I know it will give Mildred some peace of mind."

"Thank you for taking such good care of her. Please call me if Mildred needs anything."

"I will," Bonnie promised before walking back inside the house.

Anne stood on the porch for a moment, staring at the box in her hands. She still couldn't believe the scarab necklace was inside. Now she just wanted to know why the same person who had successfully pulled off the vanishing act forty years ago decided to make the necklace reappear again.

CHAPTER NINE

I don't believe it!" Wendy exclaimed, gaping at the scarab necklace. "Is Mildred sure it's the same necklace that disappeared before?"

"She's positive," Anne said. She'd returned to the library just after noon and found it empty of patrons. With nothing else to do, Wendy had found time to dust both the first and second floors of the library, as well as stock all of the returned books.

Now they sat at a table in the History Room, sharing the chicken salad sandwich that Wendy had brought for lunch and marveling over the reappearance of the necklace.

Wendy gently fingered the blue-glazed scarab pendent, marveling at the blue and green beads lining the outstretched wings of the scarab beetle. "So where has it been for the last forty years?"

"That's what I want to know." Anne picked up her half of the sandwich and took a bite. She'd contributed tortilla chips and fresh baby carrots to the meal, along with a glass of iced tea for both of them.

The library seemed oddly empty to Anne, almost lonely, especially for the middle of the day. She'd expected the sunny weather to bring patrons streaming in but, according to Wendy, only a few people had visited the library, and the majority of them were just returning borrowed books and then leaving empty-handed.

Wendy split a baby carrot in half. "So tell me who's on the suspect list again?"

"Abel Randle, Coraline Watson, Bonnie Zimmer, and Cleta Rinehart."

Wendy shook her head. "The only one I know is Coraline. But she didn't live next door to Mildred in the seventies, did she?"

"No, she and her husband moved there about twelve years ago. But Coraline's sister, Ada Coombs, owned the house previously and, apparently, Coraline was a frequent visitor."

"Interesting," Wendy mused. "So what's your opinion of Bonnie Zimmer? I know she lives in town, but I've never met her."

"She was at the diner the other day when I was having lunch with Alex and the kids, and I also ran into her once or twice at Mildred's house, but I don't really know the woman. Bonnie seems sweet, and I know she and Mildred get along very well."

"Does that mean you've ruled Bonnie out?"

Anne hesitated. Her instincts told her that Bonnie wouldn't have stolen the necklace in the first place, but her instincts might be wrong. "Bonnie's cleaned Mildred's house once a week for the past forty years, so it seems unlikely she'd return the necklace now. But I guess it wouldn't hurt to find out a little more about her, just to be sure she had nothing to do with it."

"I think that's a good idea." Wendy picked up another carrot and took a bite.

Anne kept waiting for someone to walk through the front door, but they'd sat there almost an hour without one patron arriving at the library. She held out hope the clay pot wasn't keeping them away, but after hearing that some Blue Hill residents were calling the police about the curse, she didn't know what to think.

"So that leaves Abel Randle and Cleta Rinehart," Wendy said. "Do you know anything about them?"

"Not really," Anne said with a sigh. "And neither one of them was in Mildred's house recently, so I doubt they're the culprits. Still, I'll see what I can find out."

"Let me know if I can help."

Anne smiled as she picked up a tortilla chip. "Well, you can help me figure out how to bring more people into the library. I think that clay pot might be scaring them away."

Wendy snorted. "Now, that's just silly."

"I know, but look around..." Anne gestured toward the empty rooms of the library. "Are people actually scared to come here?"

"Of course not," Wendy assured her. "It's just a lull." She popped the last bite of sandwich into her mouth and chewed thoughtfully before taking a sip of her tea. "You know," she began, "maybe you need to do a little advertising. Like hold a giveaway of some free books or something to bring people in."

"That's not a bad idea," Anne mused. "Christmas is only a few months away. Maybe I'll have a drawing for some holiday craft books."

"Perfect." Wendy rose to her feet. "Speaking of crafts, I'd better get going so I can start putting together the bean pots for Story Time on Wednesday."

They chatted for a few minutes about the upcoming story hour, and then Wendy took her leave.

Anne stood alone in the library, wondering what to do with the rest of the afternoon. She puttered around for a while, making sure books were arranged properly on the shelves. Then she ordered some holiday craft books for the drawing she planned to have this month. She knew the members of the Tea and Book Club would be excited about it, as many of them enjoyed making crafts.

To Anne's surprise, she found enough to keep her busy until it was almost time for the kids to arrive home from school. She decided to head into the library's kitchen and prepare one of Ben's favorite treats, "ants on a log," which were celery sticks filled with peanut butter and topped with raisins.

She'd just finished placing the last raisin on the plate of celery sticks when two patrons entered the library and began browsing in the Fiction Room. Then the sound of footsteps from the floor above told her that the kids were home. Ben and Liddie soon appeared at the bottom of the back stairwell, followed by Ryan and a boy she'd never seen before.

"We're starving," Ben announced walking into the kitchen with Hershey trotting along beside him.

"I've got 'ants on a log' ready for you," Anne told him, "along with some baby carrots and orange slices." Then she turned to the boy standing next to Ryan. He was shorter than Ben and a little plump around the middle, with wavy blond hair and a small scar above his left eyebrow.

"Hello, there," Anne greeted him. "You must be Carter."

"Yep, he's Carter," Ben said, reaching for a celery stick. "He just moved here from Chicago."

"Yeah, he's in our class," Ryan said, walking over to hand Anne a check. "That's from Uncle Alex."

She stared down at the amount, then she turned her attention back to their guest. "Please help yourself to some snacks, Carter."

"Thank you, Mrs. Gibson," Carter said before walking over to stand next to Ben. Carter reached for a baby carrot and took a bite, chewing thoughtfully as he looked around the large kitchen.

"How do you like living in Blue Hill, Carter?" Anne was eager to get to know Ben's new friend.

"I like it all right," Carter said between bites. "It's a lot smaller than Chicago."

Anne smiled. "It sure is."

Carter turned to Ben. "Can I see your room now?"

"Sure," Ben said, picking up another celery stick before heading to the stairs. "It's this way."

Anne watched the three boys, trailed by Liddie and Hershey, climb up the back stairs until they were out of sight. She was glad that Ben was reaching out to the new boy in his class and looked forward to meeting Carter's parents.

With the kids upstairs and no patrons who needed her assistance, Anne decided now was the perfect time to do a little computer research.

She walked over to the checkout desk and opened a search engine on the computer. Then she typed the name *Abel Randle* into the search box. The first link that appeared was for the *Randle Repair & Renovation* Web site. Anne clicked on the link and saw that the company was located in Deshler and that Abel was listed as the owner. She pulled a piece of scratch paper toward her and jotted down the address of the business.

Then she conducted a computer search for *Cleta Rinehart* but came up empty. If Cleta's husband had joined the army, the two of them could have landed anywhere in the world and never come back to Blue Hill. Anne realized now that she should have asked Mildred for Cleta's married name, since the woman would be hard to track down without it.

Moving on to the next possible suspect in the theft of the scarab necklace, Anne typed the name *Bonnie Zimmer* into the search engine, but all she found was an address in Blue Hill.

Then she tried typing in the name of Bonnie's daughter, Jillian Zimmer, hoping to find out more about Bonnie through her. The attorney Web site of Klove, Zimmer & Franklin appeared in the short list of links. Anne clicked on the Web site, and a quick scan told her that the law firm, located in State College, specialized in family law and providing legal assistance to underprivileged clients and victims of domestic violence.

Anne tapped one finger on the desk, considering the possibility that if Bonnie *had* taken the necklace forty years ago, Jill might have advised her to return it. But surely the statute of limitations for theft would have expired by now. So why take the chance of revealing yourself as the original thief? Unless the guilt had simply become too overwhelming and Bonnie wanted to make it right.

The problem was that Bonnie didn't act guilty. In fact, she was one of the most cheerful people Anne had ever met.

"Earth to Anne."

She looked up from the computer, surprised to see Alex standing on the other side of the checkout desk. "Wow, I didn't know you were here."

"Obviously," he said with a tender smile. "I've been standing here for a while, but you were so focused on whatever you were reading that I didn't want to interrupt you."

She gazed into his blue eyes, wondering if he could help her find the answers. "I'm just trying to figure out the latest Egyptian mystery in my life." Then she told him that Mildred's missing scarab necklace had suddenly reappeared after vanishing forty years ago.

When she finished explaining the story, she showed him the necklace.

Alex moved closer to her as he stared down at the scarab necklace in the box, then shook his head in disbelief. "I can't believe it showed up in her house again. That's really strange."

"That's one word for it," Anne said wryly.

The rumble of stomping feet sounded on the floor above them, reminding Anne that Alex was here to pick up Ryan. "It sounds like the boys are having fun together," she said with a smile. "Have you met Carter yet?"

Alex shook his head. "Not yet, although Ryan's told me all about him. Apparently, the fact that Carter's from the big city of Chicago makes him the new cool kid in the fourth grade."

Anne chuckled. "So that's why Ben has been so eager to invite him over. I'm just glad the boys are making him feel welcome."

"Me too."

Her mind drifted back to the scarab necklace. "Do you know what really puzzles me? Why was that scarab necklace taken in the first place? I mean, why risk a theft charge unless you're going to sell the necklace? And if you don't sell it, why keep it all these years and then secretly plant it in Mildred's house again?"

Alex shrugged. "It doesn't make any sense to me either."

Anne glanced down at the notepad in front of her. "I have the names of four people who were in Mildred's house on the day the necklace disappeared. Two of them I know, and two of them are strangers. One is a woman named Cleta Rinehart, and the other is a man named Abel Randle."

"I know Abel," Alex told her. "He's been in the construction business a long time and has made quite a name for himself over the years."

"What else can you tell me about him?"

"He's a shrewd businessman who owns one of the most successful contracting companies in the area. His two sons joined him in the business, and they're the ones who go out on jobs now."

"So Abel started out as a handyman and built his business into a family affair?"

Alex nodded. "Do you think he might have taken the necklace?"

"I doubt it," she replied, "since he wasn't in Mildred's house when the necklace reappeared. But he might know who took it forty years ago."

* * *

On Wednesday afternoon, Anne checked her watch as the group of preschool children gathered in the Children's Room began to grow restless.

Wendy was late.

She picked up her cell phone and dialed Wendy's number, but after five rings, the call went to her voice mail. *"Hi, this is*

Wendy. I can't come to the phone right now, so please leave a message after the beep."

When the beep sounded, Anne said, "Hey, Wendy, it's Anne. I'm just calling about Story Time. The kids are all here and ready for action. I just wanted to make sure you could still make it. Hope to see you here soon."

Then she ended the call, wondering what to do next.

Wendy usually arrived early for Story Time, but Anne hadn't seen or heard from her all day. She was beginning to worry, and the group of three- and four-year-olds was growing louder and more unruly.

Anne waited five more minutes, but Wendy was still a no-show. At last, Anne decided it was time for her to step in and take over.

"Hey, kids," Anne said, walking to the center of the large, braided rug where the children sat cross-legged on the floor. "Wendy's running late today, so I'm going to fill in until she gets here. Are you ready to hear a good story?"

"Yes," they shouted in unison.

Anne picked up one of Liddie's favorite books and sat down on the rug. The children all began to form a half circle around her, many of them scooting closer.

"I'm so glad to see you all here today," Anne told them, holding the book on her lap so they could see the cover. "I have a special story for you. It's called *Brown Bear, Brown Bear, What Do You See?* Have any of you ever heard it before?"

There were a few nods and varying shouts of "Yes!" or "No!"

"First, let's look at the cover. Can anyone show me where the title is?" Anne asked.

Little hands shot up all around the room. Anne chose the child closest to her, a three-year-old named Tessa. The little girl sat up on her knees and pointed at the title.

"That's right!" Anne said with an enthusiastic smile.

Then she opened the book, holding it up so all the children could see the wonderful illustrations.

"'Brown bear, Brown bear, what do you see?'" Anne began to read.

Then a woman's shout interrupted the story. "Tessa! It's time to go."

Anne looked up to see Kelly Everly, Tessa's mother, walking into the room. She was followed by Beth Wilson.

"You too, Reggie," Beth said, holding out her hand to her four-year-old son. "We have to leave right now."

"Why do we have to leave, Mommy?" Tessa said. "I want to hear the story."

"No, honey, we can't stay here." Kelly Everly looked at Anne. "I'm sorry, but I don't feel my child is safe when that *thing* is down there. When we heard that Denise brought over the preschool kids for the story hour, we had to come right over."

Denise Brown ran a daycare center in Blue Hill, accepting children who needed full-time care, as well as drop-ins. She or one of her assistants often brought children to the library so they could explore the bookshelves. Anne had always thought it a wonderful way to start planting the seeds for a love of reading, but thanks to the recent rumors about the clay pot, the library now seemed to plant seeds of fear instead.

Reggie scowled at his mother and folded his arms across his chest. "I'm staying here!"

Beth walked over and picked up Reggie in her arms. He struggled for a moment, but she held him firmly against her. "I'm sorry, Anne. I really am. But after what just happened, I refuse to risk Reggie's safety."

Anne stood up, concerned by the women's behavior. She didn't want them to upset the other children, but she had to know why they were acting this way. "What just happened?"

Kelly took Tessa by the hand. "Wendy Pyle collapsed at Newlands' Grocery Store. Beth and I both saw it."

"She fainted," Beth clarified. "It happened about an hour ago. She was only out for a few seconds."

"But she was still dizzy when she tried to stand," Kelly added. "And when I helped her to a chair, she said the curse must have gotten to her."

Anne blinked. That didn't sound like Wendy. "Are you sure she blamed the curse?"

Kelly nodded. "I'm positive."

"I heard it too," Beth said meekly. "And after what happened to Mildred Farley..."

Anne looked between the two women. "I'm so sorry that you feel this way. I can assure you that everything is perfectly safe here."

"That may be so," Kelly said. "But I think we'll be even safer at home."

"What about Wendy?" Anne asked, sick with worry for her friend. "Is she all right?"

"She was able to walk to my car, although she felt sick to her stomach," Beth said. "I gave her a ride home, since she was too dizzy to drive. She went straight to bed, and I called her husband to let him know she was ill. He planned to go straight home and take care of her."

Kelly looked down at her daughter. "Say good-bye to everyone, Tessa."

"Bye," Tessa said, her voice forlorn as she waved to her friends.

Anne watched the two worried mothers take their children out of the room, feeling a little sick herself. She was concerned about Wendy but knew that Chad would take good care of her.

"Miss Anne, is there a monster in the library?" Bobby Phillips asked her.

The question startled her. "Oh, of course not, Bobby. The only monsters here are the ones in the books."

"I like the monsters in *Where the Wild Things Are*," Shayla Beck said. "It's my favorite."

"Mine too," Bobby said. "Can you read that one to us next?"

"Absolutely," Anne said, grateful that the children didn't seem too upset by the interruption. She opened the book and resumed reading where she'd left off, keeping her voice calm and even. Soon the children were caught up in the story and no longer distracted by what had just happened.

Unfortunately, Anne couldn't say the same.

CHAPTER TEN

That evening, Anne carried a Crock-Pot full of soup up to the front door of the Pyle house and rang the doorbell. A moment later, the door opened and the four-year-old twins, Jacob and Ethan, stood on the other side.

"Hello, boys," Anne greeted them. "May I come in?"

They didn't reply but opened the door wide enough for Anne to step inside. She saw Chad emerge from the kitchen, dressed in blue jeans and a red T-shirt, a white dishtowel slung over one burly shoulder.

"Hello, Anne," he said with a weary smile. "I see you come bearing gifts."

"If you can call minestrone a gift," she said, carrying the Crock-Pot into the kitchen and setting it on the counter. She plugged the cord into the outlet and set the dial on low.

"I call it a godsend," he said with a long sigh. "Poor Wendy's been in bed all afternoon, and I've taken over the cooking duties, much to the dismay of my kids."

"How's she doing?" Anne asked him. "I've been so worried about her ever since I heard what happened."

He gave a small shrug. "She's a little better now, actually. We called the doctor and told him Wendy's symptoms. He said it sounded like a case of food poisoning. You can go on upstairs if you'd like to see her. I'm sure she'd appreciate the company."

"Thanks, I will." Anne headed for the staircase and found Christian and Emily both seated on the bottom step.

"The curse made our mom sick," Christian said bluntly, scowling at Anne.

"No, it didn't," Emily countered. "Mommy said she ate some bad food."

"She ate it because of the curse," Christian told his sister. "I heard one of the cooks at school talking about it. She said more bad things are going to happen because of that clay pot." Then he looked up at Anne, worry shining in his gray-blue eyes. "Is that true, Mrs. Gibson? I don't want my mom to be sick anymore."

Anne's heart ached for the boy, and she searched for words to comfort him. "I don't want your mom to be sick either, Christian. I'll do everything I can to help her feel better, okay?"

He gave a small nod. "Okay."

Anne continued up the stairs, wondering if the other Pyle children felt the same way as Christian. And according to Kelly and Beth, even Wendy had blamed the curse for her current illness. That thought still made Anne feel sick inside.

She approached the master bedroom door, which stood ajar. Anne peeked inside and saw Wendy reclined in the bed, a pillow propped behind her as she flipped through the pages of a magazine.

Anne tapped lightly on the door. "Are you up for some company?"

Wendy looked over at her and smiled. "Boy, am I! You're just the person I wanted to see."

Anne walked inside, relieved that Wendy looked better than she'd imagined. "How are you feeling?"

"Much better," Wendy told her. "It hit me hard and fast, but it didn't last long. I'd be up and around now if Chad hadn't insisted I stay in bed." Her smile widened. "Now, tell me about Story Time. Did the kids like planting the beans?"

Anne sighed. "I'm afraid we didn't get that far. A couple of the mothers came to pick up their kids because they saw you faint in the grocery store and were afraid of the curse. That disrupted Story Time a bit, and we ended up reading some other books and didn't have time for any crafts."

Wendy's mouth gaped. "That's ridiculous. I fainted because of some bad tuna fish, not some silly curse."

Anne hesitated, wondering if Wendy had been too ill to remember everything she'd said. "But they heard you say the curse made you sick."

Dismay swam in Wendy's blue eyes. "Oh, Anne, I was joking! I can't believe they took me seriously."

"Don't blame yourself," Anne told her. "I'm just happy *you* don't believe it. Poor Christian thinks the curse made you sick, though. He heard one of the cooks at school talking about it."

"I know. He's been having some trouble at school and is blaming the curse for that as well."

"What kind of trouble?"

Wendy sighed. "A boy in his class is picking on him. Carter Pratt? He and his family just moved here."

"I know Carter. He and Ben are friends. Why is he picking on Christian?"

"I have no idea, but Chad called the boy's parents and they were no help at all. I'm torn between telling Christian to ignore him or else give Carter a good punch in the nose."

Anne sighed. "No wonder Christian is upset."

"He acts tough," Wendy said softly, "but he's got such a tender heart. I'm sure this trouble between them will blow over eventually, but it hurts my heart to see him struggle."

"Should I say something about it to Ben?" Anne asked, wondering if her son had witnessed Carter's treatment of Christian. "Maybe he could say something to him."

Wendy shook her head. "I don't want to put Ben in the middle of it. He's only nine. As much as I want to fix it, I know from experience that the boys will just have to work this out themselves."

Anne wanted to fix it too, but she decided to follow Wendy's lead. Christian was Wendy's son and she knew what was best for him. Still, Anne intended to keep a close eye on Ben just to make certain Carter wasn't a bad influence on him.

They chatted a while longer, and then Anne took her leave. As she drove back home, she thought once more about just destroying the clay pot. The rumors about the curse seemed to be growing stronger — and when a ten-year-old boy like Christian was worried about it, then Anne felt as if she had to act.

Yet, she couldn't help but think about what kind of message that would send. By destroying the clay pot, she'd be acknowledging that the curse was real. Despite how much she wanted all this nonsense to go away, she simply couldn't let a silly superstition have that kind of power.

* * *

Liddie greeted Anne at the private entrance when she arrived home from Wendy's house. "Mommy, Mommy, guess what?"

"What?" Anne asked, already knowing the answer. Liddie's wide smile revealed a missing bottom tooth. It had been loose for so long that Anne had started to wonder if it would ever fall out.

"I tripped over Hershey and knocked my tooth out," Liddie said proudly.

"Tripped over Hershey? Are you all right?"

"Yes, it hardly hurt at all." Then she held out her hand to reveal the small white tooth she held.

"Oh my, that is something! But how about Hershey? Is he all right?"

"He's fine," Remi said, appearing at the bottom of the stairs. Anne had hired her to watch the kids while she checked on Wendy.

"I don't think Hershey even noticed," Remi continued, fingering the thick, brown braid that hung over her shoulder. "And I see Liddie told you her big news."

"She sure did," Anne said, setting her purse on the counter. "That means it's time to get out the tooth fairy glass."

Liddie started jumping up and down. "I'll do it, Mommy. I want to fill the fairy glass with water."

It was a tradition in their family to place a lost tooth in a glass of water and then set it on the kitchen counter overnight so that the "tooth fairy" could trade the tooth for a shiny new coin. "All right, you can do it."

Liddie hurried over to the kitchen cupboard and retrieved the special glass that Anne's mother had purchased during a visit to Blue Hill. It had a cartoon image of a fairy on it, complete with a wand and a tiara.

Liddie filled the glass with water and then set it on the counter. "There," she said, dropping the tooth in the glass and watching it sink to the bottom. "Now it's all ready for the tooth fairy!"

"It sure is," Anne said with a smile.

Liddie grinned and then leaned against the counter to stare at her tooth. "I can't wait until tomorrow!"

Anne treasured special moments like this and just wished she could forget about the rumors of that silly curse. But that wasn't possible, not when mothers were pulling their kids from Story Time and people were talking about it in the grocery store and at the elementary school.

Maybe it was time to remove the clay pot from public display, just to stem the growing hysteria about it. Anne refused to destroy it, since it had belonged to Aunt Edie, but putting it out of sight might buy her some time.

She believed the best way to put an end to the hysteria was to prove that the curse didn't really exist. To do that, she needed to prove that the mysterious disappearance — and reappearance — of Mildred's scarab necklace had a perfectly reasonable explanation.

And she needed to do it soon.

As the evening wore on, Anne thought about her next step. She knew where to find three of the four people listed in the original police report and planned to track down Abel Randle tomorrow. The fourth person, Cleta Rinehart, was still a mystery. She'd tried to find the woman on the Internet but came up empty. The fact that Anne still didn't know her married name was hampering her search.

After tucking both Liddie and Ben into bed, Anne walked to the living room and opened the laptop on her coffee table. Hershey padded into the room a few minutes later and jumped up onto the sofa. He settled onto the cushion next to her and rested his head on Anne's thigh.

Anne gently scratched his furry ears as she waited for her computer to warm up. She leaned back against the sofa and closed her eyes, wondering where to find Cleta Rinehart. In her mind, Cleta was the most likely suspect to have taken the necklace. She'd lived in Mildred's house, giving her twenty-four access. Cleta could have snuck downstairs in the middle of the night and taken the necklace, then hidden it someplace where Mildred — and the police — would never think to look.

"But why would she take the necklace?" Anne said out loud to Hershey.

He lifted his head and looked up at her.

"Mildred said Cleta had trouble paying the rent," Anne mused. "Maybe she'd planned to sell it."

Unfortunately, there was no way to know for sure until she learned more about the mystery woman who had rented a room in Mildred's house forty years ago.

"Of course, Cleta would have needed a license to get married, and that would be a public record." Anne logged onto the Commonwealth of Pennsylvania Web site, hoping this might be the key to discovering Cleta's whereabouts.

But to Anne's dismay, the Web site with information about vital records stated that records of marriage licenses were not available online and advised people to head to their local county courthouse in search of such records.

Since Anne didn't know where Cleta and her husband had married, she might have to search every county in the state. And it was possible they hadn't even been wed in Pennsylvania.

With a long sigh, Anne closed the Commonwealth of Pennsylvania Web site. She still planned to drive to Deshler tomorrow to meet with Abel Randle. Since the county courthouse was located there, she could stop in and search for a marriage license for Cleta Rinehart.

"Wait a minute," she told Hershey as another thought suddenly occurred to her. There was another Web site that listed marriage licenses, as well as other vital statistics. "Why didn't I think of this before?"

Anne logged onto a popular genealogy Web site she had joined several months ago when looking for some information. She still retained her membership, although she hadn't used it for so long that she'd almost forgotten about it.

Anne typed the name *Cleta Rinehart* into the Web site's search bar and a few minutes later, some names popped up. There was more than one Cleta Rinehart listed, but only one of the profiles in the list mentioned Pennsylvania.

Anne clicked on the link and saw Cleta's family tree. She started at the top, where Cleta's husband was listed as Harper Allen Kane. But before she could search any further, Anne heard Liddie calling out for her from the floor above.

Setting the laptop aside, Anne gently moved Hershey's head from her lap and then went upstairs to Liddie's bedroom. She opened the door and used the glow of the night-light to find her way to Liddie's bed.

Her daughter lay under the covers, a doll clasped in her arms. Anne could see the glimmer of tears on her cheeks. "Liddie, what's wrong?"

"Oh, Mommy," Liddie sobbed. "Ben told me."

Anne lay a gentle hand on Liddie's shoulder, wondering if she'd had a nightmare. "Told you what, honey?"

"That there's no tooth fairy!" Liddie blurted out, followed by more tears. "He said the tooth fairy is just make-believe."

"When did he tell you this?"

Liddie sniffed. "When we were brushing our teeth. I thought he was lying, but he told me that you're the one who puts the money in the fairy glass. That's not true, is it, Mommy?"

Anne swallowed a sigh, wondering how to navigate these tricky waters. She didn't want to disillusion her daughter but didn't want to lie to her. And the timing wasn't great either. She wished they could have this conversation when Liddie wasn't so tired and upset.

"The tooth fairy is a fun family tradition," Anne told her, wiping a tear from Liddie's face. "Just because she's not real doesn't mean we can't enjoy that tradition."

"So you *do* put the money in the fairy glass?"

"I do," Anne said gently. "And I have so much fun doing it. Just like I have fun putting *Finding Nemo* into the DVD player, because I know how much you're going to like it, even though Nemo is make-believe too."

"I do like Nemo," Liddie said thoughtfully. "Does that mean I can still like the tooth fairy?"

Anne smiled, relieved that Liddie understood that fictional characters often add an element of joy to their lives. "Of course you can still like the tooth fairy! I like her too."

One of the reasons Anne had become a librarian was to share the wonderful fictional worlds created by authors for both adults and children alike. Those stories enriched lives and sparked imaginations in ways that couldn't be measured.

"What about God?" Liddie suddenly asked, her expression serious. "Ben said He's make-believe too."

Anne blinked. "He did?"

Liddie nodded and then emitted a loud yawn. "I don't think God is make-believe. Is He, Mommy?"

"No, my dearest," Anne said softly, leaning down to kiss Liddie's forehead. "God is real. He's watching over us right now."

"Good," Liddie said, a smile curving her lips as she closed her eyes and cuddled with her doll.

Anne sat there for a few minutes, her heart aching as she watched her daughter sleep. How could Ben tell Liddie that God was make-believe? Did he really think that himself?

When Anne left Liddie's bedroom, she walked straight down the hallway to Ben's room and pushed the door open. Her son lay asleep on his stomach underneath the bedcovers, hugging his pillow. The moonlight through the window illuminated a stray curl of hair spilling onto his forehead.

Anne stood there for a long moment, tempted to wake him and have a conversation about God. Was this the real reason he'd skipped the youth membership class—because he no longer believed in God?

That disturbing question would have to wait until tomorrow, she told herself, stepping out of his bedroom and into the hall. She knew it wasn't unusual for kids to question the existence of

God at some point in their lives, she just hadn't expected it to happen until Ben hit his teen years.

Anne headed back to the living room, trying to figure out how to address the subject with her son tomorrow. Hershey still lay on the sofa, bathed in the glow of her open laptop. She picked up the laptop, ready to log off and go to bed, when she noticed a familiar name on one of the branches of Cleta Rinehart's family tree.

PATRICIA KANE m. LONNIE O'HANLON

Her mouth gaped as she stared at the names. Patty Kane O'Hanlon was Cleta's daughter. Before now, Anne hadn't seen any connection that Mildred's home health aide, Patty, had to the necklace. According to the genealogy Web site, Patty had been born in 1979, well after the necklace had disappeared from Mildred's house. But now that she knew Patty's mother was Cleta Rinehart, the connection became clear.

Cleta could have taken the necklace, and her daughter, Patty, could have returned it. Anne smiled as she closed her laptop, feeling one step closer to figuring this all out.

CHAPTER ELEVEN

The next morning, Anne stood at the kitchen table and put the finishing touches on the sign advertising the holiday book giveaway. She'd awakened early, still bothered by her conversation with Liddie last night. A shiny fifty-cent piece sat in the bottom of the fairy glass, waiting for Liddie to find it. She just hoped the moment wasn't tarnished now that Liddie realized Anne had put the coin there instead of the tooth fairy.

Ben walked into the kitchen, dressed in a pair of blue jeans, a purple T-shirt, and white tennis shoes. He'd combed his dark hair, wetting it down a bit to tame a few wayward spikes, and sported a dab of toothpaste on one corner of his mouth. "Morning, Mom."

"Good morning," she said, then tapped the corner of her own mouth. "Looks like you missed a spot when you brushed your teeth this morning. "

Ben stuck out his tongue and licked the toothpaste off before sitting down at the table. He reached for a box of his favorite cereal. "May I have chocolate milk too?"

"Sure," Anne said, walking over to the cupboard to retrieve a glass. "Is your sister awake yet?"

"Yeah, I heard her talking to one of her dolls, but she's still in her pajamas."

That told Anne she had a few minutes before Liddie arrived in the kitchen. She poured milk into a small glass and then added some chocolate syrup before giving it a good stir. Anne carried the glass over to the table and handed it to Ben. "We need to talk."

He reached for the chocolate milk. "What about?"

"God." She kept her tone calm and even, not wanting Ben to think she was angry with him.

Ben took a loud gulp of chocolate milk and then set it down on the table. "Liddie told you?"

"She did," Anne said, taking a seat across from him.

Ben stared down at his cereal bowl. "So what exactly did she tell you?"

Anne folded her hands on the table. "Well, first she was upset because you told her the tooth fairy wasn't real. Then she mentioned that you told her God was also make-believe."

Ben cleared his throat. "Well, the tooth fairy *is* make-believe."

"Yes, it is," Anne said. "And Liddie was so excited when she lost her tooth yesterday and got to put it in the tooth fairy glass. Why did you decide that last night was a good time to tell her about the tooth fairy?"

Ben gave a small shrug, a flush rising in his cheeks. "I don't know."

Anne could see her son was growing uncomfortable, but they needed to talk about this. She just wanted him to open up to her. "So tell me why you think God isn't real."

"Because He's not," Ben said, sputtering a little. "Carter told me that no one can prove God is real. People talk about Him, but we never see Him. Carter says that God is just like the tooth fairy or the Easter bunny—just something people made up."

Now Anne understood that Ben was listening to his new friend, Carter, and following his lead. She opened her mouth to tell him that Carter was a bad influence on him but then closed it again. Even at the tender age of nine, Ben needed to follow his own faith journey. She didn't want him to believe in God just because she told him to do so.

"I see," she said at last. "So is that the real reason you skipped the youth membership class last Saturday? Because you're not sure God is real?"

"Yes," Ben admitted, his flush deepening. "But I did see Carter playing ball in his yard, so that part was true." Then he looked up at Anne. "Are you mad at me?"

"Well, I'm not happy about the lying or about the things you told Liddie, but I'm not mad at you." Anne gazed at her son, love for him filling her heart. "What you believe about God is something you have to determine in your own heart and mind, but I'm afraid your new friend and I have a difference of opinion about this."

He lowered his head. "Okay, Mom. I just…"

Liddie burst into the kitchen before Ben could finish his sentence. "Did the tooth fairy come?"

Anne smiled at her. "Take a look in the fairy glass and see for yourself."

Liddie skipped over to the counter and looked inside the glass. "Oh, wow! It's so big and shiny!" She picked up the glass and carried it over to the sink. Then she carefully tipped the glass so the water spilled out, allowing her to catch the large coin in her hand. "How much is it?"

"Fifty cents," Anne told her. "That's half a dollar."

Liddie dried the coin off with a dish towel. "I'm going to take it to school for show-and-tell."

"All right," Anne said, rising from her chair. "I'll put it in your backpack for you while you sit down and eat breakfast."

Liddie handed Anne the coin on the way to her chair. "Did you see what I got, Ben?"

"Yeah, I saw it," Ben replied. "Pretty cool."

Liddie poured herself a bowl of cereal and added some milk from the carton. "Even if the tooth fairy is make-believe, I still like her. And I like God too."

Anne waited for Ben to reply as she walked over to Liddie's backpack and placed the fifty-cent piece inside the zippered front pocket. But when she turned around, his chair was empty and she heard his footsteps heading up the stairs to his room.

"Is Ben mad about something, Mommy?" Liddie asked, spooning up a bite of her cereal.

"No, honey," Anne replied, saying a silent prayer for her son. "He's just confused."

* * *

That afternoon, Donna Slade, a member of the Library Guild, took charge at the library while Anne made a trip to Deshler to talk to Abel Randle.

The scenic drive to Deshler gave her time to think about her conversation with Ben earlier that morning and she remembered a Bible verse in Proverbs that gave her comfort.

"Train up a child in the way he should go, and when he is old, he will not depart from it."

She also remembered her late husband, Eric, telling her about a crisis of faith he'd experienced in his mid-teens, when he'd been going through a rebellious phase with his parents. A phase he'd obviously overcome since his deep faith as an adult had been one of the reasons Anne had fallen in love with him.

Ben was so much like his father, Anne thought to herself. She just needed to rely on her own faith to see her through this latest development.

As she turned onto the street leading into the town of Deshler, Anne checked her handwritten directions to *Randle's Repair & Renovations*. The office was located just off Main Street on the south side of town. She wasn't sure yet how to approach Abel about an incident that had happened forty years ago. Although, the way the news had been spreading around Blue Hill about the cursed Egyptian clay pot, she wouldn't be surprised if he'd already heard all about it.

After driving a few more blocks, Anne turned off Main Street and saw a cement block building on the corner with a sign advertising the Randle family business. The building was painted ash gray and had a dark blue corrugated tin roof. The yard surrounding the building was sparse, consisting more of dirt and weeds than grass. A lone red rose bush stood near the front entry, a few late fall blooms beginning to droop.

Anne parked her Impala in front of the building and then walked to the front door. When she opened it, a cool blast of air hit her, making her shiver a little. Inside, a long narrow counter separated the office into two parts. On one side were a few scattered chairs, a coffee machine, and a small table stacked with old farming magazines. On the other side of the counter were two desks and a row of black file cabinets lining the cream-colored wall.

A man sat at one of the desks, his gray beard and thick glasses making him look about seventy. He glanced up when Anne approached the counter, but he didn't rise from his chair.

"Can I help you?"

Anne rested one arm on the scratched wooden countertop. "I'm looking for Abel Randle."

"You found him," the man said, still seated. "Are you here about getting some work done?"

Anne noticed the man didn't waste any time on small talk. "Actually, no," she replied. "I was hoping you might be able to help me figure out a forty-year-old mystery."

He scowled. "Come again?"

Anne sensed this conversation might be even more difficult than she'd imagined. Perhaps if she made herself at home, he'd realize that she wasn't going anywhere until she got some answers. "Do you mind if I have a cup of coffee?"

"Help yourself," he said, pushing his chair back. Then he reached for a cane leaning against his desk and stood up. "I'll take a cup too. Sugar, no cream."

Anne suppressed a smile at his treating her like a waitress. He reminded her of a great-uncle who had spoken to people in much the same manner. Uncle Clive had had a heart of gold, but his blunt manner of speaking and unawareness of social niceties had often caught strangers, and even some family members, off guard.

She had no idea if Abel Randle had a heart of gold, but she decided to give him the benefit of the doubt as she poured each of them a cup of coffee, adding a generous portion of sugar to his cup.

"Here you go," she said, setting his paper coffee cup on the counter between them. She took a sip from her own cup, pleasantly surprised at the rich, aromatic brew.

"Now, who are you?" Abel asked, leaning against the counter before reaching for his cup.

"My name is Anne Gibson and I'm from Blue Hill. I run the library there."

His brow furrowed. "Never heard of you before."

"Well, I grew up in Blue Hill but lived in New York as an adult. I moved back to Blue Hill after my great-aunt, Edie Summers, passed away."

"Her, I knew." Abel took a sip of his coffee. "Did some work on her house once."

"Oh?" Anne said, not realizing that Abel had once been hired by Aunt Edie. "Was that before or after Mildred Farley hired you to fix her washing machine?"

He arched a silver brow. "Mildred Farley?"

"Yes, she was a friend of Aunt Edie's. She hired you forty years ago, shortly before an Egyptian necklace disappeared from her home."

His face darkened. "I didn't take that necklace."

"I'm not saying you did," Anne said gently, not wanting to accuse him of anything. "I was just hoping you might be able to give me some information. You see, that necklace suddenly turned up again, and I'm just trying to figure out how that could happen."

"Ask that housekeeper of hers, if you can find her. Name starts with a Z. Ziller, Zimmer, something like that."

"Bonnie Zimmer?"

"That's the one," he said with a nod of affirmation. "As I remember it, the woman could barely scrape two nickels together. She even asked me for a job cleaning up after my construction work, but my wife did that for free, so I turned her down."

"How do you know Bonnie needed money?"

He took a long sip of his coffee, then wiped his mouth with the back of his hand. "It was common knowledge in Blue Hill back then. Her husband up and left her one day. She had to pick up any odd jobs she could find. Almost lost her house to the mortgage company, but Mildred owned some rental homes and let Zimmer and her kid stay in one in exchange for cleaning her house."

Anne stared at him, taking in this new information. She hadn't realized Bonnie had struggled so much in the seventies. The woman had such a cheerful outlook on life, it was hard to imagine her barely making ends meet. "So you believe Bonnie stole Mildred's necklace?"

"Well, if she didn't steal it, then I'd look at that Rinehart woman. She was on a manhunt for a husband and finally nabbed a bachelor in Blue Hill. Then she quit her job the day before she got married. Wouldn't surprise me if she heisted some jewelry from Mildred's house to wear to the wedding."

"It doesn't sound like you liked Cleta Rinehart very much."

He shrugged. "Didn't really know her, other than hearing her complain about the noise my tools made. She worked nights as a telephone operator and slept during the day."

"So did you see or hear anything about the necklace before it disappeared?"

He shook his head. "Not a thing. I do remember that people blamed its disappearance on some curse, which was one of the dumbest things I'd ever heard. Sounded more like a case of simple greed to me." Then he scratched his grizzled chin. "Although, if the necklace showed up again, that means the thief didn't sell it."

"That's right," Anne agreed. "And that's what has me so perplexed. I was hoping you could shed some light on the situation for me."

He scowled at her. "If you're looking to blame me, you've got the wrong man. There were plenty of things in the Farley house worth stealing, but that bug necklace sure wasn't one of them."

Even though Anne had just met the man, Abel's words had a ring of truth to them. He didn't strike her as the type to be impressed with ancient artifacts from Egypt. "Well, thank you for your time."

"Come back when you've got a job for us to do," Abel told her. "You won't find a better contractor in Blue Hill, that's for sure."

Anne gave him a small smile, certain that Alex would disagree. She didn't particularly like Abel Randle's style, but his blatant honesty struck her as genuine.

She glanced at her watch, deciding she still had plenty of time to visit one of the women Abel had accused of stealing the necklace before she returned to the library.

* * *

Anne drove back to Blue Hill and headed straight for Patty O'Hanlon's house. Patty owned a large three-story Victorian home that had been built nearly a century before.

The house was in shambles when the O'Hanlons purchased it a year ago, with most of the paint worn off and the wraparound porch practically falling to pieces. With hard work and considerable expense, they'd turned the house into a beautiful painted lady sporting three different paint colors and charming gingerbread trim. The wraparound porch had been completely rebuilt and filled with colorful plants and flowers, along with an old-fashioned porch swing.

As Anne neared the O'Hanlon's home, the reason for their extensive renovations suddenly became clear. Near the front walk was a sign that read *O'Hanlon Bed-and-Breakfast*.

As she parked her car and climbed out, Anne noticed that a pair of white wooden rocking chairs had been added to the porch, along with an old-fashioned milk crate near the front door filled with decorative gourds and pumpkins.

Anne knocked on the door, hoping either Patty or Lonnie might be home. She'd met them a few times before when they'd attended services at Blue Hill Community Church. Lonnie worked for a farmer, and Patty enjoyed her job as a home health aide for the medical clinic.

When there was no answer, Anne rang the doorbell. A few moments later, she heard the sound of footsteps approaching from the other side. The door opened and she saw Patty wearing a pair of light blue nursing scrubs.

"Hello," Anne greeted her. "I hope I haven't come at a bad time."

Patty clapped her hands together, her green eyes dancing with delight. "This is the perfect time! I was just thinking about you."

"You were?"

"Yes, please come in." Patty ushered her inside the house, closing the door behind them. "This is serendipity. I've been working on a promotional brochure for our bed-and-breakfast." She turned to face Anne. "Did you know Lonnie and I are turning this place into a B and B?"

Anne smiled as she followed Patty into a large parlor filled with antique furniture and vintage knickknacks. A baby grand piano sat in one corner with sheets of classical music displayed on the music rack. "I figured it out when I saw your sign outside."

Patty laughed. "Oh, of course. We just put the sign up last night and are planning to officially open for business next weekend." She motioned to an antique Edwardian settee upholstered in gold brocade and adorned with decorative pillows. "Please have a seat. I'm afraid we won't have long to talk. I'm due to be at a client's house in about fifteen minutes."

"So this really *is* a bad time," Anne said, sitting down on the settee. "Which means I probably should get straight to the point of my visit."

"Before you do," Patty said, perching herself on an antique piano stool, "may I ask you a favor?"

"Of course."

"Lonnie and I would love to borrow that Egyptian pot that you have on display at the library for our grand opening. You see, according to my research, the most successful B and Bs have some kind of special attraction. I think the curse of the clay pot is the perfect way to attract a certain type of tourist."

Anne stared at her. Patty was the first person she'd met who actually considered the supposed curse a *good* thing. She didn't know what to say.

"Now, we'll understand if you don't want to let us borrow the clay pot. After all, it is a valuable Egyptian artifact. But if we could even just take a photograph of it for the brochure, that would be enough. Of course, we'll add in some text about the legend of the curse and some of the strange things that have happened in Blue Hill, both back in 1975 and more recently."

It suddenly occurred to Anne that if Cleta Rinehart had stolen Mildred's scarab necklace, then Patty had the perfect motive for returning it. What better way to attract a certain kind of clientele to a B and B than by resurrecting a forty-year- old curse?

"Do you mind if I think about it and let you know?" Anne said, not certain she wanted to promote the legend of the curse when it seemed to be driving patrons away from the library.

"Yes, that's fine," Patty said with a smile. "I know it's a lot to ask."

Anne smoothed her hand over the arm of the settee. "This brocade is lovely. In fact, this parlor makes me feel as if I've stepped back in time to the late nineteenth century."

"Thank you," Patty said. "I inherited most of the antiques from my mother. She was quite a collector. My father was in the army and they lived all over the world. She'd buy antiques on all of her travels and have them shipped to Blue Hill. That's how I ended up with them." Patty breathed a wistful sigh. "Mom passed away about ten years ago, but she had a real sense of style."

"And I believe she actually rented a room at Mildred's house at one time."

Patty's eyes widened as she looked at Anne. "Yes, she did! Back in the seventies. I just discovered that yesterday when Mildred and I were chatting. I mentioned that my mother's first name was Cleta, and Mildred told me about a boarder she'd had by that name. It didn't take us long to figure out that it was the same Cleta!"

"Yes, that is a coincidence. Did your mom ever mention Mildred?"

Patty shook her head. "Not that I can remember."

Anne gave a slow nod, treading carefully now. "She must have been living there around the time Mildred took that trip to Egypt. I wonder if she got to see the scarab necklace before it disappeared."

Patty gave a small shrug. "I really have no idea."

Anne sensed that it was time to change the subject. She looked around the room, marveling at how pristine it looked. "You've done so much work to this house. I'm sure all of your future guests will love it."

"I certainly hope so," Patty said. "We're pulling out all the stops to make it a success."

Anne wondered if that included perpetuating the curse by returning the scarab necklace to Mildred's house. But before she could find a way to pose that question, Patty looked at her watch.

"Oh no," Patty cried. "I'm late! I hate to hurry you out the door, Anne, but this particular client is a real stickler about punctuality."

"I understand." Anne stood up and walked out of the parlor. "Thanks for taking the time to see me. Someday, I'd love to have the full tour."

"Of course. Just give me a call and we can arrange it," Patty said, following Anne out the front door.

They parted ways as each headed to their own car. For a brief moment, Anne wondered if Patty's sudden need to leave had been spurred by their discussion of the scarab necklace. Maybe Patty had inherited more than antique furniture and knickknacks from her mother. Maybe Cleta Rinehart Kane had also left her daughter a blue-glazed scarab necklace.

CHAPTER TWELVE

Anne tossed and turned in bed on Thursday night, thinking about her visit with Patty, as well as the fact that fewer and fewer patrons were coming to the library. A library needed readers to survive, and they were dwindling fast. Anne knew she had to find a way to turn that trend around.

By Friday morning, she had a plan. She picked up the phone and called Grace Hawkins, asking her to stop by the library when she had some free time. Then she started baking a cake, planning to serve some refreshments to the Tea and Book Club members who would be meeting at the library this afternoon.

"What are you making?" Liddie asked, walking into the second-floor kitchen.

"A chocolate chiffon cake for the book club meeting today." Anne stood at the stove, carefully melting chocolate in a double boiler. "Are you excited to have the day off from school?"

"Yes, I'm going to build a fort in my room," Liddie announced. "No boys allowed!" That's when Anne remembered that she'd given permission for Ryan and Carter to come over today. It was too late to back out now, she told herself, realizing that she already had her hands full with running the library and making refreshments for the book club.

Besides, the boys were old enough to entertain themselves. They could play outside or build forts of their own in Ben's room. She had enough leftover fried chicken from last night's supper to feed them for lunch and plenty of fresh fruit and vegetables for snacks.

Ben appeared in the kitchen, still wearing his Spider-Man pajamas. "Hey, Mom, what's for breakfast? Can we have waffles?"

"Sorry, Ben," Anne said, stirring the melting chocolate, "but I don't have time to make waffles this morning. I have to finish putting this cake together and then open the library. So you'll have to make do with cereal and toast."

"Okay," Ben said, walking over to the cupboard and pulling out a box of cereal. "Ryan and Carter are coming over at nine, so I need to be ready. We're going to build a Lego town."

"Sounds fun," Anne said, as Liddie walked over and sat at the table with her brother.

"Mommy, can I call Cindy and Becca and ask them to come over to play today?" Liddie asked.

"Sure," Anne said, figuring there'd be less trouble if Liddie wasn't trying to get the boys' attention. And the Jacobs sisters were such sweet girls. Anne knew they wouldn't be any trouble at all. "As long as one of their parents can bring them here, they can stay all day."

"Yippee!" Liddie shouted, pumping her hands in the air.

Anne finished putting the cake together while the kids ate their breakfast and made plans for their day. She glanced out the window after pouring the cake batter into the tube pan. The sun was shining in the blue sky, and a light breeze caressed the remaining leaves in the trees. "You need to call Cindy and Becca," Anne reminded Liddie. "So why don't you do that as soon as you finish your cereal and then go get dressed."

"I'm done," Liddie announced, slipping off the chair and carrying her empty bowl to the sink.

"Me too," Ben said, reaching for his juice glass and draining it. Then he followed Liddie up the stairs to the third floor, leaving Anne alone in the kitchen with Hershey.

"So which one of us is going to wash these dirty dishes?" she asked the dog. "Me or you?"

Hershey just looked up at her, wagging his tail.

"I guess I'll do it," Anne said with a smile. She carried the cake pan over to the preheated oven and placed it inside before setting the timer.

"Mommy," Liddie shouted down the stairs. "Cindy and Becca's mom is on the phone. She wants to talk to you."

Anne closed the back door and walked over to the phone extension sitting on the kitchen counter. She picked it up and said, "Hi, Yvette."

"Hello, Anne. I'm just checking to make sure you want both girls to spend the entire day at your house."

"Yes, that would be great." Anne leaned against the counter. "Ben is having some friends over, so Liddie asked if Cindy and Becca could visit as well. I'll be here all day, so the more, the merrier."

A long silence carried over the line, then Yvette cleared her throat. "So...I was just wondering. Have there been any more...problems at the library?"

"Problems?" Anne echoed, although she could guess what Yvette meant.

"I heard that both Mildred Farley and Wendy Pyle were bothered by an Egyptian artifact there. Something about a curse?"

Anne swallowed a sigh. "Well, I did find an Egyptian clay pot that my great-aunt had stored in the attic for the last forty years. Some people like to believe there's a curse attached to it, but I promise there's nothing of the sort. Cindy and Becca will be perfectly safe here."

Yvette chuckled. "I assumed it was something like that. Like I said, I've heard some rumors, so I wasn't sure what to think. I just wanted to check with you."

"I'm glad you did," Anne said, relieved that Yvette planned to let the girls visit in spite of her reservations.

They chatted for a few minutes more, and then Yvette ended the call, promising to drop the girls off around nine o'clock.

Anne wanted to get the library ready to open before the kids arrived, so she quickly washed up the breakfast dishes, then headed downstairs to prepare the library for the day.

* * *

"Oh my," Claire Daniels exclaimed as Anne set the chocolate chiffon cake on the table in the second-floor meeting room of the library. "That looks divine."

To Anne's delight, a steady stream of patrons had entered the library all morning, and this afternoon promised to be even better. Seven members of the Tea and Book Club had arrived for their meeting, and Anne's cake had turned out perfectly.

"Just help yourselves whenever you're ready," Anne told them, adjusting the stack of dessert plates on the table. She'd made a large pitcher of raspberry iced tea, along with a pot of coffee for the club members to enjoy with their cake.

"We certainly will," Gloria Parnell said with a smile. "To tell the truth, I had some doubts about coming here today given some of the recent problems, but I'm sure glad I did."

"Me too," Peggy Rey chimed. "Mary Zumfelde was supposed to come with me, but after Mildred's scarab necklace turned up out of the blue, she got a little spooked. Mary told me she doesn't believe in the curse, but she decided to play it safe by staying home today."

Anne had found that to be the case with many of the regular patrons who were now avoiding the library. She supposed it was no different than people who made it a point to never walk under a ladder or let a black cat cross their path. Sometimes, habits like that simply became second nature.

Anne just hoped avoiding the library didn't become a habit for the residents of Blue Hill.

"How is Mildred doing?" Gloria asked. "Does anyone know?"

"I saw her this morning," Claire said. "Her ankle is mending, but it will still be awhile until she's back on her feet. Thankfully, Bonnie Zimmer is there to run errands for her and make sure the house is running smoothly. I believe she's even stayed over a night or two."

Gloria nodded. "Bonnie's been a godsend for her, that's for sure. Does she have any family in Blue Hill?"

"No, but her daughter, Jill, and her brother, Garth, both live in State College."

"I remember Garth," Peggy said. "He was the star of the Blue Hill football team back in the fifties. I wonder if he's still as handsome as he was back then."

Claire chuckled. "I caught a peek of him the other day when I was driving by Bonnie's house. He must have been visiting. I'd say he's even handsomer. And better still, I hear he's single."

Anne smiled as she left the meeting room and walked up to the third floor to check on the kids. Liddie and the Jacobs girls had built a massive fort in Liddie's room, using several quilts and blankets. They were giggling together when Anne stuck her head in the door.

"How's everyone doing?"

"Good," the girls said in unison.

Anne smiled. "All right. I'll be down in the library if you need anything."

As she walked back into the hallway, Anne took a peek out the window that overlooked the backyard. Ben, Ryan, and Carter were tossing a football around while Hershey bounded back and forth between them. She'd fed them all lunch and had snacks ready for them in the refrigerator whenever they were ready.

"So far, so good," Anne murmured to herself as she headed to the first floor.

She'd chatted with a few of the patrons who were browsing through the bookshelves in the History Room. She'd removed the Egyptian display and placed the clay pot out of public view in the library's kitchen until she could decide what she should do with it. A few people had asked her about it, and she'd been truthful with them that it was still in the house. Now she just had to come up with a new idea for a display.

Anne made her way into the Fiction Room, brainstorming ideas for a display, and had just reached the checkout desk when the lights started to flicker.

"What is that?" Betty Bultman asked, her arms full of recently returned books that she was placing back on the shelves.

A feeling of dread tightened Anne's stomach as the lights began to flicker again, even faster this time. She saw several of the patrons hurrying toward the front door.

"Please, everyone," Anne called out. "There's no reason to panic. I'm sure there's just a little glitch with the electricity."

"Or it's the curse," a woman shouted, dropping the books she held in her arms onto the nearest table. "I've never seen lights do that before."

"Please, don't leave," Anne implored, hurrying toward the front door. The lights kept going on and off and back on again. She looked up and saw Claire, Peggy, and Gloria leading the way down the stairs.

"I'm sorry, Anne," Claire said, looking a little frantic, "but we've decided to cancel our book club meeting for today. Some of the members are ... concerned. I'm sure you understand."

"Of course," Anne said, forcing a smile. Suddenly, the lights stopped flickering. "There, it looks like they're back on now."

Gloria looked around her. "But why were they flickering? It's not storming outside. In fact, there's not a cloud in the sky."

Anne wished she had a reasonable explanation. "It's an old house, so it's possible there's something in the wiring that caused it. I'm going to call Alex Ochs to check it out, but I'm sure it's nothing to worry about."

"I agree with Anne," Claire said resolutely. "In fact, I think I'll stay and look for some books to take to Mildred, since she can't make it here herself."

Anne appreciated that vote of confidence, even if she was sure Mildred wouldn't step foot in the library as long as the Egyptian clay pot was still in the house.

Liddie and the girls appeared at the top of the stairs. "Mommy, what happened to the lights? They keep going off and on."

"I want to go home," Becca Jacobs cried.

Then Cindy Jacobs burst into tears. "Me too. This house is haunted!"

The front door swung open and Hershey ran inside, his feet caked with mud. The boys followed, all three of them sweaty and dirty.

"The football landed in a mud hole," Ben exclaimed, tucking the dirty football under his arm. "And Hershey chased after it."

"Yeah, he made a real mess," Carter said as he pointed to the muddy paw prints on his yellow T-shirt. "Hershey kept jumping on me and wouldn't stop."

"That's because you had a fried chicken wing in your shirt pocket," Ryan said, rolling his eyes. "I told you not to put it there."

Hershey continued to make a mess in the front foyer of the library. Muddy paw prints covered the herringbone floor as the dog paced back and forth between Anne and the three boys. Claire gave Anne a wave and weak smile as she and Gloria followed the other patrons out the door.

Anne didn't know whether to laugh or cry at the calamities that had occurred in the space of five minutes—flickering lights, fleeing patrons, bawling Jacobs sisters, and muddy paw prints all over her clean floor. The Egyptian clay pot wasn't cursed, but her day had definitely taken a turn for the worse.

* * *

"I don't see a problem here," Alex said, looking inside the fuse box in the basement.

Anne stood beside him. "Are you sure there's not a faulty fuse or two? The lights flickered for at least two or three minutes on every floor. It was really strange."

Alex turned to her. "Did you notice anything else, like a burning odor or any of the bulbs burning out?"

"No, nothing like that." She rubbed one hand over her face, wanting to find some reasonable explanation for the afternoon's events.

After most of the patrons had left, Betty Bultman agreed to watch the library while Anne drove the Jacobs sisters home. The three boys and Liddie were now all upstairs in Ben's room playing with his toys.

She looked up to see Alex staring at her.

"This has really gotten to you, hasn't it?" he said gently.

Anne forced a smile. "Is it that obvious?"

"To me, yes." He reached out and touched her hair, his hand lingering there for a moment before he pulled a dust mote from it. "But then I've known you since we were kids. You don't believe the curse caused the flickering lights, do you, Anne?"

"Of course not," she said, watching him close the fuse box door. "But you have to admit that it's more than a coincidence that all these things started to happen after I found the clay pot. Mildred breaks her ankle, Wendy gets sick, and the lights flicker on and off." Anne turned toward the stairs. "And strangest of all, a scarab necklace that disappeared forty years ago suddenly turns up again!"

"Okay," he admitted. "That does seem like more than a coincidence."

When they reached the top of the stairs, Betty approached Anne, her purse slung over her shoulder.

"I hate to run out on you, but I just remembered that I have a dentist appointment this afternoon. And since there's no one here anyway..." Her voice trailed off. "I'm sorry, that didn't sound good, did it?"

"It's the truth," Anne said with a wan smile. "The word about the flickering lights has obviously gotten out by now. But thanks for staying and helping out."

"Anytime," Betty said as she walked over and gave Anne's arm an affectionate squeeze. "And don't worry. This too shall pass."

After Betty left, Anne turned to Alex. "I hope she's right." Then she squared her shoulders, determined to make the best of the rest of the day. "How about a piece of chocolate chiffon cake?"

He grinned. "Now that's an offer I can't refuse."

Anne led him to the kitchen in her personal residence on the second floor, where she'd placed the untouched cake after the Tea and Book Club members had fled the library. She sliced off a generous piece for Alex and then cut a thinner piece for herself before joining him at the kitchen table.

"Help yourself to some raspberry tea," Anne said, motioning to the pitcher on the table.

"Thanks." Alex poured himself a glass. "Do you want some?"

"Sure." Anne picked up her fork and took a bite of the chiffon cake, letting the chocolate flavor linger on her tongue. "Wow, that's delicious, even if I do say so myself."

Alex poured a glass of tea for Anne and set it in front of her. "Too bad the book club members missed out."

Anne took another bite of cake, her thoughts on the events of the afternoon. "I wonder if someone planned it that way."

Alex met her gaze. "You think someone did it on purpose?"

She gave a small shrug. "It's possible someone could have snuck downstairs and flipped the circuit breaker back and forth to make the lights flicker. Then that person could reappear in all the chaos and act just as panicked as everyone else."

"And who do you think might do something like that?"

Anne sat back in her chair. "I have no idea. It would have to be somebody who enjoyed the curse rumors going around town. The only people I know who fit that description are Patty and Lonnie O'Hanlon, but neither one of them were here today."

"Unless they persuaded someone else to do it for them."

As Anne considered that possibility, it dawned on her how easy it was to converse with Alex. They'd known each other so long and were so comfortable together. She could easily call him one of her best friends. "That just seems so outlandish," she said at last. There has to be some other explanation." She took another bite of cake, hoping the combination of chocolate and sugar might spark her imagination.

"You know, there is one way to solve all your problems."

"I know," she said with a sigh. "I could get rid of the clay pot. Believe me, I've considered doing it."

"You don't have to destroy it," Alex told her. "You could sell it or give it away. In fact, I'd be interested in taking it if you're tired of dealing with it. Or I could simply hold it for you until you ask for it back."

She looked over at him. "You're not afraid of the curse?"

He grinned. "This chocolate cake is more dangerous to me than that old clay pot."

"You're right," she said, mentally counting the calories she'd just consumed. "I just wish other people felt that way."

"Give it time," Alex advised. "Something else will come along to grab everyone's attention. It always does."

Anne hoped he was right. In the meantime, she'd hold book giveaways and other incentives to draw people into the library. Then they'd see there was actually nothing to fear.

"Not to change the subject," Alex said, "but Ryan told me that Ben might not be going to the youth membership class at church tomorrow."

"Yes, that's the other issue I'm dealing with. Apparently, Carter Pratt doesn't believe in God, so Ben has started questioning his own faith."

Alex's dimple flashed in his cheek as he gave her a sympathetic smile. "Wow, you really do have your hands full. So what are you going to do about Ben?"

"I'm not sure. I thought I'd ask Pastor Tom for some advice. I'm sure he's dealt with this kind of thing before."

"Well, good luck." Alex set his fork on the empty plate in front of him. "I suppose Ryan and I had better get going. Let me know if you have any more problems with the electricity."

"I will," she said, rising from the table. "And thanks for coming by on such short notice."

"Hey, if more people offered me chocolate cake during service calls, I'd be the fastest handyman in town."

Anne laughed as they left the kitchen and went in search of the boys.

* * *

After she'd seen Alex and Ryan off, Anne returned to the first floor of the empty library and walked into the kitchen to look at the clay pot that seemed to be the cause of all the trouble.

Getting rid of it would be so easy, Anne thought to herself. Even Aunt Edie had hidden it away in the attic forty years ago. So why not do the same?

Before Anne could make a decision, a loud knock sounded on the front door.

CHAPTER THIRTEEN

Anne walked over to the door and opened it, surprised anyone would knock since it was a public entrance. She saw John Rey, a member of the Blue Hill town council and an avid reader, standing on the other side. He was dressed in a suit and tie, a pair of aviator sunglasses covering his eyes.

"Hello, John," she greeted him. "The library's open, so you don't have to knock."

He pulled off his sunglasses and then peered inside before stepping gingerly over the threshold. "I wasn't sure it would be open after what happened earlier. Peggy was quite upset about it."

"I'm sorry about that," Anne said, closing the door behind him. "I had Alex Ochs check out the fuse box and he doesn't think there's any sort of electrical problem."

"Well, that's good news, I guess." John looked around the empty library. "It appears that this may be a good time for us to talk."

"Of course," she said, leading him into the History Room. She saw his gaze go to the spot where the clay pot had been displayed—now empty.

"I'm happy to see you no longer have that thing on display," John said, turning his gaze to Anne. "Especially after all the trouble it's caused."

John was an accountant and had always struck Anne as a reasonable man, so his attitude surprised her.

"Are you saying that you believe the curse is real?" she asked.

He sighed. "I don't know what to think. But just look around." He motioned to the empty library. "There's obviously a problem here." He pulled out a chair at the nearest table. "Shall we sit down and talk about it?"

His tone, as well as his expression, concerned her. Did John believe in the curse? And what exactly did he want to discuss?

He cleared his throat and then folded his hands on top of the table as he met Anne's gaze. "Peggy told me there was quite a panic when the lights started flickering."

"Yes, I'm afraid so, although I think people overreacted. The flickering stopped after just a few minutes."

"I'm sure they did overreact," John said. "Just like Mildred, when she fell and hurt her ankle. The simple truth, Anne, is that the town can't afford the liability problems that could occur if these kind of events keep happening."

"Liability? But we have insurance. Surely that will cover things like Mildred's accident."

"It will, but there comes a point where the insurance company will consider the library too big of a risk and simply cancel the coverage. And someone could still try to hold the town liable if another accident occurred here. They might not win, but it would cost Blue Hill thousands of dollars just to pay for defending such a lawsuit."

His words were sobering. "So what do you suggest we do, John?"

"Close the library," he said bluntly. "At least until the hysteria about the curse fades away. I'm not sure how long that will take, but it seems like the best course of action at this time."

"We can't close the library," Anne said, indignant at the very idea. "Aunt Edie wanted it to serve the people of Blue Hill. That was her dream. Besides, closing it because of the curse will be giving in to that hysteria, won't it? I don't see how that solves the problem."

"Look, Anne," he said evenly, "I understand your viewpoint. I really do. But what happens when someone trips walking up the front step to the library and splits their head open?" He pointed to the grand staircase in the foyer. "Or falls down those stairs when they're in a panic because the lights start flickering again? Given everything that's happened recently, you know that's a real possibility, don't you?"

Anne couldn't argue with him, as much as she wanted to disagree. People *had* panicked this afternoon when the lights began to flicker. "What if I just get the pot out of the house?"

He hesitated. "That would be a step in the right direction, but this curse business has taken on a life of its own, especially since Mildred Farley's scarab necklace suddenly reappeared. I hear someone mention the curse every day — whether in fear or jest or just for shock value."

"Closing the library is not the answer," Anne insisted. "There has to be another way."

His mouth thinned. "Look, I came to you hoping for your cooperation. It would be easier if you chose to close this place on your own, perhaps even take a vacation with your kids. By the time you returned, this whole thing will probably have blown over."

"But my kids are in school," Anne said. "And I can't just take them out."

John pushed back his chair and stood up. "I'm afraid the only other alternative is for the town council to vote to close the library, at least temporarily. We meet seven days from now, on Thursday evening. And I intend to make a motion to close the library at the meeting, unless you take action first."

"This is all so silly," Anne exclaimed, trying to make him understand. "It's just a clay pot—a *harmless* clay pot. It's been in the attic for the last forty years and no one has worried about a curse during that time."

A loud, thumping noise sounded overhead.

John's brow wrinkled as he tilted his head toward the ceiling. "What's that?"

"My kids are upstairs," Anne said. "They're probably playing some kind of game."

At that moment, Ben and Liddie walked through the front door.

"What are you two doing?" Anne asked them. "I thought you were upstairs."

"We can't find Hershey," Liddie said. "I think he went outside when Carter left, but now he's gone."

Thump. Thump. Thump.

John's eyes widened at the sound. It was directly above them. "There it is again."

"Is that another yo-yo?" Liddie asked, sounding annoyed.

"I don't think so, honey," Anne replied. The strange noise had started at the worst possible time. It certainly wouldn't help convince John *not* to close the library. "But I'm sure it's something just as silly. Maybe the window is open again and the wind is blowing something around."

Thump. Thump. Thump. Thump.

"It sounds like a giant is walking upstairs," Liddie said, her eyes full of wonder. "Like the giant from *Jack and the Beanstalk!*"

"It's not a giant, silly," Ben muttered, with a nervous glance at Anne.

John looked at his watch. "Hey, I've got to go. Please think about what I said, Anne." He hurried toward the front door, giving the ceiling another concerned glance on his way. "We'll be in touch soon."

Then he was gone.

"This is ridiculous," Anne said, heading toward the stairs and taking them two at a time. When she reached the second floor landing, she stopped and listened. There was a long silence, and then she heard it again.

Thump. Thump.

The sound was coming from the Children's Room. Anne didn't hesitate. She headed straight into the library room, ready to face whatever she found there.

At first, she didn't see anything.

Thump. Thump.

Anne turned around and saw Hershey at the other end of the room. His leash was attached to his collar and a small, five-pound hand weight was tied to the end of his leash. Each time he took a step, the hand weight thumped against the floor.

"Come here, boy," Anne said, kneeling down as Hershey walked toward her and as Ben and Liddie stood in the open doorway.

Thump. Thump. Thump. Thump.

When Hershey was within her reach, Anne grabbed his leash and untied the hand weight from the end of it. The five-pound weight hadn't been heavy enough to cause any distress to the dog. In fact, Hershey was wagging his tail.

"Good boy," Anne murmured, petting his silky head. Then she turned toward the door. "Which one of you did this?"

"Not me," Liddie said.

"Well, I didn't..." Ben began, before he was interrupted by a snort of laughter coming from the far end of the Children's Room.

A moment later, a head popped up from behind a bookshelf and Anne saw Carter Pratt with a huge smile on his face.

"Wow, that was a great joke!" Carter exclaimed. "Even better than the one we planned, Ben. I bet everybody downstairs thought there was a monster up here!"

Liddie giggled "We thought it was the giant from *Jack and the Beanstalk*." She lifted her legs high in the air and began stomping across the floor. "'Fee-fi-fo-fum...'"

"'I smell the blood of an Englishman,'" Carter shouted, stomping his way toward them.

Anne glanced over at Ben. Her son pressed his lips together to keep from smiling, but amusement danced in his eyes.

"Okay, kids, the fun is over." Anne glanced at her watch. "I think it's time for you to go home, Carter. Do you want me to drive you?"

"No, I can walk." Carter headed toward the door. "Mom and Dad told me that Blue Hill is so small that I can walk all over town if I want."

Anne followed him into the hallway and down the stairs to the first floor, Ben and Liddie on her heels. Then Anne opened the front door. "I want you to head straight home, okay?"

"Okay," he said cordially. "Bye, Ben. See you at school."

"Bye, Carter," Ben said with a wave. When Carter was out of sight, he turned to Anne. "Mom, I didn't know Carter was going to tie that weight on Hershey's leash. We were just going to play a joke on Liddie and tell her that Hershey was missing."

Liddie frowned. "That's not a funny joke."

"No, it's not," Anne said with a sigh. Then another thought occurred to her. "What about the lights flickering earlier? Was that a prank too?"

Ben winced. "We just wanted to see if we could scare people. I didn't know it would make everybody leave."

Anne didn't know what to say. On the one hand, they were just boyish pranks, but Ben obviously didn't realize how harmful they could be. John Rey had practically sprinted out of the library when he'd heard the strange thumping noise coming from the second floor.

For a moment, Anne considered calling John and explaining what had really happened, but then she realized it probably wouldn't do any good. She needed to convince the whole town that the curse wasn't real, not just one man.

"We'll talk about this later," she told Ben, not ready to mete out his punishment yet. "You go up to your room and stay there until I call you for supper."

Ben's shoulders drooped as he turned around and headed up the stairs. Hershey followed along beside him, nudging Ben's hand with his nose.

Liddie looked up at Anne. "Is Ben in trouble?"

"Yes," she replied, smoothing Liddie's hair off her forehead. The library was in trouble too, unless Anne could figure out how to keep it open.

* * *

On Saturday morning, Anne opened the library at the regular time of ten o'clock, but no one appeared at the door. Ben was in the backyard raking leaves as part of his punishment for the pranks. He was also grounded for the next week, which meant no playing with friends after school, especially Carter Pratt.

However, Anne did plan to make an exception for the youth membership class this afternoon, telling Ben that she wanted him to go. To Anne's surprise, he didn't argue with her, although he didn't look very happy about it either. She prayed that she was handling his faith crisis in the right way — so that she could help Ben move toward God instead of away from Him.

The front door of the library opened, and Anne hurried to meet the only patron who had dared to cross the threshold. That's when she saw a UPS driver, a young man in his early twenties with red hair and freckles, wearing a brown uniform and holding a box in his hands.

"I've got a delivery for this address," he said, handing Anne the box.

"Thanks." She glanced down at the routing slip on the top of the box and saw the name and address of one of her favorite book wholesalers, which meant the holiday craft books she'd ordered for the giveaway had arrived.

The delivery man's wide-eyed gaze moved slowly around the library. "Gee, it sure doesn't look very scary around here. The way people have been talking, I expected something a little creepier."

"It's not creepy at all," she said with a smile, hoping to dispel the notion that the Blue Hill Library was something to be feared.

"I heard the electricity started acting all weird here," he said. "And all the lights started going on and off."

She didn't recognize this delivery man and assumed he was a weekend substitute. Still, his job brought him into contact with a lot of people, so Anne figured he might be a good conduit to spread the message that the library was safe.

"It turns out my nine-year-old son and two of his friends messed with the lights as part of a series of pranks."

The delivery man grinned. "I knew it had to be something like that. Boy, people sure do scare easily. One lady I talked to was really spooked about it."

"Well, if you see her again, you can tell her what really happened. I'm going to try and spread the word, so any help would be appreciated."

He nodded as he moved toward the door. "I can do that."

Anne watched him leave, hoping he had a lot of deliveries to make in Blue Hill today. It might be like dropping a small pebble in a pond, but hopefully the ripples of truth would soon start spreading through the town.

She carried the box over to the checkout desk and used a box cutter to open it. After removing the protective padding inside, Anne pulled out the three new books. She loved the bright colors and festive photographs on the book covers. Now she just needed to make a display with them and include a box for the drawing.

After considering different options, Anne decided to put the display on a tall pedestal table right next to the checkout desk so that patrons couldn't miss it. She moved the pedestal table into place and then retrieved some Christmas wrapping paper from the storage closet. The box the books had come in was just the right size for the table, so she wrapped it with the Christmas paper and then added a small opening for people to place their tickets for the drawing.

"Wow," Liddie said when she walked through the door from the old kitchen. "Did you buy some Christmas presents for me already?"

Anne smiled as she tied a shiny red bow on the box. "Not yet. This is for a book drawing for the library. There will be three winners who will each receive one of these books. She showed Liddie the books that had just been delivered. "Do you want to help me set them up on the table?"

"Sure!" Liddie moved toward her, eager to help. She began by placing the gift-wrapped box in the center of the table

They worked together, adding decorative Christmas ribbon to the table, as well as some star confetti that had been left over from a birthday party. Liddie's contributions to the decorations added a child's charm that created just the look Anne wanted for the display table.

"There," Anne said, adding the sign as the finishing touch, along with the tickets for the drawing. "It looks perfect."

Liddie picked up the empty cardboard roll from the Christmas gift wrap. "Can I go play with this in my room, Mommy?"

"Sure," Anne said with a smile, knowing some of the best toys were those you didn't find in a toy store.

Liddie disappeared with the long cardboard roll, leaving Anne alone in the library once more. She walked to the front door and opened it, looking at the empty parking area. The lovely October day enticed her to step onto the porch so she could enjoy the warm air that carried the crisp aroma of fall.

It was hard for her to imagine the library closing, even if only for a short while. She loved interacting with the readers who arrived each day, sharing their love of books with her and creating friendships that Anne cherished.

The sound of Hershey's barking drew her attention to the backyard. She could see several small piles of golden leaves that Ben had gathered with the rake. At the moment, he was taking a break from raking and tossing a small branch for Hershey to chase. She smiled at the two of them, wishing life were always so simple.

With a small sigh, Anne turned and walked over to one of the chairs on the porch. She sat down and starting playing the "what if?" game in her head.

What if I'd never found that clay pot in the attic? What if Mildred hadn't fallen and sprained her ankle, blaming the curse for her injury? What if Ben and his friends hadn't played those pranks that just added to the curse rumors around town?

For the first time, Anne wondered if those rumors were just too big and pervasive to fight.

What if I just get rid of the clay pot? What if I close the library? What if I just give up trying to convince people that the curse doesn't exist?

Before she could answer those questions, Anne saw a car approaching from the distance. As it neared the house, she recognized Grace Hawkins's blue Ford Fusion. She watched Grace pull her car into the parking lot, grateful that at least one person hadn't been scared away from the library.

"It looks like I came at the perfect time," Grace said as she joined Anne on the porch. "Not much business today?"

Anne smiled. "You're the first person I've talked to this morning other than Ben and Liddie."

Grace winced. "Oh dear. I'd heard about a couple of strange incidents here yesterday, but I didn't realize it was quite that bad."

"It's so bad that John Rey paid me a visit and recommended that I close the library until these curse rumors blow over. And he made it pretty clear that if I didn't close the library voluntarily, then the town council would do it for me."

Grace's lovely blue eyes widened in disbelief. "John's always struck me as a pretty sensible guy. Don't tell me he believes in this curse nonsense too?"

"Well, if he didn't, a little prank Ben and his friends played while John was here might have made him a believer." She told her about the five-pound weight tied to Hershey's leash, as well as the flickering lights debacle.

Grace chuckled. "I'm sorry, I know I shouldn't laugh, but that's pretty creative."

"Effective too," Anne said wryly. "John couldn't leave here fast enough."

"But surely once people know that those incidents were just pranks, they'll understand."

Anne smiled. "I've actually considered going door-to-door and explaining what happened, but that would take too long. That's why I called you. I'm hoping you'll do that story we talked about earlier."

Grace breathed a sigh of relief. "Actually, I've already started, so I'm glad you're on board with it. I paid Mildred a visit yesterday afternoon and got her side of the story." She sat down in the chair next to Anne. "In case you didn't realize it, she believes things will only get worse in Blue Hill until you get rid of that Egyptian pot."

"I know," Anne replied, "but I don't want to give into the hysteria. There's just got to be another way."

"Well, maybe you could offer a reward to anyone who can prove the curse isn't real?"

"Maybe," Anne mused, wondering how anyone could actually prove a negative. "I still think the key to the situation is convincing Mildred. She's certain that her scarab necklace disappearing forty years ago and now reappearing is proof of the curse. If I can find the person who actually took it, that would change everything."

Grace nodded. "Mildred Farley is well respected in this town. Her word carries a lot of weight. I think that's one reason these curse rumors have persisted. Some people think that if an intelligent, sensible woman like Mildred believes in the curse, it might actually be true."

Anne needed Grace to do her a big favor, and there was no time like the present. "Do you mind putting your story on hold for about a week? If I can change Mildred's mind by finding the thief, I have a feeling she'll want to do another interview with you."

"I can wait a week," Grace told her, "but no longer. Will that be enough time?"

Anne's stomach clenched at the thought of a one-week deadline—especially when she didn't feel any closer to solving this puzzle than when she'd started.

But what choice did she have?

"In one week, I'll either identify the thief," Anne said, taking a deep breath, "or I'll get rid of the clay pot once and for all. Either way, this so-called curse will finally come to an end."

CHAPTER FOURTEEN

That Saturday afternoon, Anne drove Ben to the Blue Hill Community Church for the youth membership class. She'd dropped Liddie off to play at the Pyle house on the way, planning to run an important errand while Ben was at his class.

She glanced over at her son, who sat in the passenger seat beside her. He'd barely said two words since they'd left the house. Anne hadn't given him the option of attending the class today, and he obviously wasn't happy about it.

Since the class wasn't due to start for another fifteen minutes, she turned onto a shady street and slowed the Impala to a leisurely cruising speed.

"Something on your mind?" Anne asked him.

Ben turned in the passenger seat and looked at her. "I'm just trying to figure something out."

"What's that?"

He sucked in a deep breath. "Well, we're going to be talking about church and God and stuff at this class. Am I supposed to lie and say I believe in God? Will I get in more trouble if I lie or if I tell the truth that I think God is make-believe?"

Despite her distress at the question, she was impressed by Ben's intellect. Even at the age of nine, he was grappling with such complicated issues.

So much like his father.

She smiled to herself as she contemplated his question. Eric had always loved to debate deep issues and had often offered a unique perspective that she'd never considered before. How she wished he were here now to talk to Ben. She just hoped the Lord would guide her in finding the right answer.

"No, I don't think you have to lie," she said at last. "But does this mean you've decided for certain that you don't believe in God?"

He hesitated. "Well, Carter doesn't believe in him."

"I'm asking about *you*," Anne said gently. "Do *you* have doubts?"

"Doubts," Ben echoed. "Yes, I have doubts."

"Well, I think that's pretty common. Your dad had doubts at one time too."

Ben's eyes widened. "He did?"

She nodded. "A long time before I met him, but he told me about it. Even some of Jesus's disciples had doubts at times. Remember the story of doubting Thomas? Jesus had to show him the nail wounds on his hands before Thomas would believe it was truly Him."

"Yeah, I kinda remember that story." Ben sighed. "I just wish I could know for sure. I feel like a fake going to this class when I might not even believe in God."

Anne understood his dilemma, even as she prayed that he'd overcome these doubts and embrace his faith. But this was Ben's faith journey, she reminded herself. And just like so many other times in a mother's life, she had to take a step back and let him find his own way.

"Well, maybe you should think of this class as a way to learn more about God and how others feel about him," Anne told him. "It never hurts to gather information, especially when we're trying to make a big decision."

Anne intended to follow her own advice by seeking more information about the scarab necklace. Despite Mildred's insistence that it was the same necklace that had disappeared forty years ago, she wanted to know for sure. Aunt Edie had often told her that information was one of the greatest gifts people could give themselves.

"I suppose I could do that." Ben looked up at Anne, nervously nibbling his lower lip. "But what if Pastor Tom asks me if I believe in God? What should I say?"

Anne leaned closer to him, placing one hand on his shoulder. "First of all, I don't think that he will ask you that, but even if someone does ask that question, what do *you* think you should say? What do you want to say?"

Ben hesitated. "I want to say that…I'm thinking about it."

Anne nodded. "That's a good answer."

She turned the corner and pulled into the church parking lot. There were a few cars there and some children about Ben's age playing outside. "I'll pick you up in about an hour," she told him.

"Okay, Mom." Ben climbed out of the car and raced over to join the other kids.

Anne sat watching her son for a long moment and then made her way into the church. Ben was only nine and wrestling with some big, adult questions. She just wanted to give Pastor Tom a heads up in case some of those questions came up in the class.

She found the pastor in his office, a book open on the desk in front of him. "May I bother you for a moment?"

He looked up and smiled. "Hello, Anne. A visit from you is never a bother."

"Well, I know the class is supposed to start soon, so I'll only be a minute. I just wanted to tell you that Ben is having some doubts about God."

Pastor Tom nodded, looking unfazed by this announcement. "That's not unusual, but it's more common when kids hit their teens."

"Well, he has a new friend at school who told him that God is make-believe."

"Ah," Pastor Tom said. "Would that be Carter Pratt?"

Anne blinked. "How did you know?"

"Just a lucky guess. I went over and introduced myself to the Pratt family shortly after they moved here. Carter's father, Mick, made it clear that he had no use for God or religion. I got the feeling that he's had some difficulties in his life, so I've been praying for him. But it doesn't surprise me that Carter has taken on the opinions of his father."

Anne nodded. "I've been struggling with whether to allow Ben to have Carter over again. I don't want to interfere in their friendship, but I'm worried that Carter might not be a good influence."

"That's a possibility," Pastor Tom said gently. "But I think there's a greater possibility that Ben would be a very good influence on Carter. Ben's an intelligent boy with good values and a big heart. I think he might be just the kind of friend that Carter needs."

His words made her smile. "You're right. I hadn't thought about it that way."

"Don't worry about Ben. He's got a good head on his shoulders. I believe he'll come through all of this just fine."

Anne nodded, taking his words to heart. "Telling me not to worry is like telling me not to breathe," she joked. "But I'll give it a try."

He glanced at his watch. "I hate to cut our conversation short, but I've got a class to teach. You're welcome to join us if you'd like."

"Thanks, but I have some errands to run. Have fun with the class."

He smiled. "I always do."

* * *

Five minutes later, Anne walked into Kepple's Jewelry Store on Main Street. Her high school classmate Hank Kepple owned the store with his wife, Heidi. Their twin boys were in the same kindergarten class as Liddie and had inherited their father's red hair, freckles, and jovial personality.

Hank stood behind the counter, his back to her as he reached inside a glass case. "I'll be right with you," he said, picking up a ring box. Then he turned around and saw Anne.

"Well, this is a nice surprise," he said, setting the ring box on the counter. His gaze moved to the box in her hand. "Did you bring me a present, or are you making a return?"

"Neither actually," she said with a smile as she placed the box on the marble counter between them and then took off the lid.

Hank's eyes widened as he looked at what lay inside. "Is this the scarab necklace? The same one that mysteriously disappeared from Mildred Farley's house all those years ago?"

"That's what I'm hoping you can tell me. Mildred is certain it's the same necklace, but I want to know if it's possible that someone is trying to fool her."

Hank pulled the box to him and then carefully picked up the jeweler's loupe that he used to magnify jewelry. The loupe was in a stainless steel case with an optical lens and an LED light. Hank had once demonstrated how to use it, explaining that it magnified objects up to forty times their size and allowed him to see the smallest detail in pieces of jewelry.

Now Ann watched him as he used the loupe to examine the scarab necklace. He stood bent over the counter, holding the jeweler's loupe against one eye as he slowly scanned the gold chain of the necklace and then the blue-glazed scarab pendent. After several minutes, he turned the necklace over and repeated the process.

Anne waited patiently for Hank to finish his inspection, the only sound in the room the rhythmic tick of the grandfather clock in the corner. At last, Hank straightened and set the jeweler's loupe aside.

"Well?" Anne asked him, eager to know the truth. If the necklace was a fake, that would be an easy way to prove to Mildred that the curse wasn't real.

"The chain is eighteen-karat gold."

She nodded. "Just like Mildred's mother's necklace."

He leaned against the counter. "Now, I'm no expert on Egyptian artifacts, but when I heard that Mildred's scarab necklace suddenly showed up in her house again, I got curious. So I did quite a bit of research on scarab jewelry, including talking to some jewelers I've met at conferences who *are* experts in these things."

"And?"

"And I think this is the real thing." He pointed to the small hole at the top of the scarab.

"This scarab was meant to be worn as jewelry and hung from a piece of string or leather. You'll notice that the hole in the scarab isn't very straight from one side to the other. That's a sign it's probably authentic. The crude tools the Egyptians used during that time period made it necessary to drill the hole from both sides. Also, the stone is made of steatite, which is consistent with that era."

"Wow, I'm impressed," Anne told him. "So you think it's the same necklace?"

"I can't be one hundred percent sure," Hank said. "There are a lot of modern fake scarabs out there, but I don't think this is one of them. I suppose someone could have tracked down a scarab that matched the description of the one Mildred had owned, but they'd have to invest a lot of time and expense to find it. In fact, you'd probably have to travel all the way to Egypt."

Anne doubted any of the possible suspects on her list would have gone to that much trouble. "I've compared this scarab to the one in a photograph of Mildred's necklace taken by Coraline Watson forty years ago. The carvings on the scarab stone are an exact match."

He nodded. "Then that confirms it. The chances of finding a duplicate scarab with the same markings and made from the same material as the one that Mildred owned back then are practically nil."

Before Anne could reply, she saw Heidi, Hank's wife, emerge from the back room. She wore a white-and-blue polka dot blouse that matched her blue skirt and shoes.

"Hello, Anne," Heidi said with a smile. Then her gaze moved to the scarab necklace. "Oh, is this the infamous necklace?"

"According to Hank, it is," Anne told her. "I thought it might be a fake, since it's hard to imagine someone stealing it only to return it to the owner forty years later."

"Sounds like a guilty conscience to me," Heidi said, and then she hesitated, her expression changing. "Or someone trying to drum up publicity."

Hank turned to his wife. "What do you mean?"

Heidi drew out a sheet of paper from the drawer in front of her. "I mean this."

Anne looked down to see a color advertisement for the O'Hanlon Bed-and-Breakfast. A photograph of their beautiful Victorian house filled the page, but it was the message at the bottom that made Anne's breath catch in her throat.

You don't have to go all the way to Egypt to find the mysteries of the Pharaohs. Come to Blue Hill, Pennsylvania, where a forty-year-old curse is alive and well.

Beneath the message was a photograph of the Egyptian clay pot that had been on display in the library. Patty or her husband had obviously taken the photograph while visiting the library, cropping out the rest of the display so that only the clay pot remained.

"Where did you get that?" Hank asked his wife.

"Patty O'Hanlon brought it in this morning, right after I opened the store. She asked me if we could hang it up in our front window. I think she was taking the flyers to every shop on Main Street, trying to drum up business for their new B and B."

"Are there really that many people who would travel to Blue Hill just because of the so-called curse?" Anne asked, baffled by the very idea.

Hank sighed. "More than you'd probably think. I participate in a lot of Internet sports forums, including one dedicated to the Steelers and another one for Flyers fans. Even some of these guys have commented on the rumors of the curse in Blue Hill. Someone even said there was a story about it in one of the Pittsburgh newspapers."

Heidi tapped the B and B advertisement in front of her. "I think we can all make a good guess on who planted that story."

On the one hand, Anne couldn't blame the O'Hanlons for advertising their business, even if she didn't quite agree with some of their marketing methods. But this certainly wouldn't make it any easier for Anne to dispel rumors about the curse.

"They might have crossed the line with using the photograph of your clay pot for promotional purposes," Hank said slowly. "But I don't think they're the ones who planted that necklace in Mildred's house."

Anne looked at him. "Why not?"

"Because about six months ago, Patty brought in a bunch of jewelry to sell," Hank explained. "She and Lonnie were deep into house renovations and, like most projects, it was costing a lot more than the estimate. She wanted to sell the jewelry to raise money."

"I'm guessing this necklace wasn't one of the pieces she wanted to sell," Anne said.

"You're right about that," Hank said. "Although, she did have some vintage jewelry that had belonged to her mother and grandmother. Nice stuff too. But no scarab necklace."

Anne thought about the possibilities. "Maybe Patty was afraid someone might remember stories about the stolen scarab necklace, or that Mildred might come into your store and see it for herself. She could have taken it to a jewelry shop out of town to sell it."

Hank shook his head. "Like I said, I'm on a lot of Internet chat forums. One is for Pennsylvania jewelers. Believe me, if a necklace like this came into someone's shop, there would have been a lot of chatter about it on the forum."

"So if Patty did have possession of this necklace," Anne mused out loud, "she might have believed it was more valuable *not* to sell it."

Heidi's eyes widened. "You mean, Patty might have placed the necklace in Mildred's house?"

"It's possible, since she's been working there every day since Mildred's accident."

"And she was there when the necklace was found," Heidi added.

Anne blinked, surprised by this new information. "She was?"

Heidi nodded. "Patty told me all about it when she brought in the flyer for her B and B this morning. She said Mildred screamed when she saw the necklace and got really upset. Patty even took her blood pressure just to make certain she was all right."

Anne let this sink in, wondering why Mildred hadn't mentioned that Patty had been present when she'd found the necklace. Then again, if Mildred had been that upset, she might have forgotten a lot of the details — especially since she blamed the curse for the necklace's return. "I didn't realize Patty was there."

"Well, Patty made sure to spread the news about the necklace far and wide," Heidi said. "I heard about it at the beauty salon, which is Rumor Central around here."

Anne nodded, realizing that Patty appeared to have the best motive for returning the stolen necklace, especially since Hank said it was so unique that it might have captured people's attention if she'd tried to sell it.

Hank placed the lid back on the necklace box and slid it toward Anne. "I don't think it's even possible to solve a crime that happened forty years ago, is it?"

"I need to try," Anne told him. "Otherwise, this curse nonsense is going to continue keeping people away from the library — unless I get rid of the clay pot."

Heidi tipped up her chin. "Don't you dare get rid of that pot, Anne. That's just giving in to ignorance. That clay pot is an ancient Egyptian artifact. It's something that should be attracting people to the library, not chasing them away."

Anne smiled, appreciating her candor. "I just wish more people in town thought like you."

"They do," Heidi assured her, "they're just not as vocal as the superstitious ones."

Anne knew she was right, but the town council tended to listen to the loudest voices. "Thanks so much for your help." She looked at Hank. "How much do I owe you for the evaluation?"

"No charge," he said with a smile. "I'm just thrilled I got a chance to examine such a rare piece of art."

"Well, I appreciate it." She picked up the box. "And thanks for your support. It means more than you know."

"Stay strong," Heidi said as Anne made her way out the door.

Anne placed the necklace in the trunk of her car and then headed to the church to pick up Ben. He was waiting with some of the other kids out in the yard. As she pulled into the parking lot, he caught sight of her. Ben waved good-bye to his friends and then joined her in the front seat.

"How was the class?" Anne asked as she turned the car around in the empty lot and headed back onto the street.

"Fun," he said, sounding enthused. "We played some games and got a tour of the church so we could see how everything works. The bell tower is really cool!"

"Did anyone ask you if you believe in God?" she inquired, knowing that had been his fear before the class started.

"No," Ben said, a note of relief in his voice. "We mainly talked about the duties of church members and all the different ways you can volunteer."

Anne drove in the direction of Wendy's house to pick up Liddie. She'd learned more about the necklace today, authenticating that it was indeed real and that it was the same necklace that had disappeared from Mildred's house forty years ago. But had Cleta Rinehart been the one to take it?

That was the question that still niggled at her, especially since none of the other names on that police report seemed to have a motive. Even Coraline, with her collection of oddities, could have returned the necklace at any time in the last twelve years. Why wait until now?

"Mom," Ben said, "can I still be a church member if I don't believe in God?"

She glanced over at him. "Why would you want to?"

"Because I really like everybody there. And Pastor Tom is nice and has interesting stories. I could still be friends with everyone, and do all the fun stuff."

"You could," Anne said, treading carefully. "But wouldn't it bother you to sit in church and not believe the words we sing in the hymns?"

He frowned. "I never thought about that. I like to sing."

"I know you do. And what about the sermons? Would you feel like Pastor Tom was lying when he talked about God and told us stories from the Bible?"

"I don't think Pastor Tom is a liar," Ben replied, sounding confused.

"Neither do I." Anne knew she was directly challenging some of Ben's doubts and wanted to be careful not to push too hard or steer him in a certain direction before he was ready. "Those are just some things to think about."

"I want to believe in God," Ben told her. "But I just need proof that He's real. Like something I can see or hear or touch."

Anne parked in front of the Pyle house. "So if there's something that you can't see or hear or touch, then it's not real?"

He hesitated for a long moment. "Well, I believe in gravity, but that's because our science teacher showed us some experiments that proved gravity is real."

Anne turned off the car engine and unspooled her seat belt. "Let's go pick up your sister. We can talk about this later."

Ben turned to her, a yearning expression in his brown eyes. "Mom, can you prove to me that God is real?"

CHAPTER FIFTEEN

Wendy opened the front door and immediately placed a finger over her mouth. "*Shh*. Do you hear that?"

Anne stood with Ben on the front porch and strained her ears for any sounds coming from inside the Pyle house. After a few moments, she shook her head. "No, I don't hear anything."

Wendy grinned. "Exactly! This is one of those very rare moments where it's actually quiet in the house."

Anne laughed. "Even with Liddie here?"

"Oh, she and Emily are in the backyard having a tea party picnic." Then her gaze moved to Ben. "Christian is back there too, playing with his remote control car if you'd like to join him."

Ben looked at Anne. "Can I, Mom?"

"Sure," Anne said and then watched him scamper off. She turned back to Wendy. "So where is the rest of the Pyle clan?"

"Chad took them into Deshler," Wendy said, waving Anne inside. "He needed to pick up some extra shoulder pads for the football team and wanted the kids to ride along with him since he's always so busy with practice and games during the season."

"Well, that sounds nice."

"Nice for me, definitely." Wendy led Anne down the long hallway. "Let's sit in the kitchen. I just made a fresh pot of coffee, and we'll be able to see the kids from the window. Not that I have to worry about yours getting into trouble. They're always good as gold."

"Not always," Anne said wryly, thinking of the pranks that Ben and his friends had pulled.

They walked into the kitchen, where Wendy retrieved two coffee mugs from the cupboard. Sunlight streamed through the lace white curtains, making the stainless steel appliances gleam. Clean dishes were stacked near the sink and two apple pies sat on trivets next to the stove.

"It smells wonderful in here," Anne said, taking a seat at the table. "Looks like you've been baking."

Wendy filled the two mugs with coffee and carried them to the table. "Those pies are fresh out of the oven if you'd like a piece."

Anne's mouth watered. "I know I should resist, but maybe I'll just have half a piece."

"Coming right up." Wendy walked over to the counter and dished up two pieces of pie. She placed them on the table, taking a seat opposite Anne. "This is nice. It's been a while since we've had a good visit."

"I'm just glad you're feeling better. No more fainting, right?"

"I'm fine," Wendy assured her. "I'm sure I did have a touch of food poisoning, but I'd skipped breakfast that morning too, which probably didn't help." She forked up a generous piece of pie. "But as you can see, I've recovered my appetite."

Anne smiled as she took a bite, enjoying the sweet treat. The three apple trees in the Pyle's backyard provided plenty of apples this time of year, and they were always delicious.

Wendy cupped her hands around the coffee mug in front of her and breathed a wistful sigh. "I can't remember when I've enjoyed such a peaceful and relaxed Saturday afternoon. It gave me time to work on my letter."

"Letter?"

"Oh, didn't I tell you?" Wendy got up from the table and walked over to the small desk in the corner of the kitchen. She picked up a piece of paper and returned to the table, handing it to Anne. "I printed out the rough draft. It's for the Letter to the Editor column of the *Blue Hill Gazette*."

Anne began to read it out loud.

Dear Editor,

An incident occurred at Newlands' Grocery Store last week involving me. I fainted, due to food poisoning according to my doctor. I am fine now, but I was quite upset to learn that a joke I told at the grocery store is now being taken out of context and spread around town.

I like to tell jokes, especially when I'm feeling stressed. Just ask my seven kids. After I fainted, someone asked me what happened and I said, "The curse must have gotten to me." It was meant to be a joke, but apparently some people took me seriously.

I want to make it perfectly clear in this letter that I have NEVER believed in these rumors of a curse connected to the Egyptian clay pot in the Blue Hill Library. In fact, I think they're rather silly, which is why I made a joke about it in the grocery store. I want to apologize to the people in the store who took me seriously. There is no curse. The library, and every other place in Blue Hill, is as safe as it has always been. That's

why I love living here so much. I hope that we can put these
rumors to rest and continue to be a great community.

Sincerely,
Wendy Pyle

By the time she finished, Anne had tears in her eyes. She looked up at Wendy. "That is such a wonderful letter. Thank you so much."

"I'm glad you like it. I just hate the fact that my stupid joke has caused these curse rumors to flourish."

"It's not your fault. Once people latch onto an idea, it seems that any excuse will do to prove that idea is true." Then Anne told Wendy about John Rey's visit to the library and his suggestion to close the library.

"What?" Wendy exclaimed. "He can't be serious."

"Well, it didn't help matters that Ben, Ryan, and Carter decided to play a prank while he was there and spooked him away. They were also responsible for the lights flickering in the library."

Wendy shook her head, even as a smile played on her lips. "At least you know why it happened."

"Yes, and that's exactly what I'm still searching for: the *whys* behind the other strange things that have been happening."

Wendy rose from her chair and refilled both of their coffee mugs. "And are you making any progress?"

"Well, I know the scarab necklace that Mildred found is the same one that disappeared forty years ago. And it seems the O'Hanlons have the best motive so far for making it mysteriously reappear, but I don't have any solid proof." Then she sighed.

"And speaking of proof, I have another problem. Ben wants me to prove to him that God is real since he's having doubts about God's existence."

Wendy blinked. "That's an interesting challenge."

"I know. I just hope I'm up to it." Anne took a sip of her coffee.

"So what are you going to do?"

"I haven't decided yet. I put him off for now, but I can tell he *wants* to believe in God. I'm going to pray about it tonight and trust that the Lord will show me the way."

Wendy nodded. "I'll pray too, for both you and Ben. It's not easy raising kids, is it?" She grinned. "If I'd known that in the beginning, I might not have had as many."

"I can't imagine your life without them," Anne said, knowing how much Wendy cherished her children.

"Neither can I," Wendy agreed. Then a mischievous twinkle lit her blue eyes. "And I'm also having trouble imagining the rest of the afternoon with no more pie. Can I talk you into one more piece?"

Anne felt her willpower slip away. "Yes, you can." Then she held out her plate and joked, "If anyone asks, just tell them the curse made me do it."

* * *

Anne sat in church Sunday morning, still grappling with the challenge Ben had issued to her.

"Can you prove to me that God is real?"

God's love and presence surrounded her every day, but how could she prove that to a nine-year-old? She could point to the long history of the church, the power of prayer, the faithful followers who had suffered persecution for their beliefs.

But Ben was nine. He didn't want a history lesson. He wanted to believe, and he'd convinced himself that proof was required.

Heavenly Father, she prayed silently as the congregation stood to sing the closing hymn, *show me the way into Ben's heart. I love him so.*

Before the song was over, Anne knew what to say to Ben. The answer came to her like a leaf floating on the wind, so simple and yet so perfect. She closed her eyes and whispered, "Amen."

An hour later, Anne sat at the kitchen table eating Sunday dinner with Ben and Liddie. She'd prepared a pot roast, complete with mashed potatoes, carrots, onions, and gravy. And, inspired by Wendy's pie and the apples that Ben and Liddie had helped gather in the Pyles' backyard, she now had an apple cake baking in the oven. The sweet aroma filled the air and brought a familiar comfort to the cozy kitchen.

Ben took a long drink of milk, draining his glass before setting it down on the table. "May I be excused?"

"Not yet," Anne told him. "I want to talk about God and proving that He's real."

Ben's eye widened in surprise. "You can prove it?"

"I can," she said, glancing at Liddie. The five-year-old had saved her mashed potatoes for last and was now shaping them into a dome.

Anne turned her attention back to Ben. "But first I have a question for you."

"Okay," Ben said, pushing his plate away. "What do you want to know?"

Anne leaned forward, placing her folded hands on the table as she looked at her son. "Is love real?"

He blinked. "Yes."

"Can you prove it?" she asked gently.

He thought about her question for a long moment. "Well, I love you," he said, then glanced at his sister. "And Liddie. And Hershey."

"But how can I be sure?" Anne asked. "How can you prove that you love us?"

Ben frowned. "I just do."

Liddie looked up from her plate. "If you love me," she asked Ben, "why did you and Carter try to play a trick on me?"

"That was just a joke," Ben said. "I love you because you're my sister. And Mom is my mom. And Hershey is our dog."

"But we can't see love, can we?" Anne asked, watching Ben's expression. She wasn't trying to stump him, but simply to expand his way of thinking.

"What about kisses?" Liddie asked, joining in the conversation. "And hugs. We can see those."

"That's right," Ben said. "Hugs and kisses prove we love someone. Love is how we feel. It's in our hearts."

Anne smiled, her own heart filling with love for her children. "You're right. Love *is* real." She rose from her chair and walked over to the counter where she'd set her Bible after coming home from church. "There's something I want you to see."

"What is it?" Ben asked her.

"Some verses in the Bible." She picked it up and carried it to the table, opening the Bible to the place she'd marked with the thin strand of ribbon attached to the binding. "I'd like you to read verses seven and eight from chapter four in the first book of John."

Ben took the Bible from her and looked at the page for a moment before placing his index finger on the correct verse. Then he began to slowly read the passage out loud.

"'Let us love one another, for love is of God; and everyone who loves is born of God and knows God. He who does not love does not know God, for God is love.'"

"So God is love," Anne said. "And we just decided that love is real."

"Right," Ben said, nodding. "Love is real."

Anne leaned forward and pointed to another verse. "Now will you read this one to us? In fact, read both verses eleven and twelve."

"Okay." Ben slid his finger down the page about half an inch and then began to read again. "'If God so loved us, we also ought to love one another. No one has seen God at any time. If we love one another, God' —" He looked up at Anne. "I don't know what this next word is."

She leaned closer to see the word. "*Abides*. That means *lives*."

"'If we love one another, God abides in us,'" Ben continued, his finger moving along the verse as he read, "'and His love has been perfected in us.'"

He looked up at Anne. "What does *perfected* mean?"

"It means to be made perfect. These verses tell us that love is the key. God loves us. He wants us to love one another. And if we love one another, God will live in our hearts with his perfect love."

"Wow," Ben said, looking down at the Bible. "It says all that?"

Anne stood up and rounded the table until she stood behind Ben. She leaned down and circled one arm loosely around his shoulders, giving him a warm hug. "It sure does. I know it's hard to understand now, but I believe the Bible has all the answers to the important questions in life."

"So love is the answer?" Liddie said, plopping a carrot in the middle of her mashed potato mountain.

Out of the mouths of babes, Anne thought to herself. "Yes, Liddie. God is love."

Ben closed the Bible in front of him, a thoughtful expression on his face. "That doesn't seem so hard."

Anne gave his shoulders another gentle squeeze. "Oh, sweetie, it's not supposed to be hard. And God doesn't expect us to be perfect in our love. Remember the story about the mustard seed that you learned in Sunday school?"

"Yeah, it was really tiny," Ben said. "Our teacher brought some mustard seeds to Sunday school class to show us what they look like."

"Well, a person's faith can start out that small and grow from there. And whether someone's faith is tiny or large, God loves us all."

Ben smiled up at her. "And love is real."

"That's right, Ben. Love is real."

* * *

That evening, Anne tucked the children into bed and then spent some time reading in the living room. Classical music played on the CD player and a gentle rain pattered against the windowpanes.

Anne pulled the crocheted afghan off the back of the sofa and wrapped it around her. Then she picked up her laptop computer from the coffee table and opened it, planning to check her e-mail before retiring for the night.

With a few clicks of the computer keys, her e-mail appeared on the screen and a new message blinked in her inbox. Her breath caught when she saw the name attached to the unopened message: *Khafra Bakari*.

Anne clicked on the e-mail and began to read it:

Dear Mrs. Gibson,

Thank you for your letter and for including your e-mail address. I was delighted to receive a message from the niece of Miss Edie Summers. She was a great lady and meant so much to my family. As to your question about the clay pot that Miss Summers found in Armana, there is more to the story than you know....

* * *

The next day, Anne worked in the library in the morning, grateful to have three patrons show up and check out books. Then she let Bella Miller take over in the afternoon so she could visit Mildred.

When she parked in front of the Farley house, she was surprised to see Mildred sitting on the front porch. She grabbed her purse and climbed out of the car, eager to show Mildred the e-mail from Khafra Bakari that she'd printed in the morning.

"Well, this is a nice surprise," Anne said as she walked up the steps to the porch. "You must be feeling better if you can be outside."

"My ankle is much better," Mildred said with a smile. "I hardly need to use the crutches anymore, although Bonnie lectures me if I walk around without them."

Anne took a seat in the chair next to Mildred. "And what about Patty? Does she think you should be up and around?"

"Oh yes. In fact, yesterday was her last day working here. I can take care of myself now."

"That must be a wonderful feeling," Anne said, seeing the contentment on Mildred's face.

"You never realize how much you value your independence until it's taken away," Mildred said. "But I feel so blessed by all the help and prayers I've received. And the food, of course. I can't forget the food."

"I'm so glad to hear you're feeling better." She looked toward the house. "Is Bonnie here with you this afternoon?"

Mildred shook her head. "No, it's her brother's birthday and she drove to State College to treat him to lunch. She's planning to come tomorrow though."

"So you're here alone?"

"Yes, and I'm perfectly fine," Mildred said. "I've been enjoying the fresh air. In just a few more days, I'll be able to drive again. I can't wait!"

Anne reached into her purse and pulled out Khafra's e-mail. "There's something I want to show you. I'm not sure if you knew that Aunt Edie helped start a school in Egypt and corresponded with the Bakari family who ran the school."

"Yes, of course," Mildred said, a spark of recognition in her eyes. "I made some donations too. It was a wonderful cause."

"Well, I found some old letters from Khafra in the attic and decided to look up the school on the Internet to see if it was still in existence."

"And?"

"And it's thriving," Anne said with a smile. "Khafra is the director there now, and I found a way to contact him by e-mail through the Web site. I specifically wanted to ask him about the curse connected to the clay pot. I was hoping he might be able to shed some light on the origins of the curse."

Mildred leaned forward in her chair. "And did he?"

"Yes, he did." Anne handed Mildred the e-mail. "It's all in there. How a souvenir shop near Armana hired people to scare tourists away from the dig sites by telling them of a horrible curse that could befall them if they walked away with one of the artifacts. Apparently, business at the souvenir shop was suffering and they wanted tourists to buy artifacts at the shop instead of digging them up. Khafra even included an old newspaper article that he translated for me, explaining how the owner of the shop had been arrested for fraud."

Mildred stared down at the e-mail. "Oh, Anne. Is this true?"

"Yes, I believe so," Anne told her. "I did some independent research on the Internet myself after I read Khafra's e-mail. I found some other stories that verified the information he told me."

Mildred fell silent, then shook her head. "Do you mean to tell me that I fell for a scam? A scam by someone trying to sell more souvenirs?" Then she looked up. "But wait a minute, we had an incident right before we left Armana! A fire started right outside our hotel room."

Anne nodded. "Apparently, it wasn't unusual for these hired scam artists to start small fires or smash windows or to do whatever it took to perpetuate the curse myths. They were really hoping to scare tourists away from the dig sites and, in many cases, they were successful."

Mildred pursed her lips. "But what about my scarab necklace and the way it just vanished? Don't tell me that someone from Armana followed me all the way to Pennsylvania!"

"No, I'm sure they didn't," Anne said. "I think it's much more likely that your necklace was stolen. Although, I still haven't figured out who stole it or why."

"But what about the power outage in 1975? The flu that closed down the school? The mayor's wrecked Mercedes?" Then Mildred held up one hand before Anne could reply, a wry expression on her face. "Wait. There's a logical explanation for all of those incidents, isn't there? Squirrels in the transformer, a very contagious virus, and Marijane Collins's horrible driving record. That woman was a menace on the road. She almost ran me down once."

Anne breathed a sigh of relief, so grateful that Mildred was starting to see past her fear of the curse. "Yes, those reasons actually make a lot more sense than an Egyptian curse. Especially since Aunt Edie had the clay pot in her attic all of these years."

Mildred shook her head. "Oh, Anne, how could I be so foolish? I was so shocked when I saw that clay pot in the library that I tripped and fell. Then I blamed my sprained ankle on the curse. I guess I didn't want to believe that I could hurt myself over a silly superstition."

"A lot of people have fallen for that silly superstition," Anne told her. "In fact, the town council may close down the library because of it unless I get rid of the clay pot first."

"Well, we can't let that happen—not now that we know the truth."

Her words were music to Anne's ears, but she knew the truth—in the form of Khafra's e-mail——probably wouldn't be enough. She needed to provide proof once more, proof that the scarab necklace had been stolen forty years ago, instead of vanishing due to a curse. "I don't want it to happen either," she told Mildred. "That's why I need you to help me catch a thief."

CHAPTER SIXTEEN

I'm not sure how I can help," Mildred said.

"Tell me everything you remember from the day the necklace disappeared. Take me through it step-by-step until the moment you found it missing."

Mildred closed her eyes for a long moment. "I awoke early that day, expecting Abel Randle to arrive at eight o'clock to fix the washing machine." She opened her eyes. "Coraline and her sister, Ada, brought over some cuttings from some of Ada's hosta plants, so I transplanted them in my garden. I invited them in for a cup of coffee, and we chatted until Abel arrived."

Anne wasn't surprised that Mildred had such a clear memory of that day—she'd probably lived it over and over in her mind. "Did anyone else stop by that day?"

"My boarder, Cleta Rinehart, came home from working as a night operator at the telephone company. She made herself some breakfast in the kitchen and then headed up to her room on the second floor. We only said good morning to each other and little else."

"And Bonnie was here too?"

Mildred nodded. "Yes, she arrived promptly at nine o'clock to begin working for the day. We'd been doing some heavy duty spring cleaning and planned to wash the windows that day. But

Abel had turned off the water to fix the washing machine, so we had to wait until he was finished."

"Did you see anyone else that morning?"

Mildred shook her head. "No, that was it. I decided to try out a new recipe I'd clipped from the *Gazette* while I waited for Abel to finish. I kept all the newspaper clippings in my office drawer — the same drawer where I'd placed the necklace. When I opened it that morning, the necklace was gone."

"And what about Bonnie?" Anne asked. "What was she doing when you realized the necklace was missing?"

"She was in the basement, looking for something. I can't remember what at the moment. It took me a while to find her and tell her what happened. Then Cleta heard all the commotion and came downstairs. I don't remember who suggested calling the police."

Anne pictured the scene, trying to imagine how she'd react in that scenario. "So Bonnie, Cleta, and Abel were all still at your house when the police arrived?"

"Yes," Mildred said nodding. "The officer talked to each one of us alone. He also searched the house, including Cleta's room, but didn't find anything suspicious. And there were no signs of forced entry, so it's doubtful anyone broke in the night before."

"And what about Coraline and her sister? Did the officer speak with them too?"

"Yes, he had me telephone them. They walked over and agreed to be interviewed, but they hadn't seen anything unusual. *Nobody* saw anything suspicious — at least that's what they each claimed."

Anne considered the possibilities, but one thing seemed clear. "If nothing was disturbed, then the thief must have acted quickly. That means they had to have known where you kept the scarab necklace."

Mildred gave a slow nod. "Well, that would exclude Abel Randle, since the man had never been at my house before. But Cleta and Bonnie both knew where I kept the necklace." She held up one finger. "And so did Coraline. It was in that same drawer when she came over to take a picture of it."

Three suspects, Anne thought to herself, all with the opportunity to take the necklace. Any one of them could have easily slipped into Mildred's bedroom and removed the necklace from the dresser drawer without being seen. "So which one do you think took it?"

Mildred tapped one finger against the arm of her chair. "If I had to choose, I'd say Cleta. She had access to all of the rooms in the house. And frankly, I never really warmed up to the girl. She just seemed a little... distant, if you know what I mean."

Anne nodded. "And since Patty is Cleta's daughter, then she could have inherited the scarab necklace from her mother."

"Maybe Patty realized her mother had stolen it," Mildred opined, "and wanted to make amends by putting it back in the same place her mother had found it."

"Maybe," Anne agreed, and then she told Mildred about the O'Hanlon's new bed-and-breakfast and how the couple was using the curse as a promotional tool for their business.

Mildred stared at her. "People amaze me. Who would choose to go on vacation to a place that they think is cursed?"

Anne had wondered the same thing. "The world is made up of all sorts of different people." She leaned forward in her chair, still trying to put together the pieces of the forty-year-old puzzle.

"When did you believe that Aunt Edie's clay pot was cursed? Was it when the Egyptian woman in Armana approached you and told you about the curse? After the fire near your hotel room in Armana? Or during the power outage in Blue Hill?"

Mildred's mouth quivered, but she squared her shoulders. "None of those incidents made me believe in the curse. It was something more...personal." She met Anne's gaze. "You see, the day before my scarab necklace disappeared, I found a lump under my arm. I thought it was simply a swollen gland or a cyst, but when I went to the doctor, he was concerned."

"Oh, Mildred," Anne breathed. "I had no idea."

"Very few people did," Mildred said softly, "but Edie was one of them. When the tests came back and the doctor broke the news that I had cancer, I looked for someone—or something—to explain why this was happening to me. Then I remembered the Egyptian woman in Armana who had warned of a horrible curse raining down on us if we took home the clay pot."

The emotion in Mildred's voice made Anne's heart break. She could only imagine the fear and uncertainty that she must have endured during that time.

"Edie stayed by my side during my entire treatment." Mildred sighed. "Even as I began to cling to the illusion that the clay pot was the cause of my cancer. That if the clay pot was gone, my cancer would be too."

"So that's why Aunt Edie put the clay pot in the attic?"

Mildred nodded. "She did it for me. I know Edie never believed in the curse herself, and she had ignored demands from people in Blue Hill who feared that a curse had befallen the town.

But all I had to do was ask once and it was gone." She smiled. "Edie never told me what she'd done with the clay pot. 'Mum's the word,' she said, and we vowed never to talk about it again. I'd assumed she'd destroyed it, which was why I was so shocked to see it in the library after all these years."

"I'm so sorry you had to go through all of that," Anne said gently. "It must have been scary."

"It was," Mildred admitted. "I felt so...out of control. I think that's why I latched on to something to blame. If the clay pot was at fault, that meant there was a reason for my illness."

"But you obviously recovered."

Mildred chuckled. "Yes, I certainly did. With God's grace and Edie's help and, of course, some excellent medical treatment. They caught the cancer in the earliest stage, and I made a complete recovery."

Anne reached out to give her a hug. "I'm so glad. Thank you for telling me. I had no idea."

"Not many people knew." Mildred folded her hands across her lap. "And now, looking back on it, I can finally see the truth. The clay pot had nothing to do with my cancer or anything else that happened in this town. Neither did my scarab necklace. I suppose it was easier to blame the curse than for me to admit that someone I knew had stolen from me."

"That's understandable," Anne said gently, "but don't you think it's time to learn the truth?"

"It's way past time." Mildred eased her leg in front of her to stretch out her ankle. "Forty years have gone by since my scarab necklace disappeared. And now it's back. I want to know who took it and why."

"So do I, but there's been so little to go on. I wish I could find out more about Cleta Rinehart. She practically disappeared after leaving Blue Hill with her husband." Anne brushed a stray lock of hair off her face, tucking it behind her ear. "Is there anyone in Blue Hill who might have been in touch with her after she left? A family member? A friend? A neighbor?"

"I wish I could think of someone. Cleta divided her time between working for the telephone company and dating the young man she eventually married. He was working on a road crew in town, but I don't believe he was originally from Blue Hill." She shook her head. "It was so long ago, Anne. I just don't remember some of those details."

"It's all right," Anne said, afraid she might be facing a dead end.

Mildred snapped her fingers together. "Wait a minute! Loretta Krambeck worked the night shift for the telephone company with Cleta. Her name is Loretta Flower now."

"Mrs. Flower?" Anne said. "The same woman who is a substitute teacher for the elementary school?"

Mildred nodded. "One and the same. Loretta's mother and I were friends, and I remember her worrying about Loretta not getting enough sleep with that night job, because the girl also worked a second job as a waitress during the day."

Anne didn't really know Loretta or her husband very well. "Where do they live?"

"Out on Hickory Lane," Mildred said. "They have acreage there and raise llamas. You can't miss it."

Anne had passed by that house before and seen a half-dozen llamas in the gated pasture, but she'd never realized the home belonged to Mrs. Flower. "Do you know if she and Cleta were friends?"

"I have no idea, but they must have known each other."

It was a start, Anne thought to herself. At least she'd finally discovered someone, other than Patty, who had known Cleta. Maybe Loretta would be able to shed some light on Cleta's character and tell Anne if Cleta would be the type of person to steal her landlady's necklace.

Mildred emitted a small groan. "What have I done, Anne? If someone actually stole my scarab necklace, did I let the thief escape because I was so convinced that an Egyptian curse was to blame?"

"The police tried to find the thief and failed," Anne reminded her, "so don't be too hard on yourself."

"I know," Mildred said, a determined gleam now shining in her eyes. "But I have to find a way to make this right."

* * *

After Anne left Mildred's house, she headed straight for Hickory Lane, which lay on the outskirts of Blue Hill. She thought about calling first just to make sure that Loretta Flower wasn't working as a substitute teacher today but decided to take her chances.

There were only three days left for Anne to prove that someone had stolen Mildred's necklace forty years ago, which would disprove any so-called evidence of a curse. Just the fact that Mildred had come to realize the truth made Anne's heart lighter as she drove over the gentle, rolling hills to the Flowers' acreage.

She saw four llamas in the gated pasture as she passed by, two brown ones and two white ones. The exotic-looking animals had always fascinated her and, now that she knew Mrs. Flower owned them, she hoped Ben and Liddie could come and see them one day.

But that was a question she would save for another time, Anne decided as she pulled into the long, white rock driveway. The white Cape Cod-style house had black shutters and a red front door. Purple and blue asters filled the neatly landscaped flower garden that bordered the front of the house.

Anne parked the Impala at the edge of the lawn, which had just begun to fade to brown with the cooler weather. Red leaves still hung from a pair of towering sugar maple trees, although small piles carpeted the grass below them. A set of silver wind chimes hung from one low branch, tinkling lightly in the breeze as Anne made her way to the front door.

She rang the doorbell and heard a dog begin to bark inside. A moment later, the door opened and a woman in her late fifties stood on the other side.

"Mrs. Loretta Flower?" Anne asked as a tiny, short-haired Chihuahua plastered itself against the woman's ankles.

"Yes," Loretta said, leaning down to scoop up the dog. "And you're Ben Gibson's mother, right?"

"Yes," Anne said with a smile, holding out one hand. "How are you doing today?"

"Very well, thank you," Loretta said, transferring the dog to her other arm so she could shake Anne's hand. "And this is Trigger," she added. "He thinks he's quite the guard dog."

Anne's smile widened as the dog began growling at her. "I can see that."

Loretta turned around in the open doorway. "Come on in while I put Trigger in his room. Otherwise, he'll bark his head off."

Anne walked into the living room, impressed by the wide-plank oak floor and the high-beamed ceilings. A brown leather sofa and a pair of matching wing chairs sat on a large paisley area rug filled with red, green, and blue threads that matched the drapes at the front window.

"There," Loretta said, walking back into the living room. "That's better."

"I apologize for just barging in like this. I know I should have called first, but I was anxious to talk to you."

"What about?" Loretta asked, motioning Anne toward a chair.

Anne sat down, certain that Loretta had probably heard about the curse and wondered if she believed in it. "Do you know Mildred Farley?"

Loretta smiled. "Of course. She and my mother were good friends. I heard she hurt her ankle at the library because of that clay pot."

"Yes, it...startled her."

"That's what I'd heard." Loretta's brow furrowed. "I still can't fathom that Mildred believes there's a curse in Blue Hill. She's never seemed like the superstitious type to me."

"Well, I think she may be changing her mind." Anne cleared her throat. "That's why I'm here today. Mildred and I were talking about the day that her scarab necklace was stolen back in

1975. She said you might know the woman who rented a room from her back then, a woman named Cleta Rinehart."

Loretta's green eyes widened in recognition. "Oh my, I haven't heard that name in years! Yes, I knew Cleta, although she was a couple of years older than me. We both worked for the telephone company."

"Were you good friends?"

Loretta's mouth curved into a wry smile. "No, not after Cleta turned me in to our supervisor for taking too long on my break."

"She did?"

Loretta nodded. "I was only nineteen at the time and smitten with a boy in town. We would meet up during my break and share a sandwich, and I'd lose track of the time. Cleta was a very by-the-book sort of girl and didn't believe in breaking the rules."

Anne sat back in the chair, taking in this new information. "So do you believe she was the type of girl who would steal a necklace?"

"Oh, goodness, no," Loretta exclaimed. "We had a vending machine at work that would sometimes drop two candy bars into the tray when you bought one. Instead of eating the second candy bar, she'd take it to our supervisor so it could be placed back in the machine." Then Loretta's expression changed. "Wait a minute. Are you thinking that *Cleta* was responsible for stealing Mildred's scarab necklace all those years ago?"

"It's possible, since she was living in the house at the time it disappeared."

212 | *Secrets of the Blue Hill Library*

Loretta shook her head. "You've got it all wrong. Cleta freaked out after that necklace disappeared."

"Did she think its disappearance was due to a curse?"

"No, she thought a thief had broken into the house, and because the police didn't catch anyone, she was afraid he might come back."

"But Mildred told me Cleta got married very shortly after the necklace disappeared."

"She did, and that's why I know Cleta didn't take the necklace. She'd been planning a big church wedding to Harper for months and was always reading bridal magazines in the break room. But after that necklace disappeared from Mildred's house, along with that strange power outage, she talked Harper into eloping just to get away from Blue Hill."

Anne had been almost certain that Patty O'Hanlon was behind the stolen necklace, but for that to be true, then Cleta would have had to be the thief. But everything that Loretta was saying contradicted that assumption. "Did you ever hear from Cleta again?"

"Once," Loretta replied. "A group of us at work had pitched in to buy her a wedding gift. She sent a card to the telephone office, thanking us for the gift and saying that she hoped we were all safe and to be sure and lock our doors at night."

Before Anne could reply, her cell phone rang. "Sorry about this," she said, reaching into her purse to turn it off. But then she saw the caller on the screen: *Blue Hill Elementary School*.

"Oh, it's the school," she told Loretta, pulling her phone out of her purse. "Do you mind if I answer?"

"Of course not," Loretta said, rising to her feet. "It will give me a chance to check on Trigger."

Anne answered her cell phone, hoping that neither Ben nor Liddie had gotten sick at school. "Hello?"

"Mrs. Gibson? This is Nina at the school."

"Yes," she said, recognizing the secretary's voice.

"I'm afraid there's been an…incident involving Ben. Principal Bailey would like you to come in right away."

CHAPTER SEVENTEEN

A nne hurried toward the school's front entrance, eager to see Ben. Nina had assured her that Ben wasn't hurt, but that didn't stop Anne from worrying.

As she walked through the door, she saw Alex in the hallway. "What are you doing here? Is Ryan all right?"

"He's fine," Alex said, walking up to her and placing a reassuring hand on her shoulder. "And so is Ben, so you can breathe now." His words made her smile.

"I *have* been a little tense ever since Nina called. She didn't give me a lot of details, other than to say that Ben got into a fight on the playground."

Alex removed his hand from her shoulder and pointed in the opposite direction. "All four boys are in the principal's office now."

Anne turned and headed toward the office, Alex walking along beside her. "Four?"

"Ryan, Ben, Christian Pyle, and that new kid, Carter... something."

"Pratt," she told him.

"Yeah, that's it."

They walked into the secretary's office and Nina waved them toward the inner office. "Go on inside, everyone else is there."

Anne opened the door and walked into Principal Bailey's office. Alex followed behind her, and they took the only two empty chairs in the room.

Ben and Ryan were already there, seated next to each other, along with Christian and Wendy. Carter Pratt sat next to a man that Anne assumed was his father. Mr. Pratt had the same plumpness around his middle and wavy blond hair as his son.

"Thank you all for coming," Principal Bailey began, taking a seat behind his desk. "Now, boys, would one of you like to tell us what happened?"

Anne glanced at Ben, who sat stone-faced in his chair, his mouth firmly closed. Ryan wore a matching expression, his gaze fixed on the linoleum floor in front of him.

Christian fidgeted in his chair but didn't say anything. Anne met Wendy's gaze, and she could see the concern in her friend's eyes.

"Well, I'm sure my son didn't start anything," Mr. Pratt said. "He's new to this school and certainly not used to this kind of roughhousing."

"Dad," Carter muttered under his breath, looking like he wanted to sink into his chair.

Principal Bailey cleared his throat. "The teacher on recess duty didn't see who started the fight, but she told me that all four boys were involved in the tussle. She broke it up right away and, fortunately, none of the boys were hurt, but we have a zero tolerance policy for fighting at this school."

Anne saw a pink flush creep into Ben's cheeks as the principal spoke, and she could tell he was embarrassed. She didn't condone fighting, no matter who had started it, but she couldn't wait to ask him what really happened.

"Well, boys?" Principal Bailey asked, looking at each one of them. "Does anyone want to tell their side of the story?"

"Nothing happened," Carter mumbled, kicking one foot against the leg of his chair. "We were just goofing around."

Christian squirmed in his chair again but didn't say anything. Anne could see the boys had adopted that age-old silent pledge not to rat out other kids.

"All right," the principal said at last. "Since no one is talking, then the punishment will be the same for each of you: four days detention after school. It starts tomorrow and ends on Friday. So when the dismissal bell rings tomorrow afternoon, you're to go straight to the detention room." His gaze slowly moved around the room, fixing on each boy until they met his gaze. "Understood?"

The boys nodded, and Anne saw Ben's shoulders slump. She didn't blame the principal for meting out that punishment and, for all she knew at this point, Ben probably deserved it.

"That seems a little extreme, doesn't it?" Mr. Pratt said, unbuttoning his suit coat as he leaned forward in his chair. "I mean, boys will be boys."

The principal turned to him, his expression pleasant but firm. "As I said, the school has a zero tolerance policy. But I'll be happy to talk to any of you privately if you have concerns."

Mr. Pratt glanced at his watch. "No, I've stayed long enough. I need to get back to work." He stood up and clapped his hand on Carter's shoulder. "A week in detention won't hurt him anyway. Might get some of that homework done that's he's always putting off."

"You boys can go back to class," Principal Bailey said as Mr. Pratt made his way to the door. "Unless your parents would like to speak to you first."

"I would," Anne and Wendy said simultaneously.

Alex nodded as he looked over at Ryan. "Count me in too."

"That's fine," Principal Bailey said. "You can stay in here to talk while I walk Carter back to his classroom."

Carter rose from his chair and glanced over at Ben as he followed the principal out the door.

Once the door closed behind them, Wendy turned to Christian. "Okay, out with it. What happened?"

"We were just goofing around," Christian said, his voice hushed and his eyes downcast. "Like Carter said."

"Yeah," Ben said, the flush in his cheeks now turning a deep red.

Wendy sighed. "Christian, I know Carter's been bothering you lately. Are you sure you don't want to tell me?"

Tears filled Christian's eyes, but he shook his head and then buried his face in his hands.

Alex moved from his chair to sit beside Ryan. He placed one arm around his nephew's shoulders. "I know you don't want anyone to get into any more trouble, but do you think the punishment is fair? Do all four of you deserve detention?"

Ryan's lower lip jutted out and he didn't say anything for a long moment. Then he looked up at Alex. "Christian started the fight, but it was Carter's fault. He kept calling Christian a sissy and said that his name should be Chrissy. Then Carter got right up next to Christian's face and started chanting *Chrissy, Chrissy, Chrissy*, in this really loud, girly voice."

Christian's shoulders shook, his face still buried in his hands as Ryan told the story.

"So then Christian tried to push him away, but Carter started pushing him back." Ryan took a deep breath, not meeting the gaze of either boy beside him. "Then Ben tried to step in between them to stop the fight, but they all just fell on the ground."

Wendy reached out and put one arm around Christian's shoulders, giving him a hug.

"So then I jumped in to try and pull everybody apart," Ryan continued. "And that's when the teacher saw us and started blowing the whistle."

Anne looked at Ben. "Is that how you remember it happening?"

He gave a quick nod, looking miserable. She knew he liked both Carter and Christian, so a fight between them must have been tough for him to watch.

"Carter never should have called Christian names," Ben said, his voice almost a whisper. "Carter said he was just teasing, but it was mean."

"I don't think that's the first time Carter's been mean to Christian," Wendy said. "Is it, boys?"

"No, it's not the first time," Ryan admitted.

Alex rose to his feet. "Well, it had better be the last time. I'm going to talk to Principal Bailey about the bullying."

Ryan's eyes flared with fear. "Uncle Alex, you can't tell him what I told you! Then he'll tell Carter, and everyone will know I snitched!"

"You didn't snitch, Ryan," Anne said gently. "You told the truth. That's never wrong."

"Anne is right," Wendy agreed. "Especially when you're doing it to help someone else."

Despite their words of encouragement, Ryan still looked a little sick.

"Don't worry," Ben told Ryan. "Nobody will be mad. All the kids on the playground saw what Carter was doing. And Christian is everybody's favorite."

Those words made Christian lift his head and open his eyes. "I am?"

"Well, yeah," Ryan said with smile. "You're always the first one picked for teams and stuff."

Ryan's words made Christian smile.

Principal Bailey tapped on the door before opening it. "Do you need more time?"

Wendy rose to her feet. "No, I think we're done." Then she turned to Christian. "I'll see you after school, okay?"

"Okay, Mom." Christian hopped off his chair and then turned to Ben and Ryan. "We should probably go back to class now."

"Okay," Ben said, giving Anne a small wave before he followed the other two boys out the door.

Alex turned toward the principal. "If you have some time, I'd like to speak to you for a few minutes."

"Of course." Principal Bailey walked into the office and rounded his desk. "Mrs. Pyle and Mrs. Gibson, you're welcome to stay too."

"That's all right," Wendy said, giving Alex a grateful smile. "I think Alex can speak for all of us."

Anne and Wendy walked out of the principal's office, closing the door behind them. Nina was on the phone and gave them a nod as they moved past her and into the empty hallway. They waited until they were outside to speak.

"Oh, Anne," Wendy said, giving her a hug. "My heart just about broke when Christian started to cry. He's so sensitive, no matter how much he tries to hide it."

"I know," Anne said softly. "I'm just sorry that he's been a victim of Carter's bullying. Hopefully it will stop after today."

Wendy nodded. "The fact that Ben and Ryan stood up for him means the world. Those two boys don't deserve detention."

"Well, we'll see what happens after Alex talks to the principal and fills him in on the details. I'm sure he'll want to get Carter's side too. Either way, I'm glad they told us what happened."

"Me too." Wendy gave her a wry smile. "After seven kids, I'm still trying to decide if my boys or my girls are harder to raise."

Anne chuckled as they headed toward the parking lot. "Well, today, I vote for boys, but I reserve the right to change my vote anytime."

She waved good-bye to Wendy when she reached her car. A dull headache began to throb in her temple as she climbed inside. Anne didn't know whether to blame the headache on the stress of being called into the principal's office or the fact that she hadn't eaten lunch today. She'd been so focused on talking to Loretta Flower that she'd forgotten all about food.

Anne headed for Main Street and pulled into Thrifty's Drugstore. She was out of aspirin at home and had meant to stock up earlier. Now she didn't have a choice if she wanted this headache to go away before it got worse.

Several customers were lined up at the cash register when Anne walked through the door. There was a soda fountain at the back of the store, and, for a moment, Anne was tempted to take a seat and have some ice cream. But she'd already been gone from the library longer than she'd planned and wanted to get back there before Bella worried.

Anne grabbed a bottle of aspirin off the shelf and then headed toward the checkout counter. On the way, she saw small bags of her favorite potato chips. On impulse, she picked one up, deciding to call it a late lunch, and then continued on her way to the checkout counter.

She stood in line behind an elderly man who held a large bag of popcorn and a bottle of cola. Anne exchanged smiles with him, her headache growing stronger. She was tempted to grab a bottle of cola for herself, hoping the caffeine might help her headache. Instead, she waited for Jerry Brown, the pharmacist, to ring up the man in front of her. Then it was finally Anne's turn.

"It looks like you're a little short-handed today," she said, setting the aspirin bottle and bag of chips on the Formica countertop, "since you're running the cash register."

"Lindsay had to run a quick errand," he explained, ringing up her purchase, "and naturally, we got busy as soon as she stepped out the door."

Anne smiled. "But busy is good, right?"

"Busy is great! I was just going to—"

Before Jerry could finish his sentence, a young man approached the counter and interrupted him. "Hey, Jerry, am I supposed to have Mr. Bartholomew sign for his order?"

"No, that's not necessary," Jerry said, and then turned to Anne. "This is Dustin, our newest employee."

The name rang a bell. "Dustin Wolfe?"

"That's right." Dustin smiled revealing a pair of silver braces. "How did you know?"

Dustin looked more like a young teen than an adult. A green polo shirt and khaki slacks both hung loosely on his slender frame. His blond hair needed a trim, and a small tuft of blond whiskers struggled to make an appearance on his narrow chin. "I heard you were working here now."

Jerry handed Dustin a piece of paper. "Here's Mr. Bartholomew's phone number. Remember, if he doesn't answer the door, give him a call, don't just walk inside."

"Right." Dustin slipped the paper into his pocket. "I've got it."

Anne watched Dustin leave the store and then turned back to Jerry, who was placing her aspirin and chips into a small sack. "Dustin seems nice."

"He is," Jerry said with a sigh, "but his training period is taking longer than I expected. "He nearly scared Nellie Brown into a heart attack one day when she woke up on her sofa and found him in her living room. He'd seen her napping through the open door and decided to sneak in and leave her order on the coffee table instead of waking her."

"I'm sure that was quite a shock for her."

Jerry smiled. "She called to let me know what had happened but made me promise not to fire him."

Just like Mildred didn't want him fired after Dustin had walked into her house, Anne thought to herself. That's why

Mildred hadn't called Thrifty's to complain. Was it possible that Dustin had seen something the day the necklace reappeared in the office drawer? He'd been in the house that day, although neither Mildred nor Anne had considered him a possible suspect.

"Where's Dustin from?" Anne asked Jerry as another customer moved in line behind her.

"California," Jerry said. "His girlfriend is attending medical school in Philadelphia and received an internship at the Blue Hill Medical Clinic."

"So Dustin doesn't have any ties to Blue Hill?"

Jerry shook his head. "None. In fact, he told me that he's never been east of the Mississippi River before he moved here."

Anne thanked him, not wanting to delay the customer waiting behind her. She headed for the door, wishing she'd had a chance to talk to Dustin before he'd left. But when she walked outside, she saw him leaning against a silver Grand Am, texting something on his cell phone.

"You're still here," Anne said, delighted to see him, although she sensed Jerry wouldn't be so thrilled if he knew his hired help was texting instead of working.

"Yeah, I don't text when I drive," Dustin told her, "so I needed to send a few messages before I left."

Anne walked up to him. "Do you mind if I ask you a strange question?"

He shrugged. "Sure, why not?"

"You made a delivery to Mildred Farley on Laurel Lane about a week and a half ago. Do you remember?"

"That was one of my first deliveries," he said, nodding. "Ms. Farley didn't hear me come in, and I think I might have startled her. She was nice about it, though."

Anne looked into his brown eyes, hoping he might be able to answer the question that would keep the library open. "Did you happen to see anyone else there besides Mildred?"

He pondered the question for a long moment, his blond brows beetled together. "Yeah, there was the lady wearing the apron. She looked about the same age as my grandma, who is seventy-five."

"That would be Bonnie," Anne explained. "Anyone else?"

"Yeah, there was another lady too. I just caught a glimpse of her when I was walking through the house trying to find the living room. She was in a small room off the kitchen. I don't think she saw me, though, since she didn't look up from the desk."

Anne could feel her pulse racing with excitement. "Can you describe her?"

He shook his head. "Not really. Like I said, I only got a glimpse of her, and I wasn't paying that much attention."

"Please think very hard," Anne said, not ready to give up. "Can you tell me her age or hair color? Maybe what she was wearing?"

"Well, she was older than you, but younger than the apron lady. And she was wearing a skirt and some type of jacket— maybe brown or gray. And her hair was kind of blondish."

Anne sucked in her breath. He'd just described someone who had the same hair color and wardrobe style as Jillian Zimmer. Could Bonnie's daughter have placed the scarab necklace in the drawer? And if so, had Bonnie known about it?

"Thanks, Dustin," Anne said. "I won't keep you any longer."

"Okay," he said, opening his car door and climbing inside. She watched him drive away, suddenly realizing that her headache was gone.

Anne had just taken one step closer to discovering the mystery behind the scarab necklace. Now she just needed to know why Jillian had placed the necklace back in Mildred's house.

* * *

Later that evening, Anne tucked Ben into bed. "I just want to tell you how proud I am of you for sticking up for Christian today. I know that was probably hard to do, since Carter is your friend too."

"Yeah," Ben admitted, looking up at her. "Carter was nicer to Christian after school today. I think he was glad that Christian didn't tell on him."

"Well, I hope he keeps being nice to Christian."

"Me too."

She kissed him good night, thanking the Lord for giving her two such wonderful children. Then she prayed for Carter, along with Christian and Ryan, asking God to give all the boys His perfect guidance.

Anne walked out of Ben's bedroom and then padded over to Liddie's room and took a peek inside. Liddie was already asleep, her arms wrapped around Cleopatra. Anne just stood there and watched Liddie for a while, so grateful for the blessings in her life.

Then she quietly closed Liddie's door and walked down the hallway toward her own bedroom, taking a moment to look out the window. Countless stars sparkled in the night sky. The beauty of it made her breath catch in her throat.

For a brief moment, she forgot all about her troubles and just enjoyed the majesty of God's handiwork. So many times she took it for granted, too caught up in her own life to notice the beauty of a sunset or the magnificence of a fiery thunderstorm. Even the changing of the seasons was a special kind of miracle, especially the way it mirrored life itself.

Anne breathed a wistful sigh, taking it all in. But soon her thoughts once more turned to matters in her own life, such as the prospect of the library closing if she didn't end the rumors of an Egyptian curse.

Tomorrow, Anne planned to confront Bonnie at Mildred's house and find out the story behind the scarab necklace once and for all. She knew Mildred would be crushed if Bonnie had betrayed her by stealing that necklace—especially when Mildred had done so much to help Bonnie all those years ago. Just the thought of it made Anne's heart hurt.

But she also knew that Mildred wanted—and deserved—to know the truth.

Anne leaned against the wooden window frame and pressed her forehead against the pane. The cool glass felt good against her skin. Perhaps finding that clay pot in the attic had been a blessing, she thought to herself. A chance for Mildred to find peace for the events that had so troubled her for the past forty years.

Anne closed her eyes and fervently prayed that tomorrow would bring peace for everyone in Blue Hill. Then she opened them again, the stars looking even brighter than before.

"Amen," she whispered into the night.

A knock sounded on the door to their private family entrance. Not expecting a visitor, Anne walked to the door and looked through the peephole. Alex stood on the other side, the full moon casting a silvery glow on his dark hair.

She opened the door. "Hello, there. I wasn't expecting to see you tonight."

He smiled. "I know. I should have called first, but...I was worried about you."

"Worried? Why?"

After what happened at school today, I could see that you were upset." He placed one hand in the pocket of his windbreaker. "In fact, I brought you something to help you feel better."

Anne watched as he drew out a candy bar. And not just any candy bar, but her favorite. "A Baby Ruth bar? For me?"

He grinned. "You always did like them."

She met his gaze. "*Like*, Mr. Ochs? That is too weak of a word to describe my affection for Baby Ruth bars. I *love* them. In fact, I once ate four Baby Ruth bars in one sitting, and the stomachache I suffered afterward was totally worth it."

He laughed. "I seem to remember that. Was it freshman year?"

"Sophomore," she said with a wistful sigh. "After Blue Hill won its football game against Deshler. So I had good reason to celebrate."

He leaned one broad shoulder against the door frame. "As I recall, I dislocated my knee in that game and spent the rest of the night at the hospital."

She winced. "That's right. They carried you off the field in a stretcher. I saw it when I was waiting in line at the concession stand to buy the candy bars." Then she waved him inside. "Come on in. We have a Baby Ruth bar to share."

"Share?" he said, sounding surprised. "I figured you'd want it all to yourself."

"I'm not as young—nor as thin—as I used to be, so half a candy bar will do me just fine."

He walked inside the kitchen and looked around. "The kids in bed already?"

"Yes, I tucked them in just a few minutes ago." Then she tilted her head to one side. "Where's Ryan?"

"At home. I just got back from finishing a job on the other side of town. The babysitter told me Ryan was asleep when I called a few minutes ago, so I thought now would be as good a time as any to deliver the candy bar."

"Well, I appreciate it," she said, taking the Baby Ruth from him. She ripped open the package and pulled out the chocolate bar. Then she split it into two equal pieces.

He took the one she offered him. "So how are you really doing, Anne? I know this curse business with the clay pot is affecting the library."

She sighed. "You know, I'd love to spend one evening talking about anything except that silly curse. Let's go sit on the porch swing and just enjoy our candy bar. Then you can tell me about your talk with Principal Bailey."

He nodded. "That sounds like a good plan."

They walked to the front of the house and stepped out on the porch. Anne led Alex to the porch swing, the full moon glowing in the night sky.

Anne sat down on the wooden swing and then took her first bite of the candy bar. She closed her eyes, enjoying the irresistible flavor combination of chocolate, peanuts, sweet caramel, and chewy nougat. "Wow, this is good," she said. "Just what I needed tonight."

"Rough day?"

"Rough week," she said with a sigh. Then she leaned back against the swing, enjoying the gentle motion as they swayed back and forth. She breathed deeply, inhaling the fresh, crisp autumn air and enjoying the unfettered view of the stars in the black velvet sky. The tranquility of small town life was something she'd always treasured but never more than this moment.

Alex finished his candy bar in two bites, then licked the chocolate off his fingers. "So I told Principal Bailey what the boys told us. He said that story seems to match what the teacher on recess duty reported."

"So will Ben and Ryan still get detention?"

Alex nodded. "Yes, the school has a zero tolerance rule about fighting. Plus, the boys refused to tell the principal what happened, so he can't just take our word for it. Especially since Carter's father is convinced that his son is the victim."

"It doesn't seem fair," Anne said softly.

Alex emitted a soft chuckle. "Things sure have changed since we were in school. Back then, you were supposed to fight back against a bully, using your words or, more often, your fists."

"I'm not sure that was better," she mused. "I'll never understand why some kids seem to delight in tormenting others."

"Who knows?" Alex replied, clasping his hands behind his head as he leaned against the back of the swing. "The kid that bullied me thought it was hilarious."

She turned to look at him. "You were bullied?"

"Sure." He met her gaze. "Back when I was in seventh grade. Jed Hardy used to try and trip me in the lunch line every day. Don't you remember?"

Anne thought about it for a long moment and then shook her head. "No, not really."

"Well, it was the biggest crisis of my life at the time," he said with a wry chuckle, "even though it only lasted a few weeks. You know how it is at that age—everything that happens to you seems so enormous. I started dreading the lunch hour because I knew Jed was there waiting for me. I even faked being sick a couple of times so I could go to the nurse's office instead of the cafeteria."

"That's terrible," Anne said, realizing she'd never thought of Alex as vulnerable to a bully before. But then she pictured thirteen-year-old Alex, tall and gangly, with his nose always stuck in a book. He'd grown into a stellar high school athlete, but as a seventh grader, he'd had two left feet. "What made Jed finally stop?"

"Well, I wish I could say that I stood up to him, like you sometimes see in the movies, and punched him in the nose. But the guy had a good five inches on me and a hundred pounds. Maybe I would have punched him eventually, but Shaun put a stop to it without even lifting a finger.

"Shaun Milhouse?" Anne said, referring to their former classmate and the current manager at Fowler's Auto Repair.

Alex nodded. "That's right."

"What did he do?"

"Well, one day when I entered the cafeteria, I saw Jed there waiting for me. Shaun was standing beside him, and Jed poked Shaun in the ribs with his elbow and said, 'Watch this.' Then, as I walked past them, Jed stuck out his foot and tripped me. When I almost hit the floor, Jed laughed and turned to Shaun, saying, 'Isn't that funny?'"

Alex paused for a long moment and Anne could hear the lone howl of a coyote in the distance. "And Shaun just looked at him and said, 'No, it's not funny.' Then he turned around and started talking to Lisa Morelli, totally ignoring Jed."

Anne waited for him to continue, but Alex didn't say anything else.

"Then what happened?" she asked at last.

He sat up on the swing. "Nothing. Jed never tried to trip me again." Alex grinned. "Although, he was the main reason I started taking karate lessons, just in case."

Anne glanced over at him. "It sounds like Jed was looking for approval from Shaun and tried to go about it the wrong way."

"I suppose so. Looking back, I can see his insecurities were probably to blame, but I still think he was a jerk."

"I wonder if he ever looks back," Anne mused. "Maybe he regrets what he did."

"He probably forgot all about it," Alex replied. "I did too, honestly, until I heard the boys talking about Carter picking on Christian. I hope the fact that they stood up for Christian will show Carter that his bully methods won't win him any friends."

"We'll see," Anne said, as a light breezed ruffled her hair. "That's one of the hardest parts of being a parent, isn't it? When you can't protect your kids twenty-four hours a day."

Alex gave a slow nod. "I never realized how tough it is to see them get hurt until Ryan came to live with me. I hope I'm doing right by him."

Anne could hear the concern in Alex's voice and her heart went out to him. "Ryan is happy, which means you're doing a great job. Besides, I heard that if you're worried about whether or not you're a good parent, that means you are. The bad parents don't worry about it."

He smiled as he rose to his feet. "Good advice and a great candy bar, all in one. I'm glad I stopped by tonight."

Anne stood up beside him, feeling a little chilled now. "Me too."

"But I suppose I'd better get going. I told the babysitter I'd be home soon, and I have a load of laundry to do tonight." He smiled. "That's another thing about kids — the dirty clothes never seem to end."

"And boys are worse than girls," Anne said, walking him to his truck.

"Now, I don't think that's true," Alex countered. He turned to face her when he reached the driver's door of his truck. "I remember a certain girl who was covered in mud from head to toe after a bunch of us seniors made an impromptu trip to the Kepple swimming hole."

Anne smiled. "Oh, that's right. Mom never did get all the mud stains out of my clothes."

"I was smart enough to stay out of the water," Alex teased.

Anne laughed. "You were just scared of the toads in the pond—admit it!"

He shook his head as he climbed into his truck. "Not in a million years."

"Thanks for the candy bar," Anne said through the open truck door, "and for the company."

"You're welcome." Alex switched on the engine. "And watch out for toads on your way back to the house. They like to come out of the water at night."

Anne waved as he backed the truck out of her driveway and took off down the road, finding herself still smiling as she turned around and headed inside. She didn't run into any toads on the way, but she appreciated Alex showing up tonight and taking her mind off the curse of the clay pot, even for just a little while.

Chapter Eighteen

The next morning, Anne stood at the pedestal table and opened the box for the holiday craft book giveaway, curious to see how many people had filled out tickets for the drawing.

Only three tickets lay in the bottom of the box.

Her heart sank, even though she knew patrons had been few and far between these last few days. Even now, the library had been open almost two hours and not one person had walked through the door.

A sigh escaped her as she placed the lid back on the gift-wrapped box, hoping that today would change everything. Betty Bultman was scheduled to come in and work this morning, allowing Anne to confront Bonnie at Mildred's house.

Her stomach twisted a little, knowing it wouldn't be an easy conversation to have. She'd been trying to rehearse it since she'd awakened this morning but couldn't seem to find the right words.

Anne walked over to a window in the Fiction Room and opened it, enjoying the gentle autumn breeze that floated in. Soon autumn would turn to winter and the windows would stay firmly closed. But for now she'd enjoy the fresh air and the bright sun shining in the sky.

The lovely day brought to mind one of Anne's favorite hymns, and she began to sing it softly under her breath as she started dusting the bookshelves in the Fiction Room:

"For the beauty of the earth
For the glory of the skies,
For the love which from our birth
 Over and around us lies.
Lord of all, to Thee we raise,
This our hymn of grateful praise."

Her heart lightened as she sang, making her worries fade. Accusing Bonnie of stealing the scarab necklace forty years ago wouldn't be easy, but just as Anne had told Ryan yesterday, the truth was never wrong. Her search for the truth about the scarab necklace wasn't wrong either—especially if it kept the library open for the people of Blue Hill.

At least Ben had gone off to school with a smile on his face, she thought to herself. Although he wasn't looking forward to his week-long detention, it seemed as if a weight had been lifted from his shoulders. He'd shown courage by facing down his friend Carter to stop him from bullying Christian. She just hoped that Carter didn't turn his hurtful teasing tactics on Ben.

After meeting Mr. Pratt and witnessing his reaction in the principal's office, she wondered if Carter's behavior reflected a need for attention. But even if it did, that was no excuse. She just hoped that Ben could be a good example for him, as Pastor Tom had pointed out to her.

A bird began to chirp through the open window, reminding Anne that the problems of today wouldn't last forever. She continued to sing:

"For the beauty of each hour,
Of the day and of the night,

Hill and vale, and tree and flower,
Sun and moon, and stars of light.
Lord of all, to Thee we raise,
This our hymn of grateful praise."

"You have a lovely voice," Betty Bultman said as she walked into the Fiction Room. She wore a coral print dress with a wide gold belt that flattered her tall frame. "I usually have to restrict my singing to the shower."

Anne smiled as she turned around. "Sometimes I get a song in my head and I just have to start singing or humming. My mother is the same way."

They headed downstairs together, and Betty set her purse behind the checkout desk. "Well, I believe if more people would sing songs like that one, the world would be a happier place."

"I think so too." Anne carried her feather duster over to the closet and put it back on the shelf. "Thanks so much for coming in today. I'm hoping you won't be too bored, since not many people are stopping in these days."

"Bored in a library?" Betty chuckled. "I think that's impossible—especially when there are so many wonderful books to keep me company."

"True," Anne said with a smile. "You can go anywhere you want in the world, and any time in history, just by picking up a book."

"That's my favorite kind of adventure," Betty said, as she settled in behind the desk. "Don't worry about me. I'll be fine."

"All right, I'll see you later." Anne walked into the old kitchen and then took the back stairs up to the second floor.

She grabbed her purse and car keys off the kitchen counter and then headed out the door, ready to step back into the past herself.

* * *

Ten minutes later, Anne stood on Mildred's front porch and rang the doorbell again. There had been no answer the first time she'd rung, and now she was starting to worry.

She reached into her purse for her cell phone and dialed Mildred's cell phone number. To her relief, Mildred answered on the second ring.

"Hello?"

"Mildred, this is Anne. Are you all right?"

"I'm fine, dear. Why do you ask?"

Anne started to breathe easier. "Well, I'm at your house, and no one is answering the doorbell. I was worried that you might have fallen."

"Actually, I'm not even there," Mildred told her. "Bonnie and I decided to take a trial run to see if I could drive my car. We're at Coffee Joe's right now, enjoying cappuccinos and apple turnovers."

"That sounds wonderful," Anne said, so happy that Mildred was now able to get out and about.

"We've got some errands to run, but we should be back home in about an hour if you'd like to stop over later. I'd love to see you."

Anne glanced at her watch to check the time. "I'll do that."

"Wonderful," Mildred said before ending the call.

Anne dropped her cell phone back into her purse and walked off the porch. She was almost to her car when she heard someone calling to her.

"Yoo-hoo! Anne!"

She turned to see Coraline Watson standing in her backyard, wearing a floppy straw hat and a pair of blue denim overalls over a man's white shirt.

"Good morning," Anne called out. Then she remembered the photograph that she'd borrowed from Coraline that was still in her purse. She started walking toward Coraline, thinking this would be the perfect opportunity to return it.

"I just wanted to let you know," Coraline began as Anne approached her, "that Mildred isn't home. She and Bonnie drove off about thirty minutes ago."

"Yes, I just called her." Anne watched Coraline pick up her long-handled pruning shears and begin to cut some of the dead wood from a rose bush. "I'm so happy that she's finally able to leave the house."

Coraline nodded. "Yes, me too. Having Bonnie there every day to help Mildred through her recovery has been quite a blessing. They've been friends for so long. I still remember, on my visits with Ada, when Bonnie and Jilly would show up at Mildred's house."

"You knew Jillian Zimmer?" Anne asked, surprised by this new bit of information. She knew Coraline had been a frequent visitor at her sister's house, but how did she come to know the neighbor's housekeeper's young daughter?

"Oh my, yes," Coraline said, setting the pruning shears on the tree stump beside her. "The poor girl was practically attached to her mother's hip after her father left the family."

"And when was that?"

Coraline lifted her shoulders in a small shrug. "It had to be 1974 or '75, because Ada went on a yearlong trip to Europe in 1976, and then my husband's job transferred him to Texas, so I didn't visit Ada much after that."

Anne was starting to think that she'd been looking at this all wrong. "How old would Jillian have been then? Eleven or twelve?"

"Yes, that sounds about right," Coraline said. "She was so cute and always so serious. I remember her coming over to Ada's house, trying to sell us some of her rocks."

"Rocks?"

"She drew ink pictures on rocks. If I remember right, she'd been inspired by the Egyptian hieroglyphics Edie had taken to the school to show the children after her trip. I bought one rock and so did Ada, because we felt so sorry for the girl. Her father just up and abandoned the family without any warning."

"That's right," Anne mused, suddenly seeing the theft in a different light. It had never really made sense to her that someone would steal such a unique necklace with the intent to sell it. As Hank Kepple had confirmed, such a sale would have caused talk among jewelers in the area. But a child might not know that—especially a child desperate enough to sell rocks to make money.

Anne reached into her purse. "Here's the photograph of the necklace. Thanks so much for letting me borrow it."

Coraline smiled as she took the photograph from Anne. "No problem. Did it help you?"

"I think so," Anne said, mentally planning her next move. Getting anyone to confess to a crime that had been committed forty years ago would be tough — so she had to play it just right.

* * *

Jillian Zimmer got to Mildred's house in record time. Given the eleven mile distance between Blue Hill and State College, Anne figured Jillian had left her office the moment after their phone call had ended. Even then, Jillian must have sped every mile of the way to get to Mildred's house so fast.

Anne sat on a white rocking chair on Mildred's front porch, still waiting for Mildred and Bonnie to return from their trip around town. She watched Jillian hurry up the front walk, a pinched expression on the older woman's face.

"I'm glad you could make it," Anne said. "Mildred and your mom aren't back from running errands yet, but they should be here soon."

"Well, I'm glad they're not here yet," Jillian said, taking a seat across from Anne. She wore a rose pink wool skirt and matching jacket, along with a white silk blouse. Her blonde hair hung in a french braid with tiny curls framing her face.

In that moment, Anne could almost picture her as a twelve-year-old.

"Now, tell me what evidence you have," Jillian began, "that proves my mother stole Mildred's scarab necklace in 1975."

"Well, it's simply a process of elimination. Bonnie had the opportunity since she was here every week. And I understand your father had left..." Anne let the words trail off, feeling bad for even bringing up such a sore subject. But she truly did want to understand what had happened forty years ago.

Jillian tipped up her chin, a gleam of defiance in her green eyes. "Yes, he left us high and dry. But we survived. I'd say we even thrived."

"I would say so too," Anne said gently, impressed at how far Jillian had come from a little girl whose father had abandoned her. She could glimpse a shadow of pain still lurking in those green eyes. "You've done very well for yourself, and you take good care of your mother."

"It's the least I can do," Jillian told her. "She worked so hard to take care of me. That's why I'm not going to let anyone railroad her now."

"But don't you think the truth should come out—especially given these renewed rumors about the curse? Look what happened to Mildred when she thought the curse was back in Blue Hill."

A flicker of remorse flashed across Jillian's face. "I feel horrible for Mildred, but her accident had nothing to do with my mother. Besides, even if she was guilty of taking the necklace, the statute of limitations has run out long ago. The thief can't be prosecuted for it now."

"I know," Anne said slowly, rocking back in forth in the rocker. "But I believe Mildred, at the very least, needs to know the truth about who stole her scarab necklace. Don't you?"

A muscle flexed in Jillian's jaw. "It was so long ago. Can't we just let it go?"

Before Anne could reply, the screen door opened and Bonnie stepped onto the porch. "No, we can't let it go."

Mildred followed behind her, a confused expression on her face. "What's going on?"

Bonnie sucked in a deep breath and then turned to face Mildred. "I'm the one who took your scarab necklace all those years ago. I should have told you before now, but I guess it was easier to just sweep it under the rug."

Mildred's mouth gaped as she stared at Bonnie, all the blood rushing from her face. "It was you?"

"No," Jillian exclaimed, rising to her feet. "It was me. It was always me."

Bonnie turned to her daughter. "Jillian, please..."

"Mom, you've protected me long enough." Her chin quivered. "I guess it's time for the truth to come out."

Mildred wobbled on her feet. "Oh dear, I think I'd better sit down."

Bonnie grabbed one of Mildred's arms while Anne jumped up from the rocker and grabbed her other arm. They steadied Mildred on her feet and then guided her toward one of the sturdy porch chairs.

"Are you all right?" Bonnie asked, after they got Mildred settled.

"Yes, I'm fine." Mildred sat back in the chair. "I think I was just on my feet too long today, and then this..." She looked up at Anne. "Did you know?"

"Yes." Anne sat back down in the rocker as Bonnie took a seat beside her daughter. "But not until this morning. Yesterday, I was convinced that Bonnie had stolen your scarab necklace, but then I realized it was Jillian."

Mildred's curious gaze landed on Jillian. "So were you the one who returned it or your mother?"

"I did," Jillian said meekly. "I didn't want Mom involved—I never wanted her involved."

Bonnie reached out to clasp Jillian's hand. "She was only eleven years old when it happened. I'd been so worried about losing our house and all the bills that were piling up, and I didn't hide it well enough from her. But I still didn't know that she'd taken your necklace until years later..."

"By then, I was in law school," Jillian said, "as ironic as that sounds. And I'd misplaced the necklace after moving several times. I found it again a few weeks ago." Jillian sucked in a deep breath. "Mom was afraid of what might happen to my career if the truth came out. So she kept my secret all these years."

"I'm so sorry, Mildred," Bonnie said, her voice almost a whisper. "You've always been so generous to us. I'll never be able to repay you."

"You don't have to repay me," Mildred said gently. "That's what friends are for." Then she turned to Jillian, compassion shining in her gray eyes. "And you don't have to apologize for being a scared little girl who tried to help her mother."

Tears filled Jillian's eyes. "My reasons for taking the necklace were more selfish than that."

Anne saw the startled expression on Bonnie's face, her hands gripping the chair as Jillian continued.

"I overheard my mom talking to my aunt Nessa. Mom told her it might be better if I went and lived with them in Minnesota." Jillian lifted her head to look at Bonnie. "I thought you were going to send me away."

"Oh, Jilly," Bonnie whispered. "It wasn't like that. I was afraid I wouldn't be able to feed you and clothe you, at least not until I got a steady income. I was never planning to send you away forever."

A ghost of a smile haunted Jillian's mouth. "I guess I'd read the book *Anne of Green Gables* too many times. I was sure I was about to become an orphan."

Anne's heart ached for that scared eleven-year-old, and she gave God thanks once more that her family didn't have to worry about food or clothing or shelter.

Jillian took a deep, shuddering breath as she turned to Mildred and Anne. "That's why I took the scarab necklace. I thought if I could sell it for enough money, Mom would let me stay with her. Unfortunately, I didn't consider how I would sell it until I'd already taken it home with me."

"You poor thing," Mildred said. "And here I was worried about some silly curse, when I had a scared little girl in my house who needed help."

"You had other things going on," Bonnie murmured, looking at Mildred.

That's when Anne knew that Mildred had confided her cancer scare to Bonnie too. Another sign of their close friendship.

Anne was so glad that it seemed to be as strong as ever—even now that the truth was out.

Jillian stood up and walked over to Mildred's chair. "Can you ever forgive me?"

Mildred reached for her hand. "Yes. And can you forgive me for not seeing the truth forty years ago and, instead, blaming some stupid curse?"

That made Jillian smile. "I really did make a mess of things, didn't I?"

Mildred squeezed her hand. "It's nothing that can't be repaired. I'm ready if you are."

Jillian's smile widened. Now that the shadow of guilt had fallen away from her face, she looked ten years younger. "Let's do it."

CHAPTER NINETEEN

T wo weeks later, Grace Hawkins walked up to Anne as people filed into the library. "Looks like the fall gala is a success."

Anne smiled as the melodic strains of a violin drifted from the Fiction Room. Mildred had gone to great lengths to remedy the damage the rumors of the Egyptian curse had caused. She'd even sponsored a fall gala at the library, complete with catered food, live chamber music, and fancy door prizes.

A donation jar in the History Room was filled almost to the brim with money for the Egyptian school that Aunt Edie had helped Khafra Bakari's family build. Anne and Mildred had put together a large display about the school, including photographs and students' personal stories that Khafra had e-mailed to Anne last week.

"You deserve some of the thanks," Anne told Grace. "The newspaper story you wrote about the legend of the cursed clay pot was wonderful. I read it three times."

Grace smiled. "Thank you, but I can't take all the credit. My interviews with Mildred and Jillian really added a human element to the story. Jillian's story really touched me—as I'm sure it did the readers. Will she and her mother be here tonight?"

"Yes, they're coming a bit later." Anne reached for a glass of apple cider from a passing waiter. "Great dress by the way."

"Thanks." Grace looked down at the black designer cocktail dress she wore. "I bought it years ago, but I love to bring it out of my closet whenever I get a chance." She patted her tummy. "I just hope it doesn't get too snug."

Anne lifted a brow, aware that Grace would look good in a gunnysack. "I don't think you need to worry."

Then Liddie came up and tugged on Anne's skirt. "Mommy, may I have another cream puff?"

Anne turned to her. "How many have you had?"

"Just this many," Liddie said, holding up two fingers. "And I shared them with Cleopatra."

Anne sighed. "Why don't you have some of the roast beef and vegetables first, and then see if you're still hungry for another cream puff." She usually wasn't so indulgent, but today was a special occasion.

"Okay." Liddie turned and began skipping toward the grand staircase. A buffet had been set up in the meeting room, along with several tables and chairs so people could sit down to eat.

When Anne turned around, she saw Grace now involved in a conversation with the Bultmans, so she moved on to mingle with some of the other guests. She saw John and Peggy Rey, along with several other members of the Tea and Book Club. Then she waved to Hank and Heidi Kepple across the room, who had their twin boys in tow. Kyler and Keithen were dressed alike and looked adorable in their little blue suits, white dress shirts, and black ties.

A moment later, Pastor Tom walked up to her, looking quite dapper in a dove gray suit and green tie. "This is quite the party. Are you having fun?"

"I'm having a blast," Anne said truthfully. "Mildred took care of everything, so all I have to do is mingle — and take charge of the drawing for the free holiday craft books later."

"Ah yes. Maggie entered the drawing and is quite excited about it."

"Which book does she want to win?"

He smiled. "All of them, but I'm sure she'll just be happy if her name is called."

Anne knew that Maggie Sloan's name had been on one of the three lone tickets in the box two weeks ago. Now that same box was full-to-overflowing with tickets. Fear of the Egyptian curse no longer kept patrons away from the library, especially since the article Grace had written had cleared away all the rumors and revealed the truth. In fact, several people had been taking pictures of the clay pot once again on display in the History Room.

"So I've been meaning to ask you," Anne said, "how is Ben doing in the youth membership class?"

"Very well. He always asks such thought-provoking questions."

"Uh-oh," Anne said with a smile. "Is that good or bad?"

"I think it's wonderful," the pastor replied. "It's led to some insightful conversations with the rest of the kids and allowed me to share some of the books from my library with them."

Anne nodded. "Yes, I've seen Ben reading one of those books. It seems to have really captured his attention."

Compassion filled his eyes. "I know you're still worried about Ben's faith and his relationship with God, but I think it will grow even stronger in the years to come."

"I hope you're right," she said, sending up a silent prayer for her son.

"Oh, and guess who came to visit me?" Pastor Tom said. "My new neighbor, Mrs. Pratt."

"Carter's mother?"

He nodded. "She asked if Carter could start attending Sunday school."

"Does her husband know about this?"

"I don't know, but I get the feeling that Mrs. Pratt might wear the pants in that family. I told her that Carter was welcome anytime, so we'll see what happens."

Wendy walked up to greet them, wearing a lovely black-and white maxi dress. "It's almost time for the drawing, Anne. Are you about ready?"

"Yes, I think so."

She followed Wendy into the Fiction Room, where the drawing would take place. At Anne's silent cue, the string quartet finished their song and then took a break.

"Gather around everyone," Wendy announced, her voice carrying throughout the library. "It's time for the drawing."

More people crowded into the room. Bella and Remi Miller were there along with their parents. The four of them were chatting with Coraline Watson and the Gundersons. Anne glimpsed Alex talking to Chad Pyle while Ryan and Christian each indulged in a cream puff.

"How is Christian getting along with Carter?" Anne whispered to Wendy as they approached the pedestal table with the gift-wrapped ticket box.

"Much better," Wendy said with a smile. "They even played catch together at recess yesterday."

"I'm glad to hear it."

Anne and Wendy moved behind the pedestal table as more people gathered around them. Wendy picked up the three books to be given away while Anne pulled the box toward her for the drawing.

"Is everybody ready?" Anne asked.

An enthusiastic cheer went up in the room. She'd never imagined, when she'd ordered the holiday craft books, that her free giveaway would be such a success. Anne knew she owed much of it to the wonderful fall gala that Mildred had put together, and she was so thankful that the dark days of the so-called curse had finally passed and the library was once again full of enthusiastic readers.

Anne closed her eyes and dug her hand into the box full of tickets. She pulled one out and then called out the name. "Edwin Flower."

Loretta's husband, wearing a pair of blue denim overalls and a plaid shirt, clapped his hands together as he walked up to choose his book from the three that Wendy held in her hands. He grinned as he plucked one from the pile. "Now I don't need to go shopping for Loretta's birthday!"

The crowd laughed, including Loretta, who accepted the book with a delighted smile.

Maggie Sloan won the next book, and Anne chuckled as Pastor Tom give his wife an enthusiastic hug of congratulations.

Then Anne pulled out the last ticket, surprised by the name she saw there. "Dustin Wolfe."

Dustin emitted a loud whoop as he walked up to claim his prize, with Remi and another young woman following behind him.

"I can't believe I won," Dustin said, taking the last book from Wendy and looking at the cover. "This is so cool."

"Do you like to do crafts?" Anne asked him.

He shrugged. "I don't know, but I'll give it a try." Then he turned to Hannah Pyle. "She's the one who talked me into entering."

"Oh?" Anne raised a brow. "I didn't realize you two knew each other."

"I introduced them," a young woman said. "I'm Tina, Dustin's fiancée. I met Hannah at Coffee Joe's. She was scolding her laptop at the time."

Hannah smiled. "Tina told me that Dustin did some computer repair work on the side, so I had him take a look at my laptop since it kept shutting off."

"The power cord was defective," Dustin explained. "So it was an easy fix."

"I'm glad to hear it." Anne turned to Hannah. "And I'd still love to read your English paper."

Hannah nodded. "I'll e-mail it to you. It might even be a little better than the one I lost."

Anne chatted with some of the other guests, leisurely making her way through all the rooms on the first floor and then heading up the stairs to the second. She saw Liddie playing with Emily Pyle in the Children's Room but realized that she hadn't seen Ben for a while.

As Anne walked down the second-floor hallway, she thought she heard Ben's voice coming from the family kitchen. She continued down the hallway and then peeked into the kitchen.

Ben sat on his knees near the private entrance, Hershey sitting in front of him. Mud covered all four of the dog's paws and was smeared halfway up all four legs.

Muddy paw prints dotted her beige tile floor like a patchwork quilt. Anne swallowed a groan at the sight, ready to walk through the door and say something. Then she realized that Ben was talking to Hershey, so she stayed silent in the doorway, listening to their conversation.

"You need to learn to stay out of that mud hole," Ben told the dog. "I know it's fun, but mud is supposed to stay outside, remember?"

The dog wagged his tail once and then stopped, as if remembering he was in trouble.

"I know you didn't mean to make a mess," Ben said, scratching behind one of Hershey's ears. "I'm not mad at you, so don't be sad. God loves us, no matter what."

Then Ben slipped his arms around Hershey's neck and gave him a gentle hug.

Anne quietly closed the kitchen door, stepping back into the hallway. She wiped the tears from her eyes, so very thankful to have witnessed that sweet scene.

"God loves us, no matter what."

Anne couldn't help but smile, joy filling her heart. "Amen."

About the Author

Emily Thomas is the pen name for a team of writers who have come together to create the series Secrets of the Blue Hill Library. *Mum's the Word* was written by Kristin Eckhardt. Kristin is the author of more than forty books, including twenty books for Guideposts. She's won two national awards for her writing, and her first book was made into a TV movie. Kristin and her husband have three adult children and live in central Nebraska. Kristin enjoys quilting, traveling, and spending time with family.

A Conversation with the Author

Q. *Aunt Edie doesn't appear to believe in curses or superstitions but many of the residents of Blue Hill do. Do you have any personal superstitions or good luck customs?*

A. I personally don't have any superstitions, but I'm fascinated by the superstitions in sports—especially professional baseball. I enjoy watching the games with my husband and seeing players adhere to certain superstitions—such as a pitcher taking care not to step on the foul line when leaving the field. Or players wearing their caps on backward in the dugout to rally their team for a win. It adds to the fun of the game, especially when it gets a little silly.

Q. *What is your most prized family heirloom? Why?*

A. My favorite family heirloom is an antique piano stool that once belonged to my great-grandma Hattie. My sister and I used to spend a week every summer in her home and the old piano had a prominent place in the living room. Best of all, the top of the piano was filled with framed photographs of the family. I loved looking at those photos and learning about my extended family. The antique piano stool now has a prominent place in my home and it always reminds me of that special time in my life.

Q. *Anne moves back to her hometown after years in New York City.*
What do/would you miss about your hometown?

A. I grew up in Omaha, Nebraska, and miss the family and
friends who still live there. Fortunately, I can drive there in just
under three hours, so I'm able to visit fairly often. Moving
from city life to my husband's farm thirty years ago was the
biggest adjustment for me as a young wife. At that time, I
missed fast-food restaurants, movie theaters, and most of all,
the large, city library. But farm life introduced me to some
wonderful new experiences and new friends. And with no
fast-food restaurant within forty miles, I learned to be a much
better cook!

Q. *Aunt Edie loved to travel. What's your favorite vacation or tourist*
destination?

A. My favorite place to vacation, so far, is Phoenix, Arizona. My
daughters and sister live there, so that's a big part of the reason
I love to visit so much. There's something about the desert that
is so peaceful to me and I find the scenery breathtaking. My
husband and I have big plans to travel more in our future, so I
can't wait to discover my next favorite spot!

Q. *What's the most interesting fact you've learned while researching*
and writing the Secrets of the Blue Hill Library series?

A. While writing *Mum's the Word*, I enjoyed researching Egypt
and Egyptian artifacts. One of the most interesting things
I learned was that scarab beetles were considered sacred in
ancient Egypt. Jars with beetles in them were even buried

with the deceased since, to some, the scarab beetles represented transformation. Many Egyptians wore jewelry made of stone or jewels that were carved in the shape of scarab beetles and considered amulets. You can still find centuries-old jewelry like this in museums worldwide.

Q. *Who is your most interesting relative?*

A. There are so many to choose from! I have always been fascinated by the life of my great-grandma Viola. When she was eleven years old, she was placed on an orphan train and charged with looking after her three-year-old brother. Their parents were no longer able to care for them due to their mother's debilitating, chronic illness.

   After several train stops, where Viola had to tell interested couples that she and her cute, little brother were a package deal, they were eventually taken in by a farm couple in Nebraska. She had a loving relationship with her foster parents, although she used to joke that they'd only wanted her for milking cows. After her marriage, Great-Grandma Viola brought her ailing mother to Nebraska and cared for her for the next two decades. My great-grandma's unwavering faith, courage, and strong family values still resonate with me today.

Recipes from the Library Guild

Anne's Good-For-What-Ails-You Minestrone

3 tablespoons olive oil

1 cup onion, chopped

4 teaspoons minced garlic

4 cups vegetable broth

1 (14-oz) can, undrained,
   diced tomatoes

2 (15-oz) cans, undrained, red
   kidney beans

2 (15-oz) cans, undrained, white
   beans

½ cup carrots, shredded

3 cups hot water

1 ½ teaspoon oregano

½ teaspoon ground pepper

½ teaspoon basil

¼ teaspoon thyme

1 (16-oz) bag small shell
   pasta

Heat olive oil over medium heat in a large soup pot. Sauté onion and garlic for five minutes or until translucent. Add vegetable broth to pot, along with diced tomatoes, beans, shredded carrots, hot water, and spices.

Bring soup to a boil, then reduce heat and simmer for twenty minutes. Add pasta and cook for an additional twenty minutes.

Enjoy!

From the Guideposts Archives

This article by Terry Francona originally appeared in *Guideposts* magazine.

The curse. The Boston Red Sox had no chance—no chance!—of ever winning the World Series because of the dreaded "Curse of the Bambino." The Sox had foolishly traded Babe Ruth to their bitter rivals, the New York Yankees, in 1920. That's all I heard when the Red Sox hired me as their manager in November 2003. The team hadn't won a title since 1918. All because of the Curse.

Folks pointed to 1978, when the light-hitting Yankees shortstop Bucky Dent improbably slugged a game-winning home run to knock the Sox out of the playoffs. They talked of the ground ball that rolled, heartbreakingly, through first baseman Bill Buckner's legs, triggering the team's 1986 World Series defeat.

But I don't believe in curses, not even one that had tormented the Red Sox Nation for eighty-six years. "To win we have to be loyal to each other," I told my players before the start of the 2004 season. "We have to have faith. We have to stay positive. We have to believe."

For six months they had. Now it was October, playoff time. The Red Sox were four victories away from reaching the 2004 World Series and a chance at winning the championship for the first time in nearly a century. Millions of New Englanders—four generations' worth—were counting on us. All that stood in our way was a best-of-seven league championship series against, naturally, the Yankees, for the right to go to the Series.

What a time to play our worst baseball! We came off the field after game three at Fenway Park that October down three games to none. The Yanks had just hammered us 19–8. The Boston fans were moaning. No playoff team in baseball history had come back from three such losses. I don't doubt some of the fans were thinking: the Curse!

The clubhouse was very quiet. Still, I had this funny feeling and thought, We can still win this thing. I eyed each and every one of the guys. "We've won ninety-eight times this year," I said. "We're pretty good at it. Just win tomorrow and we'll be on our way."

If I'd said that to any other group of people I'd have been laughed out of the room. But looking at Kevin Millar, our first baseman; Manny Ramirez, our star outfielder; Johnny Damon, our leadoff hitter; and the rest, I could sense they believed too. Professional athletes are trained to think positive. In our hugely competitive world it's the only way to succeed. You must believe. You must have faith.

I was proof of that, I suppose. The day the Montreal Expos selected me in the first round of the 1980 player draft, the last thing I thought I needed was more determination. All I'd ever wanted in life was to be a ballplayer. My dad, Tito Francona, was a longtime major leaguer who once almost won the batting title. My final season at the University of Arizona I'd been named college player of the year. I figured I'd vault to the majors and tear up the league. Sure enough, less than two years later I was playing left field for Montreal. I was on my way. Then in my fourth season I swung at a pitch and everything changed.

The ground ball was like a thousand others I'd hit. A high hopper up the first base line, an easy out. It was June 1984 and we were playing the Pittsburgh Pirates. The Pirates hurler raced from the mound and grabbed the ball. He reached to tag me and I ducked, trying to elude him. That's when I heard my left knee pop. I went down like I'd been shot. I knew right away it was bad. The guys had to help me off the field.

Why now? I thought, as they helped me to the dugout. I was twenty-five years old, leading the league with a .346 batting average, playing left field for a pennant contender. Then just like that I was done for the season.

I worked like crazy to rehab my knee. Hours and hours in the gym, all through fall and winter. By the start of the 1985 season I was back on the field. But something had changed. I wasn't hitting home runs, not driving runs in. I couldn't steal bases. I wasn't helping the team win. One day I checked the lineup. My name wasn't on it. I didn't have to ask why.

I was a twenty-five-year-old benchwarmer. That was the worst. To be so young and have the game taken away. It just killed me.

I lived with a lot of frustration that year. I'd get home from a game and my wife, Jacque, would talk to me. She'd try to steer the conversation away from baseball. "Are your knees feeling better?" she'd ask.

I'd barely answer. Yeah, wins were what baseball was all about. But how had I contributed, sitting nine innings on the bench? I'd turn on the TV and stare at the screen, trying not to show my frustration.

I wasn't any happier at the ballpark. I'd get there early and run. I took extra infield practice. I worked out. Anything to get rid of my pent-up energy from not playing.

Baseball is a team sport, but a lot of stuff you have to figure out yourself. Our best player was Andre Dawson, our slugging all-star outfielder. Andre was a man of professional dedication, someone I admired. He had two damaged knees. Before each game he spent hours in the trainer's room getting treatment. I was in there too. I watched what he went through daily in order to suit up and play. Reporters would ask him, "Why do you do it?" And he'd answer, "If you love it enough, you find a way."

Andre's words stuck with me. *What do you really want?* I thought. I tried to be realistic — not an easy thing to be when your ego is on the line. I was through as an everyday player. But I still loved baseball. What I wanted more than anything was to stay in the game. Find a way, I told myself. So I did. I tried to become a valued pinch hitter. I played solid defense. Anything to contribute.

It wasn't enough. A few days before the start of the 1986 season the Montreal manager called me into his office. "I'm sorry," he said. "We're releasing you."

I was through at twenty-six.

Everyone is tested in his own way, I thought. I chose to approach this as an opportunity: I could prove myself to a new team. I hooked on as a "utility player" with a succession of teams: the Chicago Cubs, the Cincinnati Reds, the Cleveland Indians, the Milwaukee Brewers. I didn't allow a negative thought to enter my mind, even when each of those teams later released me. "A fresh opportunity," I'd tell Jacque. I found a way to stay in the game I loved, playing another five seasons despite not being able to run well and averaging just two home runs a year. I retired on my terms when I was ready to move into coaching.

I never doubted the power of positive thinking after that. Not even after my first experience managing in the majors, in Philadelphia. I was thirty-seven, a young, inexperienced leader running a young, inexperienced team. We took our lumps. Last place in 1997. A distant third in 1998 and 1999. Last again in 2000. Then I was fired. Friends said they were sorry. I wasn't. I'd learned a lot. I'd worked out my philosophy for running a baseball team. How to manage and motivate players, confront pressure, make decisions, deal with the media. Most of all, how to handle adversity. And there's only one way—to treat it positively, as an opportunity.

I was ready in late 2003 when the Red Sox called. I may not have been the popular choice. The Red Sox were one of the best teams in baseball. The media and fans had expected the club to hire a proven winner. I was anything but.

The team got off to a slow start. The critics had a field day. They didn't like my laid-back approach. They didn't like that I gave the players a lot of freedom. They thought I'd lost control of the clubhouse. I just gritted my teeth.

Late one night after a tough loss the phone rang. It was John Henry, the team owner. "I want you to know I believe in you," he said. "I think we're going to be okay."

I fed the players the same kind of support Mr. Henry gave me. I believe in you. That is one of the most powerful things you can say to someone. A few weeks later we made some key trades for infield help. A couple of injured players came back. We went on a roll, winning sixteen of seventeen. We beat Anaheim in the first round of the playoffs.

And then we went down three games to none against the Yankees, and our faith, confidence, and determination came into play. Everybody felt it. The guys didn't need any words from me the next night when they took the field. We played every pitch in those next four games like it was our last breath. Everyone on the team contributed. A stolen base. A key hit. A critical fielding play. After the final out, after we'd won our fourth straight to defeat the Yankees and go to the World Series, we had such a feeling of release. I don't even remember how I got out onto the field. But I do remember guys telling me, "The Curse is dead!"

What curse? Two weeks later we beat the St. Louis Cardinals and became World Series champions for the first time since 1918.

Yes, eighty-six years is a long time to go between championships. I can see where it might prompt some superstition among fans, especially ones as long-suffering and seemingly snakebit as Red Sox fans. But, I don't believe in curses. I believe in meeting adversity as a challenge and an opportunity. I believe in faith, self-confidence, and determination. After all, look how far it got a benchwarmer like me.

Read on for a sneak peek of another exciting book
in Secrets of the Blue Hill Library!

Sidetracked Suspicions

On a Monday morning in early June, the front door of the Blue Hill Library flew open and Wendy Pyle, in all her five-foot-one glory, stepped through, raised one hand in the air, and sang out loud, for the benefit of anyone within earshot, that she "had a fever that was hard to bear."

Anne Gibson was seated behind the circulation desk processing the books that had been returned over the weekend. She glanced calmly up at her friend, who held her pose, awaiting a reaction. "Good morning, Peggy Lee," Anne said and returned her gaze to her computer terminal.

Appearing somewhat deflated by Anne's mild response, Wendy shut the door behind her and stepped over to the circulation desk, heaving a canvas shopping bag onto its surface. "I suppose you want me to shush," she said.

"I've told you before that librarians don't shush," Anne replied. "That's a stereotype." A smile tugged at one side of her mouth, and she glanced over her glasses at her friend again.

Recovering her enthusiasm, Wendy leaned forward and asked, "Don't you want to know what 'fever' I'm singing about?"

"I'm guessing," said Anne, shifting a pile of books, "that, like last week and the week before, it's auction fever."

"Auction fever, baby!" Wendy cried, pumping her fist into the air. "All of Blue Hill is catching it. It's an epidemic. An epidemic of community spirit. You need to catch the fever too, Anne."

"I'm feeling sufficiently feverish, thank you. But I gather..." she gestured toward the shopping bag, "...that your current bout of fever has a specific cause?"

"I was just at the bank," Wendy replied, pulling an old shoe box from the bag and removing the lid, "and Rita Sloan came out from her office to give me this." She carefully unfolded some tissue paper to reveal three small beaded purses. "They originally belonged to her grandmother before she gave them to Rita, but she says that she never uses them." Wendy ran her fingers lightly over the beads. "Aren't they gorgeous?"

Despite their obvious age, the bags appeared to be in excellent condition. Wendy carefully lifted them from the box, and the nacre and glass beads seemed to change color as Wendy moved the purses in the light.

"They're mad-money bags," Betty Bultman said from behind Wendy. Anne looked up to see Betty Bultman looking over Wendy's shoulder with a book in her hand. "When my grandmother used to go to formal dances, her mother always made sure that she had enough cash in her mad-money bag for cab fare to get her home in case her date turned out to be a lout." She looked down at the three purses. "For the auction?" she asked, and Wendy nodded.

Taking Betty's book from her, Anne said, "That's very generous."

"Lots of people have been generous," Wendy said with a satisfied smile.

"That's what Bob says too —" Betty's husband was the mayor of their town. " — but I haven't been down to the museum yet to see all the donations that have been collected." Betty retrieved the book that Anne had checked out to her.

"You should come down this afternoon," said Wendy. "The committee will be doing some sorting. It would be a good time to see everything."

Betty paused for a moment as if mentally reviewing her schedule, then smiled and said, "I believe I will." She wished Anne and Wendy a good day and, as she left, Wendy began to repack the purses in the tissue paper.

"Can I put this behind the desk for safe keeping?" asked Wendy, now intent on her work.

"What? Why?" Anne spoke a bit sharply. "Aren't you taking them to the museum?"

Wendy looked up with a puzzled expression. Gesturing to the room around them, she said, "I've got my shift." She was one of Anne's most dedicated volunteers.

Anne frowned. "I'll be fine here alone for the few minutes that you'll need to take them down to the museum," she said, adding after a slight hesitation, "I don't think I want the responsibility of having them here."

Wendy shrugged. "Well, if you don't mind..."

Anne shooed Wendy toward the exit, but the library door opened before Wendy could turn the handle.

"You're back!" Anne exclaimed.

Douglas and Marian Pauthen stepped into the expansive foyer, and Wendy repeated Anne's exclamation. "You're back!" She paused, apparently trying to recall where they had gone.

"California, right?" She continued after a beat. "To see your old Army buddies?"

Douglas nodded and Marian added, "And to see nieces and nephews."

"How was it?" Anne asked.

"Well, funny thing…" Douglas slowly shook his head. "I can't tell just quite how it happened, but you know all those young fellas I told you about? The ones I was in the service with? They've all gotten *old!*" He shook his head again as if befuddled, but he had a twinkle in his eye.

Marian poked her husband and shook her head. "We had a lovely time, dear, thank you."

Anne and Wendy asked them a few more questions about their two-week trip then brought them up to date on some of the news in Blue Hill.

"Railroad Days? Auction?" Douglas asked after Wendy referred to them a couple of times. "What auction?"

"Douglas, you know they started the planning for Railroad Days before we even left," his wife said.

"I know, Mare," he responded in an apologetic tone, "but I wasn't paying that much attention. And now, even though we've only been gone for two weeks, it seems to have become the only topic in town. Besides, I don't remember hearing much about this auction."

Anne and Wendy looked at one another. "Wendy, you're the committee member," Anne said, offering a "you explain it" gesture. Anne knew that, while Wendy had reluctantly been pressed into service on the ad hoc planning committee for Blue

Hill's Railroad Days events, she had come to really enjoy the experience.

"So you know that the basic idea is to celebrate the 150th anniversary of the arrival of the railroad in Blue Hill, right?" Wendy began with a gleam in her eye.

Douglas nodded. "Yes, I attended the talk that Mr. McCollum gave last month," he said, referring to the director of the Blue Hill Railroad Museum. "It was fascinating. I hadn't realized how important the railroad was to the early development of the town."

"Yes," said Wendy, nodding vigorously, "that was our first event. And we have others scheduled over the next few weeks. But the idea that has really exploded has been the Antique Appraisal Fair and Auction." Wendy beamed.

"Ask her whose idea that was," Anne interjected.

Wendy, never one to take the credit, waved that comment away. "It was a team effort," she said, "but the point is, in the past couple of weeks, people have started to get really excited about it."

"And what will that involve?" Douglas asked.

"This will be the culminating event of the whole Railroad Days celebration," Wendy said. "That Saturday we're going to have a day-long antique appraisal fair, so that anyone can bring in any antique they want and have it appraised for free."

"Like on that television show," Marian said.

"Yes," Wendy continued, "like that. Do you know Miles Bridges, who runs Midtown Antiques?"

The Pauthens nodded.

"He's coordinating all the appraisers. Everyone recognizes that Mr. Bridges is the foremost authority in these parts on antiques. He'll do a lot of the appraising himself, but he has also rounded up a number of other specialty experts. Of course, he'll also be drawing on the knowledge of our local antique authorities, such as George Franklin from Franklin's Antiques, and Harriet and James Zelinski who run Minnie's Doll Hospital. And then that evening, he will cry the Charity Benefit Auction!"

"Wendy is very proud of her new auction jargon," Anne interjected.

Wendy chuckled and shook her head but continued talking. "People are donating all kinds of wonderful things for the auction. The proceeds will be divided so that half will benefit Blue Hill's Railroad Museum and half will go to the town council to distribute to other worthy causes. Oh, and before the auction, we're displaying all of the donated items at the museum. More things are going on display all the time." Once again, she pulled out the beaded purses so the Pauthens could admire them.

"How did you come to be so involved with all this, Wendy?" asked Douglas. "Are you a railroad buff?"

Wendy responded with a laugh. "I'm not, although it's been interesting to learn about." She shook her head and laughed again. "It's my children's fault. They're involved in another Railroad Days project. Hal McCollum's brainchild actually. He dreamed up the idea of collecting oral histories from older Blue Hill residents about the railroad and about the history of the town.

"He wanted to use high school students as the interviewers, so a few months ago he gave a presentation at the school looking to recruit volunteers. Well, my daughter Hannah signed on, the other Railroad Days activities started to come together—and yours truly found herself drafted for the steering committee." Wendy smiled as she spread her hands and shrugged.

"An inspiring tale of selfless dedication," Anne said with a wink.

"Oh, shush, you," Wendy retorted. She turned back to the Pauthens. "Anyway, that's what happened while you were away, and I really hope you'll plan to come to the fair and the auction."

"Oh, we'll be there," said Douglas, "and if I know that look on my wife's face, we'll be donating something as well."

Marian glanced up at her husband and smiled. "Oh, I have some ideas," she said. "But at the moment, I still need to find something to read."

The two of them moved off to scan the shelves for new releases.

"And what about you?" Wendy asked Anne. "Have you decided what you're going to donate yet?"

Anne had been trying to think of an appropriate choice, but she still hadn't settled on anything.

When she didn't respond immediately, Wendy continued, "You know, you don't have to donate to the auction at all. You could just register to have something appraised. We've already got a hundred people signed up for the appraisal slots, and Mr. Bridges is talking about bringing in a few more experts because of the interest."

"As a matter of fact," Anne said, "I do have something I'm curious about. Aunt Edie had a collection of *matryoshka* dolls..." She paused at the quizzical look on her friend's face. "You know, those Russian nesting dolls?" Wendy nodded in recognition, and Anne continued. "Aunt Edie had some really nice ones. I'm sure they're in the attic someplace, but I haven't tried to dig them out yet. I figured I'd wait until Liddie is a little older. When I was a child, I wasn't allowed to play with them unless Aunt Edie was supervising." She smiled at the memory. "I'd pester her to show them to me often. They were a lot of fun. There was a set of Russian peasant dolls, I remember, and the smallest was a tiny little baby. And a set of Soviet political figures. And a religious-themed set that Aunt Edie said was very old. And some others. She wrote a small book about matryoshka dolls once, did I ever tell you?"

"No, not that I recall," Wendy said, shaking her head. "And I think I'd remember if I'd heard your aunt Edie had written a book."

"I should find my copy of that," Anne said. "Anyway, I've wondered whether those dolls might have some real value, aside from sentimental value, of course. It would be interesting to learn more about them."

Wendy nodded. "I'm sure someone at the appraisal fair can tell you all about them—what they're worth, how to take care of them." She hoisted her canvas bag over her shoulder. "All right, I'm off to the museum. I'll be back in ten minutes, if you think you can handle the crowds until then."

As she watched Wendy breeze out the door, Anne reflected that her friend was right about the level of interest that had developed around the Antique Appraisal Fair and Auction. Anne had seen a steady stream of patrons at the library to review whatever reference materials she had about antiques. The Kovels' guides were particularly popular, and at the end of the day, Anne would find them bristling with Post-it notes that had been used as bookmarks. She'd made a little game out of guessing which items were being investigated. The sections covering Depression glass, silver serving sets, and antique tools seemed to be in great demand, but toys of all sorts, watches, and vinyl records were also being investigated.

The Appraisal Fair was a popular topic of conversation as well, and many of her patrons were eager to tell Anne about the items they intended to have appraised. Mostly, it seemed to her, people were curious about things that held more sentimental than monetary value. One woman had a set of letters her great uncle, a professional calligrapher in the 1920s, had penned in that beautiful, flowing script. Another had a Civil War era locket with a lock of hair in it and a tiny picture of a stiffly posed young soldier. Each item came with a story, and Anne had quickly recognized the wisdom in Hal McCollum's idea of tapping this event for an outpouring of Blue Hill's living history.

* * *

Later that afternoon, Anne was behind the circulation desk when she was surprised to see Wendy, whose shift was long over, once again come through the front door of the library. "No musical entrance this time?" she asked with a smile.

Wendy ignored this and instead asked, "Is he here?" Anne's puzzled expression and a quick glance around the room answered Wendy's question. Shrugging, she stepped up to the desk. "Miles Bridges called me and asked if I could meet him here. I guess I got here first."

Anne's puzzled expression deepened. "Here? Why?" Surely he wasn't coming to do research, she thought. He had his own, more specialized resources.

Wendy shook her head. "Don't know." But before she could say more, the antiques dealer came through the door wearing a broad grin and cradling a box in the crook of his arm.

"Good afternoon, ladies," he said, a twinkle in his eye. "I have something here that I think will be of interest to you."

The two women exchanged a glance as he set the box on the circulation desk with great care.

He seemed to be trying to control his own excitement before continuing. "I should explain that I have been approached by a certain individual who wishes to make a donation to the auction." He gestured toward the box. "But this generous person had two requests to make. Before I share those requests, however, let's just have a look." He removed the lid of the box and gently parted several layers of bubble wrap and tissue.

Anne and Wendy crowded in close behind Miles and looked over his shoulder. Nestled in the box was a vase that appeared to be of oriental design. It looked very old and was a little over a foot tall, with a scene of flowers and birds showing in the narrow section exposed.

Anne glanced from the vase to Miles, who gazed down at it with an expression akin to a new grandfather.

"I'm going to leave it in the box," he said, even speaking in a hushed tone. "I don't want to handle it unnecessarily."

"It's lovely," Anne offered, feeling that some praise was called for, but after Mr. Bridges had remained silent for a few moments, she finally prodded, "Who is the donor?"

"Ah well," said Miles, recovering himself, "that's the first of the requests. The donor wishes to remain anonymous."

He looked at Wendy as he said this, and she shrugged. "I guess that's okay. We hadn't really made provision for something like that, but I don't see a problem. *You* know who the donor is and can, you know, vouch for it." Wendy gestured toward the vase.

Miles nodded again but said, "I'm not an expert in Chinese porcelain, but yes, I'm arranging to have it examined by someone who's a specialist in this area."

There was another moment of silence, and Anne asked, "You said the donor has two requests. What's the other?"

"The donor has asked," said Miles, "to designate a specific beneficiary for the proceeds of this particular piece." He looked at Anne. "In fact, he wants it auctioned to benefit the Blue Hill Library."

When neither Anne nor Wendy responded immediately, Miles continued, "The thing is, this vase is likely to be the most valuable piece we have in the auction—by far. As I say, this isn't my area of expertise. But I've seen enough to be fairly confident that the donor is correct when he estimates its value at ten thousand dollars."

A Note from the Editors

We hope you enjoy Secrets of the Blue Hill Library, created by the Books and Inspirational Media Division of Guideposts, a nonprofit organization that touches millions of lives every day through products and services that inspire, encourage, help you grow in your faith, and celebrate God's love in every aspect of your daily life.

Thank you for making a difference with your purchase of this book, which helps fund our many outreach programs to military personnel, prisons, hospitals, nursing homes, and educational institutions. To learn more, visit GuidepostsFoundation.org.

We also maintain many useful and uplifting online resources. Visit Guideposts.org to read true stories of hope and inspiration, access OurPrayer network, sign up for free newsletters, download free e-books, join our Facebook community, and follow our stimulating blogs.

To learn about other Guideposts publications, including the best-selling devotional *Daily Guideposts*, go to ShopGuideposts .org, call (800) 932-2145, or write to Guideposts, PO Box 5815, Harlan, Iowa 51593.